Emma

Emma

by
Charlotte Brontë
and
"ANOTHER LADY"

New York EVEREST HOUSE *Publishers*

Emma

Chapter One

We all seek an ideal in life. A pleasant fancy began to visit me in a certain year, that perhaps the number of human beings is few who do not find their quest at some era of life for some space more or less brief. I had certainly not found mine in youth, though the strong belief I held of its existence sufficed through all my brightest and freshest time to keep me hopeful. I had not found it in maturity. I was become resigned never to find it. I had lived certain dim years entirely tranquil and unexpectant. And now I was not sure but something was hovering round my hearth which pleased me wonderfully.

Look at it, reader. Come into my parlour and judge for yourself whether I do right to care for this thing. First you may scan me, if you please. We shall go on better together after a satisfactory introduction and due apprehension of identity. My name is Mrs Chalfont. I am a widow. My house is good, and my income such as need not check the impulse either of charity or a moderate hospitality. I am not young, nor yet old. There is no silver yet in my hair, but its yellow lustre is gone. In my face wrinkles are yet to come, but I have almost forgotten the days when it wore any bloom. I married when I was very young. I lived for fifteen years a life which, whatever its trials, could not be called stagnant. Then for five years I was alone, and, having no children, desolate. Lately Fortune, by a somewhat curious turn of her wheel, placed in my way an interest and a companion.

The neighbourhood where I live is pleasant enough, its scenery agreeable, and its society civilized, though not numerous. About a mile from my house there is a ladies' school, established but lately — not more than three years since. The conductresses of this school were of my acquaintances; and though I cannot say that they occupied the very highest place in my opinion — for they had brought back from some months' residence abroad, for finishing purposes, a good deal that was fantastic, affected and pretentious — yet I awarded them some portion of that respect which seems the fair due of all women who face life bravely, and try to make their own way by their own efforts.

About a year after the Misses Wilcox opened their school, when the number of their pupils was as yet exceedingly limited, and when, no doubt, they were looking out anxiously enough for augmentation, the entrance-gate to their little drive was one day thrown back to admit a carriage — 'a very handsome, fashionable carriage,' Miss Mable Wilcox said, in narrating the circumstance afterwards — and drawn by a pair of really splendid horses. The sweep up the drive, the loud ring at the door-bell, the bustling entrance into the house, the ceremonious admission to the bright drawing-room, roused excitement enough in Fuchsia Lodge. Miss Wilcox repaired to the reception-room in a pair of new gloves, and carrying in her hand a handkerchief of French cambric.

She found a gentleman seated on the sofa, who, as he rose up, appeared a tall, fine-looking personage; at least she thought him so, as he stood with his back to the light. He introduced himself as Mr Fitzgibbon, inquired if Miss Wilcox had a vacancy, and intimated that he wished to intrust to her care a new pupil in the shape of his daughter. This was welcome news, for there was many a vacancy in Miss Wilcox's schoolroom; indeed, her establishment was as yet limited to the select number of three, and she and her sisters were looking forward with anything but confidence to the balancing of accounts at the close of their first half-year. Few objects could have been more agreeable to her than that to which, by a wave of the hand, Mr Fitzgibbon now directed her attention — the figure of a child standing near the drawing-room window.

Had Miss Wilcox's establishment boasted fuller ranks — had she indeed entered well on that course of prosperity which in after years an undeviating attention to externals enabled her so triumphantly to realize — an early thought with her would have been to judge whether the acquisition now offered was likely to answer well as a show-pupil. She would have instantly marked her look, dress, &c., and inferred her value from these indicia. In those anxious commencing times, however, Miss Wilcox could scarce afford herself the luxury of such appreciation: a new pupil represented 40*l*. a year, independently of masters' terms — and 40*l*. a year was a sum Miss Wilcox needed and was glad to secure;

6

besides, the fine carriage, the fine gentleman, and the fine name gave gratifying assurance, enough and to spare, of eligibility in the proffered connection. It was admitted, then, that there were vacancies in Fuchsia Lodge; that Miss Fitzgibbon could be received at once; that she was to learn all that the school prospectus proposed to teach; to be liable to every extra; in short, to be as expensive, and consequently as profitable a pupil, as any directress's heart could wish. All this was arranged as upon velvet, smoothly and liberally. Mr Fitzgibbon showed in the transaction none of the hardness of the bargain-making man of business, and as little of the penurious anxiety of the straitened professional man. Miss Wilcox felt him to be 'quite the gentleman'. Everything disposed her to be partially inclined towards the little girl whom he, on taking leave, formally committed to her guardianship; and as if no circumstance should be wanting to complete her happy impression, the address left written on a card served to fill up the measure of Miss Wilcox's satisfaction — Conway Fitzgibbon, Esq., May Park, Midland County. That very day three decrees were passed in the new-comer's favour:—

1st. That she was to be Miss Wilcox's bed-fellow.

2nd. To sit next to her at table.

3rd. To walk out with her.

In a few days it became evident that a fourth secret clause had been added to these, viz. that Miss Fitzgibbon was to be favoured, petted, and screened on all possible occasions.

An ill-conditioned pupil, who before coming to Fuchsia Lodge had passed a year under the care of certain old-fashioned Misses Sterling of Hartwood, and from them had picked up unpractical notions of justice, took it upon her to utter an opinion on this system of favouritism.

'The Misses Sterling,' she injudiciously said, 'never distinguished any girl because she was richer or better dressed than the rest. They would have scorned to do so. *They* always rewarded girls according as they behaved well to their schoolfellows and minded their lessons, not according to the number of their silk dresses, and fine laces and feathers.'

For it must not be forgotten that Miss Fitzgibbon's trunks, when opened, disclosed a splendid wardrobe; so fine were the various articles of apparel, indeed, that instead of assigning for their accommodation the painted deal drawers of the school bedroom, Miss Wilcox had them arranged in a mahogany bureau in her own room. With her own hands, too, she would on Sundays

7

array the little favourite in her quilted silk pelisse, her hat and feathers, her ermine boa, and little French boots and gloves. And very self-complacent she felt when she led the young heiress (a letter from Mr Fitzgibbon, received since his first visit, had communicated the additional particulars that his daughter was his only child, and would be the inheritress of his estates, including May Park, Midland County) — when she led her, I say, into the church, and seated her stately by her side at the top of the gallery pew. Unbiassed observers might, indeed, have wondered what there was to be proud of, and puzzled their heads to detect the special merits of this little woman in silk — for, to speak truth, Miss Fitzgibbon was far from being the beauty of the school: there were two or three blooming little faces amongst her companions lovelier than hers. Had she been a poor child, Miss Wilcox herself would not have liked her physiognomy at all: rather, indeed, would it have repelled than attracted her; and, moreover — though Miss Wilcox hardly confessed the circumstance to herself, but, on the contrary, strove hard not to be conscious of it — there were moments when she became sensible of a certain strange weariness in continuing her system of partiality. It hardly came natural to her to show this special distinction in this particular instance. An undefined wonder would smite her sometimes that she did not take more real satisfaction in flattering and caressing this embryo heiress — that she did not like better to have her always at her side, under her special charge. On principle, Miss Wilcox continued the plan she had begun. On *principle*, for she argued with herself: This is the most aristocratic and richest of my pupils; she brings me the most credit and the most profit: therefore, I ought in justice to show her a special indulgence; which she did — but with a gradually increasing peculiarity of feeling.

Certainly, the undue favours showered on little Miss Fitzgibbon brought their object no real benefit. Unfitted for the character of playfellow by her position of favourite, her fellow-pupils rejected her company as decidedly as they dared. Active rejection was not long necessary; it was soon seen that passive avoidance would suffice; the pet was not social. No: even Miss Wilcox never thought her social. When she sent for her to show her fine clothes in the drawing-room when there was company, and especially when she had her into her parlour of an evening to be her own companion, Miss Wilcox used to feel curiously perplexed. She would try to talk affably to the young heiress, to draw her out, to amuse her. To herself the governess could render no reason why her efforts soon flagged; but this was invariably the case. However, Miss Wilcox was a woman of courage; and be the *protégée* what she might, the patroness did not fail to continue on *principle* her system of preference.

A favourite has no friends; and the observation of a gentleman, who about this time called at the Lodge and chanced to see Miss Fitzgibbon, was, 'That child looks consummately unhappy': he was watching Miss Fitzgibbon, as she walked, by herself, fine and solitary, while her schoolfellows were merrily playing.

'Who is the miserable little wight?' he asked.

He was told her name and dignity.

'Wretched little soul!' he repeated; and he watched her pace down the walk and back again; marching upright, her hands in her ermine muff, her fine pelisse showing a gay sheen to the winter's sun, her large Leghorn hat shading such a face as fortunately had not its parallel on the premises.

'Wretched little soul!' reiterated the gentleman. He opened the drawing-room window, watched the bearer of the muff till he caught her eye and then summoned her with his finger. She came; he stooped his head down to her; she lifted her face up to him.

'Don't you play, little girl?'

'No, sir.'

'No! why not? Do you think yourself better than other children?'

No answer.

'Is it because people tell you you are rich, you won't play?'

The young lady was gone. He stretched out his hand to arrest her, but she wheeled beyong his reach, and ran quickly out of sight.

'An only child,' pleaded Miss Wilcox; 'possibly spoiled by her papa, you know; we must excuse a little pettishness.'

'Humph! I am afraid there is not a little to excuse.'

Chapter Two

Mr Ellin — the gentleman mentioned in the last chapter — was a man who went where he liked, and being a gossiping, leisurely person, he liked to go almost anywhere. He could not be rich, he lived so quietly; and yet he must have had some money, for, without apparent profession, he continued to keep a house and a servant. He always spoke of himself as having once been a worker; but if so, that could not have been very long since, for he still looked far from old. Sometimes of an evening, under a little social conversational excitement, he would look quite young; but he was changeable in mood, and complexion, and expression, and had chamelion eyes, sometimes blue and merry, sometimes grey and dark, and anon green and gleaming. On the whole he might be called a fair man, of average height, rather thin and rather wiry. He had not resided more than two years in the neighbourhood; his antecedents were unknown there; but as the Rector, a man of good family and standing and of undoubted scrupulousness in the choice of acquaintance, had introduced him, he found everywhere a prompt reception, of which nothing in his conduct had yet seemed to prove him unworthy. Some people, indeed, dubbed him 'a character', and fancied him 'eccentric'; but others could not see the appropriateness of the epithets. He always seemed to them very harmless and quiet, not always perhaps so perfectly unreserved and comprehensible as might be wished. He had a discomposing expression in his eye; and sometimes in conversation an ambiguous diction; but still they believed he meant no harm.

Mr Ellin often called on the Misses Wilcox; he sometimes took tea with them; he appeared to like tea and muffins, and not to dislike the kind of conversation which usually accompanies that refreshment; he was said to be a good shot, a good angler. — He proved himself an excellent gossip — he liked gossip well. On the whole he liked women's society, and did not seem to be particular in requiring difficult accomplishments or rare endowments in his female acquaintances. The Misses Wilcox, for instance, were not much less shallow than the china saucer which held their teacups; yet Mr Ellin got on perfectly well with them, and had apparently great pleasure in hearing them discuss all the details of their school. He knew the names of all their young ladies too, and would shake hands with them if he met them walking out; he knew their examination days and gala days, and more than once accompanied Mr Cecil, the curate, when he went to examine in ecclesiastical history.

This ceremony took place weekly, on Wednesday afternoons, after which Mr Cecil sometimes stayed to tea, and usually found two or three lady parishioners invited to meet him. Mr Ellin was also pretty sure to be there. Rumour gave one of the Misses Wilcox in anticipated wedlock to the curate, and furnished his friend with a second in the same tender relation so that it is to be conjectured they made a social pleasant party under such interesting circumstances. Their evenings rarely passed without Miss Fitzgibbon being introduced — all worked muslin and streaming sash and elaborated ringlets; others of the pupils would also be called in, perhaps to sing, to show off a little at the piano, or sometimes to repeat poetry. Miss Wilcox conscientiously cultivated display in her young ladies, thinking she thus fulfilled a duty to herself and to them, at once spreading her own fame and giving the children self-possessed manners.

It was curious to note how, on these occasions, good, genuine natural qualities still vindicated their superiority to counterfeit artificial advantages. While 'dear Miss Fitzgibbon', dressed up and flattered as she was, could only sidle round the circle with the crestfallen air which seemed natural to her, just giving her hand to the guests, then almost snatching it away, and sneaking in unmannerly haste to the place allotted to her at Miss Wilcox's side, which place she filled like a piece of furniture, neither smiling nor speaking the evening through — while such was her deportment, certain of her companions, as Mary Franks, Jessy Newton, &c., handsome, open-countenanced little damsels — fearless because harmless — would enter with a smile of salutation and a blush of pleasure, make their pretty reverence at the drawing-room door, stretch a friendly little hand to such visitors as they knew, and sit down to the piano to play their well-practised duet with an innocent, obliging readiness which won all hearts.

There was a girl called Diana — the girl alluded to before as having once been Miss Sterling's pupil — a daring, brave girl, much loved and a little feared by her comrades. She had good faculties, both physical and mental — was clever, honest, and dauntless. In the schoolroom she set her young brow like a rock against Miss Fitzgibbon's pretensions; she found also heart and spirit to withstand them in the drawing-room. One evening, when the curate had been summoned away by some piece of duty directly after tea, and there was no stranger present but Mr Ellin, Diana had been called in to play a long, difficult piece of music which she could execute like a master. She was still in the midst of her performance, when — Mr Ellin having for the first time, perhaps, recognized the existence of the heiress by asking if she was cold — Miss Wilcox took the opportunity of launching into a strain of commendation on Miss Fitzgibbon's inanimate behaviour, terming it ladylike, modest, and exemplary. Whether Miss Wilcox's constrained tone betrayed how far she was from feeling the approbation she expressed, how entirely she spoke from a sense of duty, and not because she felt it possible to be in any degree charmed by the personage she praised — or whether Diana, who was by nature hasty, had a sudden fit of irritability — is not quite certain, but she turned on her music-stool:—

'Ma'am,' said she to Miss Wilcox, 'that girl does not deserve so much praise. Her behaviour is not at all exemplary. In the schoolroom she is insolently distant. For my part I denounce her airs; there is not one of us but is as good or better than she, though we may not be as rich.'

And Diana shut up the piano, took her music-book under her arm, curtsied and vanished.

Strange to relate, Miss Wilcox said not a word at the time; nor was Diana subsequently reprimanded for this outbreak. Miss Fitzgibbon had now been three months in the school, and probably the governess had had leisure to wear out her early raptures of partiality.

Indeed, as time advanced, this evil often seemed likely to right itself; again and again it seemed that Miss Fitzgibbon was about to fall to her proper level, but then, somewhat provokingly to the lovers of reason and justice, some little incident would occur to invest her insignificance with artificial interest. Once it was the arrival of a great basket of hothouse fruit — melons, grapes, and pines — as a present to Miss Wilcox in Miss Fitzgibbon's name. Whether it was that a share of these luscious productions was imparted too freely to the nominal donor, or whether she had had a surfeit of cake on Miss Mabel Wilcox's birthday, it so befell, that in some disturbed state of the digestive organs, Miss Fitzgibbon took to sleep-walking. She one night terrified the school into a panic by passing through the bedrooms, all white in her night-dress, moaning and holding out her hands as she went.

Dr Percy was then sent for; his medicines, probably, did not suit the case; for within a fortnight after the somnambulistic feat, Miss Wilcox going upstairs in the dark, trod on something which she thought was the cat, and on calling for a light, found her darling Matilda Fitzgibbon curled round on the landing, blue, cold, and stiff, without any light in her half-open eyes, or any colour in her lips, or movement in her limbs. She was not soon roused from this fit; her senses seemed half scattered; and Miss Wilcox had now an undeniable excuse for keeping her all day on the drawing-room sofa, and making more of her than ever.

There comes a day of reckoning both for petted heiresses and partial governesses.

One clear winter morning, as Mr Ellin was seated at breakfast, enjoying his bachelor's easy chair and damp, fresh London newspaper, a note was brought to him marked 'private', and 'in haste'. The last injunction was vain, for William Ellin did nothing in haste — he had no haste in him; he wondered why anybody should be so foolish as to hurry; life was short enough without it. He looked at the little note — three-cornered, scented, and feminine. He knew the handwriting; it came from the very lady Rumour had so often assigned him as his own. The bachelor took out a morocco case, selected from a variety of little instruments a pair of tiny scissors, cut round the seal, and read:— 'Miss Wilcox's compliments to Mr Ellin, and she should be truly glad to see him for a few minutes, if at leisure. Miss W. requires a little advice. She will reserve explanations till she sees Mr E.'

Mr Ellin very quietly finished his breakfast; then, as it was a very fine December day — hoar and crisp, but serene and not bitter — he carefully prepared himself for the cold, took his cane, and set out. He liked the walk; the air was still; the sun not wholly ineffectual; the path firm, and but lightly powdered with snow. He made his journey as long as he could by going round through many fields, and through winding, unfrequented lanes. When there was a tree in the way conveniently placed for support, he would sometimes stop, lean his back against the trunk, fold his arms, and muse. If Rumour could have seen him, she would have affirmed that he was thinking about Miss Wilcox; perhaps when he arrives at the Lodge his demeanour will inform us whether such an idea be warranted.

At last he stands at the door and rings the bell; he is admitted, and shown into the parlour — a smaller and a more private room than the drawing-room. Miss Wilcox occupies it; she is seated at her writing-table; she rises — not without air and grace — to receive her visitor. This air and grace she learnt in France; for she was in a Parisian school for six months, and learnt there a little French, and a stock of gestures and courtesies. No: it is certainly not impossible that Mr Ellin may admire Miss Wilcox. She is not without prettiness, any more than are her sisters; and she and they are one and all smart and showy. Bright stone-blue is a colour they like in dress; a crimson bow seldom fails to be pinned on somewhere to give contrast; positive colours generally — grass-greens, red violets, deep yellows — are in favour with them; all harmonies are at a discount. Many people would think Miss Wilcox, standing there in her blue merino dress and pomegranate ribbon, a very agreeable woman. She has regular features; the nose is a little sharp, the lips a little thin, good complexion, light red hair. She is very business-like, very practical; she never in her life knew a refinement of feeling or of thought; she is entirely limited, respectable, and self-satisfied. She has a cool, prominent eye; sharp and shallow pupil, unshrinking and inexpansive; pale irid; light eyelashes, light brow. Miss Wilcox is a very proper and decorous person; but she could not be delicate or modest, because she is naturally destitute of sensitiveness. Her voice, when she speaks, has no vibration; her face no expression; her manner no emotion. Blush or tremor she never knew.

'What can I do for you, Miss Wilcox?' says Mr Ellin, approaching the writing-table, and taking a chair beside it.

'Perhaps you can advise me,' was the answer; 'or perhaps you can give me some information. I feel so thoroughly puzzled, and really fear all is not right.'

'Where? and how?'

'I will have redress if it be possible,' pursued the lady; 'but how to set about obtaining it! Draw to the fire, Mr Ellin; it is a cold day.'

They both drew to the fire. She continued:—

'You know the Christmas holidays are near?'

He nodded.

'Well, about a fortnight since, I wrote, as is customary, to the friends of my pupils, notifying the day when we break up, and requesting that, if it was desired that any girl should stay the vacation, intimation should be sent accordingly. Satisfactory and prompt answers came to all the notes except one — that addressed to Conway Fitzgibbon, Esquire, May Park, Midland County — Matilda Fitzgibbon's father, you know.'

'What? won't he let her go home?'

'Let her go home, my dear sir! you shall hear. Two weeks elapsed, during which I daily expected an answer; none came. I felt annoyed at the delay, as I had particularly requested a speedy reply. This very morning I had made up my mind to write again, when — what do you think the post brought me?'

'I should like to know.'

'My own letter — actually my own — returned from the post-office, with an intimation — such an intimation! — but read for yourself.'

She handed to Mr Ellin an envelope; he took from it the returned note and a paper — the paper bore a hastily-scrawled line or two. It said, in brief terms, that there was no such place in Midland County as May Park, and that no such person had ever been heard of there as Conway Fitzgibbon, Esquire.

On reading this, Mr Ellin slightly opened his eyes.

'I hardly thought it was as bad as this,' said he.

'What! You did think it was bad then? You suspected that something was wrong?'

'Really! I scarcely knew what I thought or suspected. How very odd, no such place as May Park! The grand mansion, the oaks, the deer, vanished clean away. And then Fitzgibbon himself! But you saw Fitzgibbon — he came in his carriage?'

'In his carriage!' echoed Miss Wilcox; 'a most stylish equipage, and himself a most distinguished person. Do you think, after all, there is some mistake?'

'Certainly a mistake; but when it is rectified I don't think Fitzgibbon or May Park will be forthcoming. Shall I run down to Midland County and look after these two precious objects?'

'Oh! would you be so good, Mr Ellin? I knew you would be so kind; personal inquiry, you know — there's nothing like it.'

'Nothing at all. Meantime, what shall you do with the child — the pseudo-heiress, if pseudo she be? Shall you correct her — let her know her place?'

'I think,' responded Miss Wilcox, reflectively — 'I think not exactly as yet; my plan is to do nothing in a hurry; we will inquire first. If after all she should turn out to be connected as was at first

15

supposed, one had better not do anything which one might afterwards regret. No; I shall make no difference with her till I hear from you again.'

'Very good. As you please,' said Mr Ellin, with that coolness which made him so convenient a counsellor in Miss Wilcox's opinion. In his dry laconism she found the response suited to her outer worldliness. She thought he said enough if he did not oppose her. The comment he stinted so avariciously she did not want.

Mr Ellin 'ran down', as he said, to Midland County. It was an errand that seemed to suit him; for he had curious predilections as well as peculiar methods of his own. Any secret quest was to his taste; perhaps there was something of the amateur detective in him. He could conduct an inquiry and draw no attention. His quiet face never looked inquisitive, nor did his sleepless eye betray vigilance.

He was away about a week. The day after his return, he appeared in Miss Wilcox's presence as cool as if he had seen her but yesterday. Confronting her with that fathomless face he liked to show her, he first told her he had done nothing.

Let Mr Ellin be as enigmatical as he would, he never puzzled Miss Wilcox. She never saw enigma in the man. Some people feared, because they did not understand him; to her it had not yet occurred to begin to spell his nature or analyse his character. If she had an impression about him, it was that he was an idle but obliging man, not aggressive, of few words, but often convenient. Whether he were clever and deep, or deficient and shallow, close or open, odd or ordinary, she saw no practical end to be answered by inquiry, and therefore did not inquire.

'Why had he done nothing?' she now asked.

'Chiefly because there was nothing to do.'

'Then he could give her no information?'

'Not much: only this, indeed — Conway Fitzgibbon was a man of straw; May Park a house of cards. There was no vestige of such man or mansion in Midland County, or in any other shire in England. Tradition herself had nothing to say about either the name or the place. The Oracle of old deeds and registers, when consulted, had not responded.'

'Who can he be, then, that came here, and who is the child?'

'That's just what I can't tell you: an incapacity which makes me say I have done nothing.'

'And how am I to get paid?'

16

'Can't tell you that either.'

'A quarter's board and education owing, and masters' terms besides,' pursued Miss Wilcox. 'How infamous! I can't afford the loss.'

'And if we were only in the good old times,' said Mr Ellin, 'where we ought to be, you might just send Miss Matilda out to the plantations in Virginia, sell her for what she is worth, and pay yourself.'

'Matilda, indeed, and Fitzgibbon! A little impostor! I wonder what her real name is?'

'Betty Hodge? Poll Smith? Hannah Jones?' suggested Mr Ellin.

'Now,' cried Miss Wilcox, 'give me credit for sagacity! It's very odd, but try as I would — and made every effort — I never could really like that child. She has had every indulgence in the house; and I am sure I made great sacrifice of feeling to principle in showing her much attention; for I could not make any one believe the degree of antipathy I have all along felt towards her.'

'Yes. I can believe it. I saw it.'

'Did you? Well — it proves that my discernment is rarely at fault. Her game is up now, however; and time it was. I have said nothing to her yet; but now ——'

'Have her in while I am here,' said Mr Ellin. 'Has she known of this business? Is she in the secret? Is she herself an accomplice, or a mere tool? Have her in.'

Miss Wilcox rang the bell, demanded Matilda Fitzgibbon, and the false heiress soon appeared. She came in her ringlets, her sash, and her furbelowed dress adornments — alas! no longer acceptable.

'Stand there!' said Miss Wilcox, sternly, checking her as she approached the hearth. 'Stand there on the farther side of the table. I have a few questions to put to you, and your business will be to answer them. And mind — let us hear the truth. *We will not endure lies.*'

Ever since Miss Fitzgibbon had been found in the fit, her face had retained a peculiar paleness and her eyes a dark orbit. When thus addressed, she began to shake and blanch like conscious guilt personified.

'Who are you?' demanded Miss Wilcox. 'What do you know about yourself?'

A sort of half-interjection escaped the girl's lips; it was a sound expressing partly fear, and partly the shock the nerves feel when an evil, very long expected, at last and suddenly arrives.

'Keep yourself still, and reply, if you please,' said Miss Wilcox, whom nobody should blame for lacking pity, because nature had not made her compassionate. 'What is your name? We know you have no right to that of Matilda Fitzgibbon.'

She gave no answer.

'I do insist upon a reply. Speak you shall, sooner or later. So you had better do it at once.'

This inquisition had evidently a very strong effect upon the subject of it. She stood as if palsied, trying to speak, but apparently, not competent to articulate.

Miss Wilcox did not fly into a passion, but she grew very stern and urgent; spoke a little loud; and there was a dry clamour in her raised voice which seemed to beat upon the ear and bewilder the brain. Her interest had been injured — her pocket wounded — she was vindicating her rights — and she had no eye to see, and no nerve to feel, but for the point in hand. Mr Ellin appeared to consider himself strictly a looker-on; he stood on the hearth very quiet.

At last the culprit spoke. A low voice escaped her lips. 'Oh, my head!' she cried, lifting her hands to her forehead. She staggered, but caught the door and did not fall. Some accusers might have been startled by such a cry — even silenced; not so Miss Wilcox. She was neither cruel nor violent; but she was coarse, because insensible. Having just drawn breath, she went on, harsh as ever.

Mr Ellin, leaving the hearth, deliberately paced up the room as if he were tired of standing still, and would walk a little for a change. In returning and passing near the door and the criminal, a faint breath seemed to seek his ear, whispering his name —

'Oh, Mr Ellin!'

The child dropped as she spoke. A curious voice — not like Mr Ellin's, though it came from his lips — asked Miss Wilcox to cease speaking, and say no more. He gathered from the floor what had fallen on it. She seemed overcome, but not unconscious. Resting beside Mr Ellin, in a few minutes she again drew breath. She raised her eyes to him.

'Come, my little one, have no fear,' said he.

Reposing her head against him, she gradually became reassured. It did not cost him another word to bring her round, even the strong trembling was calmed by the mere effects of his protection. He told Miss Wilcox, with remarkable tranquillity, but still with a certain decision, that the little girl must be put to bed. He carried her upstairs, and saw her laid there himself.

Returning to Miss Wilcox, he said:

'Say no more to her. Beware, or you will do more mischief than you think or wish. That kind of nature is very different from yours. It is not possible that you should like it; but let it alone. We will talk more on the subject tomorrow. Let me question her.'

Chapter Three

Miss Wilcox granted Mr Ellin's request, though with visible reluctance. Leaving her to dismal ponderings on the duplicity of mankind, he made his way to my house, Silverlea Cottage, and asked me to do a certain charitable deed. Its nature astonished me not a little, yet it was necessary that I should give my consent at once; for the matter was urgent.

The prospect was so disturbing that it was fortunate I had small leisure to think during the rest of the day; for my time was fully occupied in making certain preparations. These at last completed, I waited apprehensively for what the future might bring.

Soon after breakfast on the morrow Mr Ellin again walked to Fuchsia Lodge in the keen December air. He had a short interview with Miss Wilcox, after which he sat waiting till the child should be brought to him.

She came, wearing the plainest of her dresses, her eyes red with weeping, her fingers twitching uneasily. He had already made sure that there had been no further questioning by Miss Wilcox; but he now perceived that he had not been able to protect the young impostor from a silence that had been, all too evidently, as alarming as the inquisition that had preceded it. At once he made up his mind how to deal with the situation.

'My dear,' he said, 'is there anything that you would like to tell me?'

She shook her head.

'Then I have a little plan to propose,' said Mr Ellin. 'You know that the other young ladies are going home for the holidays, and I believe the Misses Wilcox would like to make holiday too, with no pupils to care for. So a good friend of mine has offered to let you spend the holiday season in her pleasant home, where no one will ask you any questions that you do not wish to answer. The lady is known to you by sight; for her pew in church is near yours.'

As if painfully taken aback, she asked timidly, 'Is that the lady who has never seen her stepchildren?'

Mr Ellin recollected having heard gossip during one of the Misses Wilcox's tea-parties at which the petted parlour boarder had been present, a silent listener to a conversation that he, thinking it injudicious and injurious, had done his best to suppress.

'Do not be afraid,' he said. 'Mrs Chalfont is kindness itself. She was in no way to blame for her stepchildren's unwarrantable behaviour. Will you come?'

Almost inaudibly she murmured, 'Yes.'

Rising, he took her hand. The twitching fingers lay still. They left the house together, and together they came to my door.

'Why, what is this?' I cried as I welcomed them; 'Mr Ellin, I declare you have brought this poor child here without waiting for her to put on her bonnet and cloak!'

'Upon my word, I believe I have!' said Mr Ellin. 'Have her to the fire as quickly as you can, Mrs Chalfont. Dear, dear, what a consummate piece of carelessness! Will you forgive me, Matilda?'

She looked up at him, and something resembling a smile quivered on her swollen and disfigured countenance. There was no answer in words; but she suffered herself to be placed in a chair, and Mr Ellin and I sat down beside her. Hot soup had been prepared in advance. It was now brought in, and we all partook of it. I was pleased to see that the child's face presently assumed a more composed expression; and she showed amusement at the antics of my cat, an animal so much indulged that it ventured to display indignation at the sight of Mr Ellin seated in its favourite chair. Finally, when glaring eyes and waving tail had failed of their purpose, Mrs Pussy must needs jump into the chair behind the usurper; and with paws pressed firmly into his back, she did her feline best to push him off.

'Ah, it is plain that I have outstayed my welcome,' he said as he rose.

The child also started to her feet. She uttered no word, but stood trembling, with one little hand put out as if to detain him. Her eyes, though not her lips, told her dread of being left alone with me.

He patted the hand gently. 'My dear, you are safe now, quite, quite safe. Mrs Chalfont has kindly promised that I may look in this afternoon to drink tea with you both. In the meantime I shall ride to Barlton Market to make important purchases in the fine shops there. Have you any commands for me?'

Uncertain of his meaning, she remained silent.

'Would you like me to buy you sugar-plums or burnt almonds or white peppermints?'

He had no answer, other than a doleful shake of the head.

'What! do you prefer those huge black aniseed balls that Dame Pettigrew sells in her little shop?'

Now he won first a shudder of distaste and then a genuine childish smile. 'Not aniseed balls, if you please,' she said in a whisper.

He was gone. I drew my young visitor back to the fire, feeling at a loss how to open and maintain a conversation. She seemed, however, content to sit without speaking. Her dress, I noticed, though of fine material, had recently been badly stained by some mishap with an ink-bottle. Taking up my work, I busied myself with it; and for a while no sound was heard save the crackling of apple logs and the purring of Pussy as she sang her song of triumph over the foe she believed herself to have vanquished.

The hour for our mid-day repast was approaching. I stood up and summoned Matilda. 'Come,' I said, as cheerfully as I could. 'You will like to see your room.'

She obeyed, moving like a mechanical toy.

A small guest room had been prepared over-night for her reception; one of its two doors opened into mine. Her dull eye kindled as she beheld pink curtains, snow-white bed, pictures and ornaments. A hanging bookshelf held some of my childhood's favourites. I took one down at random. 'Have you read *A Puzzle for a Curious Girl*, Matilda?'

'No, Ma'am.' The voice, gruff and low, had become distinct.

'If you like, I will read it to you this afternoon. It is no weather for a walk, even had not that naughty Mr Ellin brought you here without any outdoor clothes.'

I was delighted to hear a whispered protest. 'No, no, not naughty! Kind and — and *quick!*'

So might one exclaim who had escaped from a prison-house. I did not answer, but smiled an acceptance of the reproof. As we were about to leave the room, I caught sight of an object that had formed no part of my preparations for the visitor: it was a small old travelling-trunk.

'Miss Fitzgibbon's things,' said Eliza, appearing. 'Miss Wilcox sent the box an hour ago, and I got Larry to carry it upstairs.'

I concealed my surprise at the excessive shabbiness of the

receptacle, agreeing as it did so ill with Miss Fitzgibbon's finery and fandangles. Turning to her, I said, 'Shall we unpack the box together, my dear, and arrange your clothes in nice order? Then you will feel quite at home.'

A suppressed cry broke from the child. 'That is not my box!' I raised the lid. 'Nor are those my clothes!'

Her face was grey; her hands were tightly clasped. Eliza drew me aside. 'I did hear, Ma'am, from Jemima, her that is servant at the school, that one of the young ladies has grown so fast that her mamma, coming this morning to take her home for the holidays, left some cast-off clothes behind for Miss Wilcox to give to a poor child.'

Eliza and I looked at each other, and I saw that she knew the whole story of Miss Fitzgibbon's downfall. It was manifest to us both that in the absence of other payment, Miss Wilcox had impounded the heiress's wardrobe to supply her lawful dues.

'They are Miss Diana Green's clothes,' Eliza whispered.

If anything could have added to my embarrassment, it was the sight of my young visitor forlornly examining the contents of the box in the vain hope of finding something of her own among the discards of her schoolfellow. The unrewarding search revealed a scanty dole of such garments as were strictly necessary. They included a nightgown with a long rent in it, evidently the result of some heedless frolic. Like the other articles of clothing, it was as much too big for Matilda as it was too small for Diana.

I took the child's hand and led her from the room. 'We shall have to talk to Mr Ellin about this,' I observed. 'There is a mistake somewhere, but Mr Ellin will set it right, never fear.'

In so speaking, I confess to a measure of duplicity; for I did not well see what Mr Ellin could do to remedy matters. Matilda's faith was greater than mine. Her countenance relaxed, the dark shade of misery left it.

I brought her downstairs and once again established her in a chair by the fire for the short time remaining before my early dinner.

With a book of engravings on her lap, she sat gazing into the flames, and only roused herself now and then to turn over a page on which she did not bestow a glance. However, we dined together more sociably than might have been expected from two persons whose subjects of conversation were strictly limited. She had already heard the names of Jane and Eliza and of my man-servant-gardener, Larry; but I was able to make small talk about a third maid, the aged Annie, who, after many years of faithful service in our family, lived a retired life in her own little parlour and bedchamber. Like my own mother, Annie hailed from distant Cornwall, and she was one of the few remaining speakers of the Cornish language. Did Matilda know that Cornwall had once a language of its own, which was now lost because English had taken its place?

No, Matilda had never heard of the submerged land of Lyonesse or of the forgotten language of Cornwall. I quoted two or three words to her, having picked them up from Annie in my childhood. Annie's name for a frog, 'quilquin', led naturally to mention of my garden, where, I said, we should at present find nothing save fragrant wintersweet, spotted laurels and scarlet holly-berries. But it would not be long before we should be looking for golden aconites, fair maids of February, hyacinths, crocuses, violets, primroses. I met a questioning frown.

' "Fair maids of February"?' the child repeated.

'It is another name for snowdrops,' I told her, adding on I know not what impulse, 'Are you, then, a fair maid of February? I mean, my dear, does your birthday fall in that month? I understand that you are not far off ten years old.'

She hesitated, as if uncertain whether she was permitted to answer. At last — 'Yes, I shall be ten on February the eleventh. But I am not fair. I have brown hair and brown eyes.'

'That does not matter,' I said lightly. 'Any nut-brown maid born in February is entitled to rank as one of February's fair maids.'

The faint dawning of a smile showed itself on her face; and I felt thankful that I had refrained from uttering the first thought that came into my head: I have seen you looking like a snowdrop. It would have been cruel to remind the child that in church only last Sunday she had been resplendent in white furs, whereas she now possessed but an inkstained frock and the outworn, outgrown clothes of her less-than-friend Diana.

During the rest of the meal my mind was at work on the problem presented by those same articles of clothing. Obviously I could not, without an unseemly altercation, demand of Miss Wilcox that the child's own clothes should be returned to her; but neither could I force the poor victim of circumstances to be metamorphosed into Diana Green. Might not such a proceeding cause her to fall once more into that strange trance-like state that had twice disrupted her school life? On the other hand, could I be expected to provide a complete set of new clothes for a little girl who might shortly be removed from my care by the appearance of either the missing parent or of some other responsible person? I came at last to the conclusion that it would be well to take counsel with Eliza and Jane, on whose native wit I knew I could depend.

I kept my promise to read aloud *A Puzzle for a Curious Girl*. At first Matilda listened with some show of interest; but as soon as her head drooped over the arm of her fireside chair, I slipped away to the kitchen, where Eliza and Jane lent a ready ear to my perplexities. Both were willing — nay, eager — to help me in the shortening and repairing of the various articles of clothing. Eliza promised that, using some magic remedy of her own, she would so deal with the inkstained frock that nobody would be able to detect the damage. Jane had an aunt in the village who could do wonders with dyes extracted by a secret formula from blackberries, onions and such common plants as the willow herb. Holding up a tumbled and dirty white muslin dress, she declared that it would emerge a thing of soft pink beauty after it had been treated with aunt's dye culled from the roots of lady's bedstraw.

Much relieved in mind, I left the two good creatures busy over the bundle of garments. Returning to my charge, I found her fast asleep.

My entrance did not rouse her from what was all too plainly the slumber of exhaustion. I sat long in the twilight of that December afternoon, studying the child so strangely committed to my keeping. Her attitude, now deprived of her stiff finery, was one of careless grace.

The curtains were drawn and the tea equipage placed on the table before Miss Fitzgibbon awoke and started up in alarm and bewilderment. I hastened to reassure her; and she sank back contentedly as she felt the warmth of the glowing fire, saw the lamplight gleaming on silver and china, smelt the aroma of teacakes toasting on the hearth, and heard the kettle hissing and Pussy purring.

Prompt to the hour entered Mr Ellin, a paper of sugar-plums in his hand and two parcels under his arm. Depositing his burdens on a chair, he accepted a cup of tea. Miss Fitzgibbon ate and drank and watched him with a very bright eye.

When the tray had been carried off, he directed our attention to the two parcels, which, he averred, had been the reason for his taking a ride to Barlton Market on such a cold frosty afternoon. Handing the sugar-plums and the smaller parcel to Miss Fitzgibbon, he told her that he had found a young friend for her in the town.

She guessed at once what manner of 'young friend' this must be, and her fingers trembled with eagerness as she pulled off the wrappings. Behold, then, a particularly choice specimen of doll-anity, a splendid waxen beauty, airily clad in a long white chemise. 'Oh!' cried little miss, in a rapture. 'Oh-h, Mr Ellin! Thank you, thank you a thousand times!'

'And here,' said Mr Ellin, patting the larger parcel, 'is stuff to make the little lady a dress and cloak. I told the shop people to put up what she would require.'

I opened the parcel, which contained, as may be surmised, enough material to clothe someone much bigger than Miss Dolly. Out came blue velvet for a dress and blue cloth for a cloak. Miss Fitzgibbon stared, and then her features relaxed in the second real smile we had seen. Still hugging her doll, she turned to me: 'Mrs Chalfont,' she cried, 'see what Mr Ellin has done! He can have had no notion how much a doll would need for her frock and cloak — and he has bought enough for me as well as for her!'

'I am but a poor ignorant bachelor,' said Mr Ellin, with a droll look at me. 'However, it was a fortunate mistake; for now mamma and daughter will be dressed alike, and the effect should be very pleasing.'

Plainly, Miss Fitzgibbon thought so too. She sat gently cradling her doll, all smiles.

'What name shall you give her?' Mr Ellin asked. 'Louisa, Georgina, Arabella, or ——?'

It struck me — and my guess proved to be correct — that Mr Ellin's motive for purchasing the doll was two-fold. It was to be used in a crafty attempt to find out whether Matilda Fitzgibbon was the false name Miss Wilcox took it to be. There would be, Mr Ellin thought, some slight self-consciousness on Matilda's part if he should chance to include her own Chrstian name in the list he was preparing to rattle off.

He was immediately thwarted in his cunning device. Without the smallest hesitation, Miss Fitzgibbon answered, 'Either Ellen or Elinor.'

'Oho!' quoth Mr Ellin, disconcerted, but with a laughing glance in my direction. 'So you are going to saddle the poor doll with my ugly name?'

'It is not an ugly name,' protested Miss Fitzgibbon; 'it is the best name in the world.'

'Mrs Chalfont's is prettier,' said bold Mr Ellin.

'What is it?'

'Arminel.'

I did not choose to inquire how he came to know that. Miss Fitzgibbon considered the matter. 'My doll shall have two names: Arminel and Ellen or Elinor. Which shall I choose?'

He decided in favour of Elinor, which — as I noted thankfully — was a trifle further removed from his own name. Then he tried another way of obtaining the desired information. 'By the way,' he said carelessly, 'I remember that in my schooldays I was allowed to take a "playbox" to school with me. It was always crammed with everything I thought likely to be useful to me, from a cake to a catapult. But perhaps young ladies do not take playboxes to school?'

She said, with a sudden catching of the breath, 'Diana, Mary, Jessy, they all had playboxes.'

'But not you?'

She hesitated, flinched, looked dolorous enough.

'Because,' said Mr Ellin, watching her closely, 'I hardly think Miss Wilcox would wish to retain your playbox if you had one. How could she dispose of it — what dealer in second-hand goods would be likely to purchase a little girl's playthings?'

(He had earlier been informed by Miss Wilcox that Diana Green's old clothes had been sent to Silverlea Cottage and Matilda's finery and trinkets kept back to be sold as soon as was legally possible.)

'I — I do not know,' Matilda faltered.

'Perhaps,' he suggested, 'she would sell it to me. Then you could have it back again.'

Matilda's eyes filled with tears. 'Miss Wilcox has not got it. She never had it. He said I must leave it ——'

There was a sound of sobbing, as over the memory of a long-past grief.

'At home?'

'No, at ——' Again the pause, the hesitation. Then, dashing away the tears, she spoke in evident breach of the rule of secrecy that had been imposed on her. — 'At an inn on the journey to school. Because the carriage was overloaded, he said. But it was not heavy. It was a little box.'

Impossible to judge whether the excuse given had been the

true one, or whether the box had been abandoned because it contained clues to the child's identity. Mr Ellin went on with his questioning

'Oh, at an inn? Do you recollect the name?'

It was evident that she did. We saw her sorely tempted to reveal it; but mingled fear and prudence kept her from speaking. Mr Ellin asked no more. Of what use to trouble the child when the landlord of the inn had doubtless sold or thrown on the rubbish-heap the goods left behind by a passing traveller?

She had evidently understood what would be the fate of her treasures; for she turned her face away and sat pensively looking into the red-gold fairy castles and mountains of the fire, her whole person expressive of resignation. Mr Ellin and I chatted awhile on indifferent subjects till he took his leave.

The winter night closed in. Matilda rose submissively when I proposed her early retirement. She was soon bestowed in the little white bed where I left her, not without secret misgivings that she might run away in the night. But whither could she flee, homeless fledgling that she was?

I need not have feared. When I went to her later, there remained traces of the tears she had shed but the child was sleeping peacefully. Elinor-Arminel was seated on a chair drawn close to the bedside, clad now in a knitted neck-shawl of mine, lest she should take cold in her chemise.

Chapter Four

Eliza had been all impatience for the moment when Miss Fitzgibbon's frock should be handed over to her for the process of restoration, and by some hidden art Matilda breakfasted next morning in a dress as good as new. I thought then, and have continued to think, that this was a vital step in giving her back a sense of self-respect, although it could not contribute to solving the puzzle of her identity.

After breakfast I asked her help in packing up Christmas gifts for the old and poor among our neighbours, and I left her pleasantly employed in stitching a petticoat I had cut out for Elinor while I went out to deliver them. I returned two hours later to hear a hectoring voice in my parlour. Jane, much distressed, informed me that Miss Wilcox had, as she expressed it, 'pushed her way in', insisting that she be allowed to speak to Miss Fitzgibbon.

I entered the room to find Miss Wilcox haranguing the terrified child. In her hand she held a magnificent gold serpent-bangle, a costly but somehow unpleasing object with flaming ruby eyes. 'Now,' she was declaiming, 'you cannot hope to escape by lies or sullen silence. Here is your Christian name engraved on this bangle, which you had deliberately concealed in the secret drawer of your jewel case. You are Emma, Emma, Emma — you cannot deny it! What is your surname, and where do you live? Speak! Do you wish me to call the constable?'

The child screamed out in a panic, 'Mr Ellin, Mr Ellin — oh, come!'

'None of that!' the woman said coarsely. 'He is not here to defend you — he has ridden out beyond reach of your wailings. Tell me —'

'What is this?' I exclaimed indignantly. 'Miss Wilcox, pray restrain yourself. I cannot tolerate such behaviour in my house.'

She turned on me. 'See here,' she cried, showing the snake-bracelet. 'It was pushed cleverly out of sight, but I found it, engraved with her name, Emma. I shall insist on hearing the truth, whether in your house or out of it. Now, Emma, speak!'

'I am not Emma,' gasped the child. 'Not — not — not!' She beat her hands together, sobbing and screaming. Miss Wilcox towered above her, implacable as ever. Short of taking our unwelcome visitor by the shoulders and forcibly ejecting her, I could do nothing save draw Matilda protectingly to me, while trying in vain to hush the strident sounds proceeding from the mouth of the girl's ex-preceptress.

Powerless also was the child, who, seeing no way to free herself from her tormentor, cried out in partial surrender. 'Not Emma! I am *Martina* ——'

And there she stopped in terror and dismay. Not a word more would she utter; I think no power on earth could have forced her to reveal the surname. I felt the shaking and quivering of her frame; and with a resolution of which I had not believed myself capable, I bade Miss Wilcox leave us. She marched off, bracelet in hand, pale with anger, baffled when she thought victory was within her grasp.

I sank down on the sofa, my arm about the child, calming her as best I could. When her agitation permitted, I slipped away to pen a note to Mr Ellin, informing him of what had taken place. He came as soon as he had returned from his ride.

'Well,' he said cheerfully, 'so there has been a mighty tempest in a tea-cup, has there not? And so your Christian name is Martina? Don't be frightened — Mrs Chalfont and I are not going to ask what your surname is. I'll tell you a piece of news — we both like the name "Martina" a great deal better than "Matilda". And I will venture a guess that at home you were usually called "Tina". Whether you were or not, that's what I intend to call you in future.' He turned to me, 'Mrs Chalfont, I'm sure you are not one of those disagreeable people who disapprove of nicknames and pet names and shortened names. I had an old aunt who never would address me as "Willie" when I was a little boy. She always called me "William", which she pronounced as "Will-yum". I did not like it. Little girl, shall you object if we call you "Tina"?'

Martina looked up. Her wet eyes were shining. 'No, I like to be "Tina".'

'And you won't cry any more for your snake-bracelet?'

Drawing herself up, the mite answered proudly, 'I never did cry for it. I hated the horrid thing. It was hidden because I disliked it, not because I tried to hide it from Miss Wilcox.'

'Ah, that is good hearing. Forget what has happened as fast as you can. If you find yourself thinking about it, try to remember that Miss Wilcox is sadly in need of money just now. She has to pay the salaries and wages of a good many persons, besides the rates and taxes and household bills — and I am afraid that you will find money troubles are apt to make grown-up people very cross!'

Tina drew a small purse from the pocket of her frock. 'See, I have six shillings. It would have been more, but all the Misses Wilcox had birthdays one after the other, and the school had to give them presents. Diana said I was the richest, so I must give most. Would six shillings help to pay the bills?'

'Undoubtedly it would,' Mr Ellin answered gravely, 'but your papa would not wish you to be deprived of your pocket-money, my child. Until we hear from him, I am well able to advance what Miss Wilcox may require to meet her immediate liabilities. Put away your purse, forgive those harsh words, and be glad in the remembrance that tomorrow is Christmas Day when everybody is or should be joyful. Do you know why?'

She had been well taught, whether by Mr Cecil or some other did not appear. 'We are joyful because on Christmas Day we celebrate the birthday of our Saviour, the Lord Jesus Christ.'

'Very good,' said Mr Ellin. 'Now you must put away sad thoughts and prepare to celebrate. A joyous Christmas to you both!'

He withdrew, leaving sunshine where there had been gloom. The recovery of Tina's spirits was materially aided by the unexpected arrival of a cumbersome wicker basket, brought to my door in a wheelbarrow by a boy messenger, who thus delivered himself, 'Please, Ma'am, Mrs Smyly's compliments and she regrets she has been obliged to send you the missionary basket a fortnight too soon as she has been summoned away of a sudden to nurse a sick relative.'

With tugging and puffing, the huge object was deposited in the parlour; it was tall enough and capacious enough to have housed one of Ali Baba's forty thieves. I saw the unspoken question in Tina's eyes and explained to her that the missionary basket was a useful means of providing money to be used for the benefit of the heathen in countries far away. It was filled with saleable articles by the ladies of the parish, whose duty it was to keep, by turns, the basket for one month. During this time the basket-keeper sold what she could to her friends before sending the basket to the lady whose name stood next on the list.

I rose and took from a cupboard my own contributions to the basket. These I laid on a large round table, congratulating myself on the forethought that had made me prepare them in advance. 'Come,' I said to Tina, 'the books and ornaments must be cleared from the table to make room for a display. If we leave everything in the basket, nobody will know what there is for sale. I have no doubt the basket has been seen trundling down the road from Mrs Smyly's house. That means the ladies will soon be arriving here to buy last-minute Christmas gifts. Will you help me?'

Nothing could have pleased Tina better than to dive head-first into the basket and fetch out the miscellanea it contained. Dolmans, night-caps, egg cosies, dahlia pen-wipers, mittens, aprons, bouquets of paper flowers — all had to be judged by us as to their fitness for making a show on the big table or on a smaller one over which I asked Tina to preside. A distinct look of gratification answered my request; and she lost no time in setting afoot a grand process of rearrangement, in the course of which she discarded almost everything she and I had previously selected, in favour of new treasures fished up from the basket. Leaving her to her own devices, I sought advice from Jane and Eliza about the provision of refreshment for an unknown number of customers. So near Christmas, they would certainly expect to be hospitably entertained — but how were we to know whether their numbers would be large or small? The unlooked for arrival of the missionary basket had left scant time for providing the kind of fare they would expect: we could only hope that the pastry cook had not sold everything he had. Jane went flying down the road and returned, beaming, with a bountiful supply of shortbread and fancy cakes; Eliza baked scones with a will; Larry hastened to the farm for more milk.

I need not have feared that we should be left with a surplus of food on our hands. Early in the afternoon the doorbell began to ring, nor did it cease ringing till darkness fell. But before the first tinkle was heard, old Annie, leaning on her silver-topped ebony stick, had ensconced herself in a fireside chair; and Jane and Eliza — as they well deserved — were enjoying 'first pick' of the array on the tables. Tina watched them for a minute or two; then I heard a timid, 'Mrs Chalfont, pray might I buy some things too?'

On my assenting, she choose five articles, the total cost of which amounted to the six shillings in her purse. I wondered what she could want with two embroidered needlecases, one particularly hideous pincushion, an elaborately worked watch-pocket and a box decorated with painted and varnished sea-shells. She vouchsafed no word as to their destination, but put them out of sight on a shelf in the bookcase, and went to stand in readiness behind her table. Hardly had she reached her station when the first instalment of my fellow-parishioners came flocking in, so powdered with snow that I inwardly rejoiced at my own forethought in protecting the parlour carpet with newspapers. I hope I do not wrong my friends by a suspicion that some of them were prompted not so much by missionary zeal as by a desire to inspect at close quarters the erstwhile heiress, rumours of whose story had already begun to circulate. Many curious and significant glances were exchanged; many whispered comments were heard. The latter, I was happy to note, were without exception favourable. Indeed, Mrs Runnacles went so far as to say that nobody would have believed that the sulky grandee of Fuchsia Lodge could change herself into the demure little saleswoman of Silverlea Cottage.

Happily, Tina heeded not the glances and the whispers: her whole attention was given to the satisfying of her customers' wants, diversified by dips into that Aladdin's cave, the basket, for the purpose of replenishing her stores. Only the entrance of Mr Cecil and his friend Mr Ellin proved to be a magnet powerful enough to distract her from her duties. Her eyes followed them as they made their way across the room.

Like the other buyers, they had come to fill gaps in their supply of Christmas gifts, and Mr Cecil was especially anxious to find a warm wrap for a needy widow in the village.

They moved on to Tina's table after I had provided a red and black crossover for the widow and sundry fleecy comforts for the old people in the almshouses. A set of collar-and-cuffs worked by me in perforated linen had been much admired but rejected as too expensive by the frugal-minded. This, with a flower-vase mat in blue and crystal beads, now formed the table's principal adornments. When Mr Cecil bought the mat, I caught a sibilant whisper of *Miss Mabel Wilcox* issuing from I know not whose lips. Tina heard it too. With deft movement she concealed the collar-and-cuffs under a chairback cover in drab and claret Berlin wool. I was not slow to appreciate the meaning of this manoeuvre. Obviously she had been the silent listener to gossip in which Mr Ellin's name had been mentioned as well as Mr Cecil's; and she had resolved in her small mind that my collar-and-cuffs should not go to grace Miss Wilcox's person.

I hoped that Mr Ellin had not seen what she did or guessed why she did it. His chameleon eyes warned me that my hopes were vain. A green gleam of intelligence was shot forth from them, and they then became very blue and merry. 'What are you hiding under that woolly creation, Tina?' he asked. 'Fetch it out, whatever it is. I am looking for a gift for my sister, whose birthday is on New Year's Day.'

Tina could not quite hide her look of relief at which his eyes twinkled more merrily than ever. She drew the chairback cover aside. 'Mrs Chalfont made them. They are very beautiful and quite suitable for your sister — but they are rather costly, the ladies say.'

'And you think I have spent all my money?' said Mr Ellin. 'I have a little left, and with great care I believe I shall be able to afford the price.'

He carried off the collar-and-cuffs, wrapped in silver paper; and from that moment I was convinced — if indeed I needed any convincing — that he had never attended Miss Wilcox's social occasions in the character of suitor, but only as a sociably-disposed lonely man who had undertaken to keep his friend, Mr Cecil, in countenance.

Before he left us, I was pleased to see him greeting Annie in friendly fashion as she sat surveying the lively scene. On his asking how she felt, she answered, a little strangely, 'Well in health, Sir, well in health, but puzzled. Aye, puzzled. I am old, and old folk are easily bewildered. Tell me, is that one of Mrs Chalfont's nieces that I see yonder? Little Miss Margaret, say, or Miss Bertha?'

'Why, no,' Mr Ellin answered, 'you are forgetting, Annie. That is the child who is staying with Mrs Chalfont till her father claims her. Martina Fitzgibbon is her name.'

'So it is, so it is,' assented Annie. 'Like enough, the noise of people talking has confused me. As I said, I puzzle easily, being old.'

She was soon restored to the quiet of her own parlour; for in no long time the last cake had been eaten, the last cup of tea drunk, and the basket was standing completely empty. Amid laughter and clapping Mr Cecil counted twelve pounds into a black silk shoe-bag, one of his purchases. Mr Ellin, who had remained to the end, offered to act as police-escort to Mr Cecil's lodgings, lest any robbers should be lying in wait to snatch so magnificent a sum.

Much merriment had been caused by my buying the last three articles in the basket, these having remained unsold — as we all knew — for some years. One was a squat strip of crochet about eighteen inches long, serving no useful purpose that anyone could detect. Equally useless were a broad piece of yellow ribbon and an extraordinary contraption of fur, felt and feathers, the nature of which remained a mystery.

'What are you going to do with them?' Tina asked, when the parlour had been restored to order after the departure of the guests. I was adjusting the sprigs of holly in a great bowl of Christmas greens; and she, having fetched her purchases out of hiding, was wrapping them in left-over scraps of silver paper.

'Wait and see,' was my answer. 'It is a Christmas secret.'

'I like *Christmas* secrets,' said Tina, with a marked emphasis on the word.

She went on with her work. The pincushion, I guessed, was for Annie, the needlecases for Jane and Eliza; and the watch-pocket and shell-box could only be meant for Mr Ellin and me. A shade of anxiety showed in her face as she stood contemplating the results of her labours. 'Shall I see Mr Ellin tomorrow?'

'No, I think not. You cannot come to Church with me as your cloak will not be ready for at least a week. But you have a gift for him, have you not? If you entrust it to me, I will ask one of the servants to deliver it.'

She gave one of her little parcels into my hand. The others we bestowed on a table where my household gifts were awaiting the simple festivities of Christmas Day.

These were heralded, according to custom, by the arrival of the carol-singers with their bobbing lantern. In they presently came, muffled to the ears, in hearty voice, to be regaled with mince pies, sausage rolls, cheesecakes and cocoa, and to be rewarded with silver coins. A little later, I was alone.

Chapter Five

I was sorry to be alone. Ever since the visit of Miss Wilcox with the snake-bracelet I had been troubled by an inrush of the disturbing thoughts, the dismal unwanted recollections which for five years I had been striving to bury deep within me; I could not hope to banish them forever. While in congenial company I had been able to keep these memories at bay; but in the silence of the night they pressed hard on me and I had little strength against them.

To defeat the enemy, I called in my grand ally, Work. Doll Elinor's blue velvet frock had been begun the night before, but I had doubts whether I could finish it in time to ensure that she should present a respectable appearance on Christmas Day. It was wise, therefore, to provide a quickly-made substitute; and this I proposed to do with the aid of the last three articles from the missionary basket. The strip of crochet needed no more than a seam and a threaded waist-ribbon to turn it into a skirt; the broad yellow ribbon could be folded into the semblance of a bodice, all deficiencies being concealed under my neck-shawl; and a few stitches, cunningly placed, would transform the fur-felt-and-feathers into a jaunty hat.

The task was accomplished in less than twenty minutes, after which I set about the making of the blue frock with a will. But though my fingers never ceased to fly throughout those hours, my grand ally miserably failed me in my bitter need. It could do nothing to drive from my mind the word that tortured me. That word was *Emma! Emma! Emma!* pronounced in tones of triumph by Miss Wilcox, and by Martina in shuddering repulsion and despair.

Emma! Emma! Emma!

The name rang out like a knell.

In vain I tried to shut my eyes to the intruding visions that were thereby called into life. My pleasant holly-trimmed parlour faded from my sight; it resolved itself into an open chaise in which I, a seventeen-year-old bride of a few hours, was being driven by my husband to my future home. Mr Ashley Chalfont was a widower, twenty-five years older than I, awe-inspiring in his stern composure. Never having met unkindness from living soul, I was quite undaunted by the knowledge that four stepchildren would be waiting to greet me. Indeed, I looked on them almost in the light of playfellows, so young was I, so pitifully young.

Night was closing in ; dark clouds were hanging above the vast dreary moorland over which we were passing, its purples and duns and olives all subdued to a universal grey. Suddenly, from behind a belt of wind-swept trees, I saw a great black object emerging. A moment later it had taken shape as a ponderous coach, driven at a reckless pace, swaying to left and right as it came. With a horrified exclamation my husband drew the chaise close to the side of the road, where he had much difficulty in controlling the horses, which, like ourselves, had been startled by the apparition. Lurching and plunging and almost scraping us, the great clumsy vehicle went by. I had a momentary glimpse of the driver, an oafish grinning fellow, by whose side stood rather than sat a young girl with dark hair wildly waving as she urged the horses on.

My husband saw neither the girl nor the driver: his attention was wholly given to mastering our own horses and soothing their fears. Having succeeded in quieting them he turned to look at the vehicle, now almost out of sight. 'Upon my word, I believe it is the old funeral coach that serves Grewby and the neighbouring villages,' said he; 'and driven, it seems likely, by the undertaker's son, who is not much better than a half-wit. What can Jones be thinking of, to let that dolt of a Billy loose on the roads at this hour? I shall speak to him tomorrow. A girl with him, do you say? Nothing more likely! — and she'll be lucky if she returns home with a whole bone in her body! If I were her father, I would give her — as the country folk say — "a word of a sort".'

The funeral coach went swaying, bumping and rattling into the darkness. As he gave the horses the signal to proceed, I heard a short, angry laugh from Mr Chalfont. I saw nothing to laugh at. A violent fit of shivering had seized me, and with it came a curious, inexplicable sense of desolation. What was I doing, I asked myself, driving over a lonely moor with this man, this stranger?

For I had listened to my parents' assurances that Ashley Chalfont was an excellent man. Universally respected, known far and wide as a humane landlord, he was the very man to whom they, elderly and infirm, could safely entrust their beloved youngest child. I knew nothing of love other than the love of family and friends — how should I, so recently a denizen of the schoolroom, the playfellow and companion of my eldest brother's children? Desiring to please and gratify my dearest father and mother, I had found it easy enough to persuade myself that a mixture of awe, admiration and respect was all that was required of a wife. I was flattered, too, by Mr Chalfont's choice of me — why, none of my sisters had been married as young as seventeen! Now, in the twinkling of an eye, the sight of that funeral coach had rendered me a prey to doubts, uncertainties, nervous fears. My husband did not appear to remark my depression of spirits; he drove on without speaking, save when from time to time he roused himself to point out some noticeable feature — historical, architectural or geographical — of the scene before us. Perhaps he, too, had been perturbed by the almost spectral vision of the funeral coach, taking it for an ill omen — I do not know.

We left the moor at long, long last, and entered a neat, orderly village with an aspect of pervading grey. Roads, house walls, garden walls, the very trees bore the same sombre hue. Greyer still were the dark slate roofs, this material being — as my husband observed with satisfaction — healthier and cleaner than thatch. At the end of the village stood the grey church in a churchyard well supplied with yews and other doleful trees. Among them, I dimly perceived a white building, semi-classical in style. 'The family mausoleum, built by my grandfather,' said my husband, who then went on to tell of his difficulty in persuading the older villagers to stop drawing water from a well in the churchyard. Though many years had passed since he provided a proper and ample alternative, they crept back with their pails as soon as a venturesome spirit had removed his sealing devices. 'I have given up my padlocks in despair,' said he. 'They must poison themselves if they choose.'

Pleasant topics these, for a home-coming conversation! I was thankful that at this moment the road curved to shut out church and churchyard. Before us, pillared entrance-gates were swung wide by the lodge-keeper. 'Grewby Towers, my dear,' said Mr Chalfont.

A stately pile confronted us, its towers and turrets gilded by the light of a moon unpleasingly orange rather than silver. As we drew up in front of the pillared portico, an owl hooted again and again.

Starting back affrighted, I saw to my horror, the dusky wings of bats wheeling and whirring about us.

A groom ran forward to take charge of the horses. Opening doors revealed brightness and glow within. But there was no sound of welcome in the babel of agitated voices that met us as we made our way into the vast hall. The assembled servants were not drawn up in line to greet us, but huddled together in groups. 'O Sir,' I heard on all sides, 'O Sir, the children have run away!'

My husband's voice rang out above the hubbub. 'Run away? *Run away?*'

Again the babel, with one word predominant — Emma — Emma — Emma!

Miss Emma led her brothers on, Sir. They would never have thought of it, much less done it, but for her. She commanded Gregson to bring out the coach and drive them to their grand-parents; but he refused flat, saying he would do nothing without your orders, Sir . . .'

'Miss Emma stamped her foot, Sir, and called Mr Gregson all manner of names . . .'

'When Miss Emma found she could not get her way with Gregson, she ran off in a passion. We thought that was the end of the affair . . .'

'But Miss Emma wasn't to be defeated. She stole down secretly to undertaker Jones's place and bribed Billy to take out the funeral coach unknown to his father. Mr Jones was almost beside himself when he found out what had happened. He came up here, trembling all over, to tell us what his lad had done . . .'

'They left the house casual-like and went down to Pennyquick Lane. Goody Norkins saw them getting into the coach, but she reckoned it wasn't her place to stop them having a bit of fun. The truth, of course, she did not know. And when we found out, it was too late . . .'

They gabbled on like machines set in motion, now defending themselves against possible charges of negligence or inactivity, now assuring their master that no power on earth could have prevented those children from doing as Miss Emma bade. 'Where are the tutor and the governess?' thundered my husband as soon as he could make himself heard above the din. 'Did Mr Harland and Miss Lefroy know nothing of all this? Why are they not here?'

All speaking at once, the servants reminded him that he had sent word that the children were to enjoy a whole holiday on the day of his marriage. Miss Lefroy was visiting friends at a distance, and the tutor had taken himself off, no one knew where.

Mr Chalfont did not waste time in multiplying questions and apportioning blame. His decision was instantly taken. 'Fresh horses for the chaise at once!' he directed. There followed a pushing and scampering in the little crowd. The old butler pressed forward, urging the wisdom of taking some refreshment before setting forth in pursuit. Mr Chalfont waved him aside. Addressing me, he said, 'If I start at once, it is possible that I may be in time to avert the otherwise inevitable accident.'

'Take me with you,' I cried. 'Yes, yes, we will go together. They shall see that a stepmother is not such a very formidable being —'

He cut me short in my eager pleadings. 'No, I shall go alone. Pray do not argue. Expect me some time tomorrow, I cannot say precisely when.'

'Expect you — you only? Not the children? Surely you will bring them back?'

'Only if they wish to come.'

His manner was aloof, his speech abrupt: it was as though he held me in some way responsible for the children's flight. Hostile also were the faces around me. Panic-stricken, I recoiled from the prospect of being left solitary in this great house where the stags' heads on the walls glared maliciously at me with their brown glassy eyes and the suits of armour had a monstrous life of their own. 'Oh, Ashley, do not leave me!' I implored. 'Do not leave me — stay, oh stay!'

His face became rigid. He would not rebuke me verbally in the presence of the gaping domestics; but his silence was the sternest of reproofs. After a long pause had marked his displeasure — 'Mrs Noble will attend you,' he said, indicating the housekeeper. 'I must not delay — the loss of a minute may make the difference between life and death.'

The servants' faces, the stags' heads, the ghostly suits of armour, all looked as if they would put in their word: *She should have known it.* Mortified and humiliated, I shrank back. I suppose Mrs Noble must have suggested that she should show me my room; for I found myself mounting the grand staircase in her wake, having first further disgraced myself by uttering a scream of dismay at the sight of a replica of Flaxman's hideous group of statuary, *The Fury of Athamas*, planted down most inappropriately among the sporting trophies and medieval weaponry in the huge entrance hall. She threw open a door and announced in sepulchral tones, 'Madam, the principal bedchamber.'

It sounded for all the world like a formal introduction. Yesterday the whimsical thought would have made me laugh. That night I felt that I would never laugh again. I did not accept her offer to send a maid to help me; for I preferred to await the coming of Annie, who was following the chaise in the luggage cart.

I waited in vain. When a maidservant brought hot water, I inquired whether the luggage cart had arrived. 'No,' said the young girl, staring, 'and we can't make out why, unless ——'

'Unless what?' I asked, uneasiness changing suddenly to dread.

'Well, Ma'am, unless horses had cast a shoe or summat of that kind,' she stammered, in such confusion that I could guess a collision with the funeral coach to be in her mind. I asked no more questions, but made myself ready for the festive meal that no other would share. No heart had I to change my travelling dress — my bridal gown remained within my valise. How could I wear it now?

Summoned by a clanging gong, I sat under the hard stare of family portraits of an older generation, persons remarkable chiefly for their bulbous eyes. A succession of dishes was presented to me; but I could touch none of them. After leaving the table I sat for a while in the stately drawing-room, where I looked for the first time on the pictured faces of my stepchildren. The three-year-old Guy was hardly more than a round, rosy baby, with no marked individuality as yet. Very different were his elders. Laurence, who was nearly twelve, had a bold, resolute but good-natured look. At thirteen, Augustine was cold and self-contained. Emma, aged ten, seemed older than her years. She was strikingly handsome, in a dark, imperious way. Her eyes, though not bulbous like those of her ancestors, had the same hard stare. I was so unpleasantly impressed by it that I moved to another part of the room, where those eyes could no longer rest on me. There I sat waiting with ever-increasing impatience for news of Annie. It did not come; and Mrs Noble, when summoned to my presence, had nothing comforting to say. She hoped that there had not been an accident — 'But with that Billy Jones on the road, who could tell? It was plain *something* had occurred to delay the cart, and that being so, Annie, Oakes and Blunt would put up somewhere for the night.'

Picturing all three lying senseless on the road, I begged that searchers should be sent out. Mrs Noble deemed this proceeding unnecessary. She reminded me that Mr Chalfont was bound to pass the scene of any accident and that he would provide for the welfare of the sufferers. Having repeated her comfortable conviction that Annie and the two men were safely lodged in an inn, she withdrew to her own domain.

After she had left me, I delayed as long as possible the hour for retiring. It could not be postponed for ever; and at last, slowly and reluctantly, I made my way to a room for which I already felt an unaccountable dislike. For some minutes I stood at the door, peering into a gloom that was but dimly relieved by the light from two tall candlesticks on the dressing-table. I knew that the room's four doors led only to dressing-rooms or wardrobes; but I could not help wondering whether the said dressing-rooms and wardrobes were tenanted by ghostly personages who might perchance emerge. As for the state bed with its close-drawn curtains, I was none too sure that it did not hold an invisible occupant. Simultaneously with this apprehension came the thought: *Doubtless my predecessor died in that bed.*

To speak truth, I do not know how I compelled myself to go into that room and shut the door behind me. All I can recollect is my sinking on to a sofa and crouching there till dawn peeped palely through the windows and a housemaid knocked at the door. I may have fallen asleep briefly from sheer fatigue, but my impression is that I remained awake the livelong night: my eyes continually on the bed-curtains that reached from floor to ceiling, my hands convulsively clutching the carved woodwork at the head of the sofa, my body ready at any moment to fly screaming from the place. Has any bride, I have often wondered, experienced so strange a wedding-night as I?

Morning found me white as the whitest of phantoms; and it was well for me that I had so much to occupy the daylight hours that I paid small heed to the nods and whispers of those around me, to whom the housemaid had duly carried the news of how I had spent the night. A message informed us that the luggage-cart had indeed had the worst of an encounter with the funeral coach, which drove on without stopping after toppling it into the ditch and causing it to lose a wheel. Robert Oakes had escaped with cuts and bruises, my poor Annie was sadly shaken, and James Blunt had broken his arm. They arrived at twelve o'clock, full of indignation and in much need of sympathy. My time was fully occupied in preparing to receive them, in commiserating their woes and in doing all I could to provide for their needs. The tutor and the governess, having returned from their holiday, demanded almost as much sympathy as the funeral coach's victims.

They spoke of the two older boys as completely dominated by Emma, for whom 'headstrong', 'wilful', 'violent', were their mildest epithets; and again and again they assured me that it was by no fault of theirs that their charges had been left to their own devices. It had been Mr Chalfont's express command that the children should have one day without adult supervision, twenty-four hours of glorious freedom before falling under a step-mother's yoke!

Mr Harland and Miss Lefroy were not to be comforted by my repeated assurances that no blame could justly be attached to them. They moped persistently, going about with long faces in a manner not calculated to raise my drooping spirits.

The endless day dragged to a close. At nightfall, my husband stepped out of the chaise alone.

Actively supported by their grandparents, the children had flatly refused to return to Grewby Towers as long as I was in it. True to his word, Mr Chalfont had left them at Parborough Hall with Mr and Mrs Grandison, who were delighted to obtain custody of their darling grandchildren, having themselves, as I was now to discover, bitterly resented their son-in-law's second marriage.

Brief and cold were the few words of explanation given to me by Mr Chalfont; and indeed he spent the greater part of the evening with the tutor, governess and Guy's nurse, making arrangements for the children's welfare and hunting out the playthings, sporting gear and books that they wished to have sent down to them in the coach on the following day. A lengthy list it was! and a fine search had to be made for at least a hundred items that had gone a-missing.

Coming back at last to the drawing-room where I sat alone, Mr Chalfont silenced me peremptorily when, in tears, I began falteringly to express my regrets and my hopes that even yet the children might experience a change of heart.

'It is over, all is decided, and we will say no more about the matter,' he said, with such authority in his voice that I dared not gainsay him, but remained in a state of mute distress. He paced the room restlessly for some minutes, then spoke again.

'It is my wish that, as far as is reasonably possible, the children shall not be mentioned between us. I will of course inform you of anything you ought to know; and I beg you will not harass me by unnecessary inquiries or allusions. The children will naturally expect to spend their holidays here; and during those weeks you will be set free to visit the members of your family or any of your friends. My Godmother, Mrs Verity, is willing to receive you into her house if for any reason it is inconvenient for your relations to take you. On my way back, I called on her and explained the position ——'

'But what have I done that I should be treated like this?' I cried, finding, momentarily, a sort of desperate defiance. 'I ask you, what have I done? You are blaming me for what has happened — but how can you in justice blame me? It is unfair, it is cruel, it is *wrong* to do so.'

'I am not blaming you,' Mr Chalfont answered coldly. 'I am merely endeavouring to provide for the happiness of my children.'

'And what do you care for the happiness of your wife? It is intolerable that you should have "explained the position" to some old woman of your acquaintance. Think of "the position" in which you are placing me! — the whispers and scandals that will make my whole life a misery! You ought never to have allowed yourself to be ruled by an untamed little hoyden of ten years old as if you were one of the brothers whom she keeps in subjection ——'

'That is enough — I will hear no more,' said Mr Chalfont, his eyes flashing in a way that awed and subdued me, child that I was. 'The matter is closed.'

And so it proved to be. On the next day tutor, governess and nurse drove off with their coach-load of children's possessions; and I had to face the sour looks of a household and neighbourhood whose alternate terror and delight those children had always been. When the shock of my husband's decree had worn off, I wrote letters of remonstrance to the Grandisons and of pleading and entreaty to the children. As soon as Mr Chalfont found out what was going on, he prohibited all correspondence and assured me that means would be taken to ensure that the children did not receive any letters I might write in breach of his edict. There was, at that time, anxiety for the health of the little Guy, who did not flourish when transported to his new home. I summoned up courage to propose that he, unconscious participant in his elders' rebellion, should be brought back to Grewby Towers. My request was refused in no uncertain terms. When Guy was seven years old, a chance remark of Mrs Noble's told me that the anxiety was renewed. A portrait of Guy had recently been installed in the picture-gallery (to console himself, I suppose, for their absence, my husband was in the habit of ordering portraits of his children at all stages of their growth). It showed a child with serious brown eyes and sensitive lips; and the wistfulness of the little oval face suggested he was missing something in life, perhaps a mother's care. Again I asked that he might be brought back to me and again I was refused, and that with an anger that put an end to all further pleadings on my part. Never again! was my resolve as well as my husband's.

O fifteen years, O fifteen years, how did you pass? A goodly proportion of each of them had perforce to be spent away from Grewby Towers; for surely never did children demand as many holidays as were clamoured for by the young Chalfonts and readily granted by their fond papa. Though they had every luxury in Parborough Hall, they were never so happy as when they were let loose on their native moors, those vast gloomy acres that had no charm for their stepmother. I could scarcely endure the sight of the sullen dun and purple masses that stretched far as the eye could see, to lose themselves at last in the mists that shrouded the imprisoning ring of hills. But the moors had been the children's playground — so Granny Norkins was later to tell me — from the time they were old enough to toddle thither, when they would fill their little hands with blue harebells, birds' feathers, bright pebbles, banded snail shells and other trifles such as children love. So, throughout the fifteen years they skated on the moor pools, hunted, shot wild fowl, fished, explored the dangerous bogs, climbed the grey-black forbidding guardians of the horizon. Not all the social diversions of their adult life could in any degree lessen their appetite for the moors.

And while they revelled, where was I and what did I? Sometimes — as Mr Chalfont had suggested — I spent those holidays with my brothers and sisters or with my parents. At other times I stayed with Godmother Verity, an ancient lady, very deaf, whose attitude to me was one of silent disapproval. I never knew what explanation my husband had given her or how much of it she had understood. I was too proud to inquire, nor would it have been possible to arrive at the truth without such use of my vocal powers as would have given her entire household the history of my woes.

Four years after my marriage my beloved parents died within a month of each other. I am not without hopes that I succeeded in concealing the truth from them. Certainly my father never knew it: during my visits he would frequently speak of Mr Chalfont's kindness in sparing me to them. I am not so sure that my mother did not guess that something was seriously amiss; she would look at me often with a kind of sorrowful perplexity in her eyes. I can, however, be quite sure that nothing went amiss during the only visit that their infirmities allowed my parents to pay to Grewby Towers. My husband showed them every attention, and the children's absence was easily accounted for. Augustine and Laurence were by that time at school, Guy was staying with a Grandison aunt, and Emma was studying the violin under a celebrated music-master chosen by her grandparents. Fortunately for my husband's peace of mind, the visit was over before it became known that the celebrated music-master had quitted Parborough Hall in a rage, having flatly refused ever again to teach the most unruly and insolent pupil it had been his ill-luck to meet.

Although I concealed — or so I hope — my unhappiness from my parents, it is not to be supposed that I could hoodwink my brothers and sisters, who were so hot and outspoken in my defence that the consequent breach between them and Mr Chalfont was never entirely healed.

I cannot claim — what mortal could? — that I was faultless throughout those fifteen years. True, there were not many outward signs of rebellion against my lot — my husband could always put down mutiny with a few severe words — but there were broodings, inward chafing and resentment. Gradually these states of mind gave place to resignation won by prayer; and thereafter — save for occasional relapses into old habits — I lived what presented itself to the world as a happy life, ordering the household, entertaining the neighbourhood as my husband wished, and occupying my leisure with books, music, drawing, needlework and vain endeavours to make the bleak grounds of Grewby Towers blossom like the rose. But I could never be without the dreary apprehension that my life was lived entirely for myself. I had no friends or allies in the house save my dear Annie and the two men who had been injured by the funeral coach. In the village, Robert Oakes's grandmother, Goody Norkins, was my staunch supporter — and my only one. The people on my husband's estate were a hardy, independent race, prosperous, suspicious of strangers, fervent champions of my stepchildren. By my husband's circle of acquaintances I was received with a formal courtesy that never broke through into friendship, since I knew not how to convince them that I was in no way responsible for what Emma and her brothers spoke of, most unjustly, as their 'banishment'. My brothers and sisters were wealthy, needing nothing that I could give.

As I have said, I had moments of weakness but still, during those years, I did what I could to mend matters. I was diligent in prayers for peace, understanding, reconciliation; I tried hard to bear with my own enforced and my husband's voluntary absences from home, and I strove to bear with the continual courteous aloofness and occasional moodiness that made a grey monotony of my life. In a manuscript book I recorded everything I could glean about the children's lives; their progress in their studies; the details of their schooling; their successes in sport; the college careers of Augustine and Laurence; Augustine's marriage; his home on his father-in-law's estate, where he was working as an agent until the time should come for him to inherit Grewby Towers. When Mr Chalfont read aloud in the evening — as was his custom — he would in later years select the exploits of famous travellers, not knowing or even suspecting that I was well aware he had chosen them because Laurence was showing signs of a passion for travel and exploration.

In these endeavours after reconciliation I was not encouraged by the incumbent of Grewby parish church, an elderly recluse who, like the rest of the world, suspected me of nefarious designs on my stepchildren's happiness. Conscious of his unspoken antagonism, I obtained little spiritual benefit from his ministry. But on one ever-memorable Sunday a stranger officiated during the Reverend Mr Blackton's temporary absence. I did not hear the stranger's name, nor did he again visit Grewby; but I shall always be grateful for the words that kept faith and hope alive in my heart through many a despairing hour.

For he spoke of God as the Fountain of light, life, truth, love, peace and joy. He quoted, I recollect, some lines by an unknown versifier. Simple as they were, I could not forget them.

> Thou art the Fountain, mighty King,
> Whence light and life and all joys spring.
>
> Thou art the Fountain, royal Son,
> By Whom alone our peace is won.
>
> Thou art the Fountain, holy Dove,
> Pure radiance of eternal love.
>
> Thou art the Fountain, One in Three,
> We thank, we praise, we worship Thee.

Nor could I forget the prayer at the end of a discourse in which he had begged his hearers constantly to seek those sparkling iridescent waters that could alone bring refreshment to the thirsty soul. It was an ancient collect that I was afterwards able to find and make my own:

Almighty God, we invoke Thee the Fountain of everlasting Light, and entreat Thee to send forth Thy truth into our hearts, and to pour upon us the glory of Thy brightness, through Christ our Lord.

My husband was an ardent book-lover, widely and deeply read, as his father and grandfather had been before him; and theological and devotional treatises were not lacking on the shelves of the library at Grewby Towers. It was not long before I had found and added to my store other prayers and passages wherein mention was made of the Fountain glowing in all its myriad colours, its celestial 'brightness' for one soul that had been near to deeming itself forsaken and forlorn. . . .

Twice in the fifteen years the invisible barrier between myself and my husband seemed to melt away, both times as the result of certain information that I had in fear and trembling felt bound to lay before him. What wretchedness of mind did I undergo when Mrs Noble disclosed to me that Emma, then aged seventeen, had secretly engaged herself to a man whose bad character was well known.

'Are you sure of this, Mrs Noble?'

'As sure as I can be, Madam' — and forthwith out came a torrent of irrefutable evidence.

'Then will you speak to Mr Chalfont?'

'No, Madam, I could not undertake to do so. It is not my place.'

From this position she was not to be shaken. Not for Mrs Noble was the role of sacrificial lamb!

During the seven years since the children left home, the conduct of Augustine had never given his elders a moment's anxiety . Nor had any complaint been brought against Guy, a quiet child now ten years old. It was far otherwise with Laurence and Emma, whose numerous mad escapades and frequent defiance of authority had caused their father great uneasiness. Never before had I deliberately told him of any misdemeanour that had come to my knowledge but not to his. On this occasion I held that Emma's perverse behaviour could not by any right-thinking person be concealed from her father.

Although grievously vexed and at first incredulous, Mr Chalfont was grateful to me for putting him in possession of the facts. He went immediately to Parborough Hall to tell the grandparents what was afoot; and after a succession of stormy scenes he and they succeeded in obliging Emma to renounce the engagement. I heard, without much heeding, a report that reached me by roundabout sources, that she had vowed to take revenge on me for my share in her disappointment.

Between two and three years later the situation repeated itself in an even worse form; for this time I heard nothing until Emma was on the point of eloping with a young blackguard compared with whom her former suitor appeared as an angel of light. Her father was only just in time to avert the disaster. I cannot tell how she came to learn that I had once more been forced to play the spy and informer. All I know is that, her affections having been more deeply engaged than before, her threats against me were correspondingly more bitter, even though her father brought such cogent arguments to support his case that at last she was brought to submission. She promised obedience — and she kept her word. The threats I heeded not; for at that time I had my own secret, unlooked for cause of joy to shield me against words however hateful. Besides, thought I, what could she do that she had not done already? Had she not, by her youthful cruelty, erected the barrier between my husband and myself, the barrier that was now lessened by our common concern for her welfare? . . .

The fire dimmed on my hearth, the carol-singers had long since dispersed to their several homes, and all sound was hushed save the wailing of the Christmas wind. I dared not dwell on what came next in my mournful history: for the thousandth time I tried to drive away the ever-recurring superstitious fear that Emma had ill-wished me. For I nearly died at the birth of my child, and recovered only to be told that the babe had been still-born. It was buried, poor nameless thing, in the family mausoleum, that place of dread, pale-glimmering among the yew trees of that windswept, dank churchyard. With the quenching of my joy, went all hope that my husband and I would be fully reconciled. We reverted to the life of distant mutual courtesy that we had always known. Whispers and rumours reached me of Laurence's debts and the audacious pranks in which Emma took a full share whenever possible. From steeple-chasing at midnight to stolen visits to the gaming-tables of Europe, there was no wildness that those two bold spirits did not essay; and it was with unconcealed relief that in those last five years Mr Chalfont witnessed his son's successive departures to explore the tombs of the Pharaohs, the caverns of Styria, and the site of ancient Troy. I lived on as best I might.

O those fifteen years, those fifteen years!

The end came suddenly while I was lying ill at the house of my sister Mary, whither I had gone at the request of my husband, to give him, as he said, a chance to enjoy his children's company. To the family reunion came Death, an unwelcome guest. My husband's horse stumbled and threw him as he rode out hunting with Emma and two of his sons.

I was not bidden to the funeral, nor could I have obeyed the summons had it come. Augustine wrote a frigid letter of condolence, regretting that illness would no doubt render it inadvisable for me to attempt any return to Grewby Towers. This epistle was shortly followed by a letter from the lawyer, informing me of the provision made for my future under the terms of my husband's will. My personal possessions would be packed and forwarded to whatever destination I should be pleased to indicate.

No one could ever accuse Mr Chalfont of niggardliness in money matters. I had ample means at my disposal; and my kind brothers quickly found me a desirable residence far, very far from Grewby Towers. In Silverlea Cottage I had found peace, tinged indeed with unavailing regrets, but nevertheless peace. Why on this night of all nights should I have been troubled by remembrances of Emma . . . Emma . . . Emma, with dark hair streaming as she urged on the driver of that hideous funeral coach? It was unlikely that I should ever see any of my stepchildren: why, oh why must I think of them now?

Throughout the whole of my mournful retrospect my fingers had not stopped flying, and now Elinor's blue frock lay finished before me. I wrapped it up and fastened the parcel with a gay bit of ribbon. Then I gathered up the miniature hat, skirt and bodice and wended my way to Tina's room. As on the previous night, the doll sat on the bedside chair wearing my neck-shawl. Cautiously I set down my candle, took off the shawl and dressed Elinor in her missionary-basket clothes, placing her Christmas parcel on her lap.

Tina did not wake. Shading the candle, I looked down at

her. Strange, stern little face! — what secrets did it hide? what joys and sorrows had this child from nowhere known?

I stole from the room and betook myself to prayer and sleep.

Chapter Six

After the stormy winds of Christmas Eve, the Day dawned clear, serene and cold. I found Tina standing by her window, which was silvered with frost ferns; she was pointing out their beauties to an unresponsive Elinor. 'Look, Elinor, look!' I heard her say. 'Did you ever see such plumes and feathers and fairy grasses?'

'Jack Frost has drawn some of his best designs for you,' I observed.

Her grave brown eyes sought mine. 'It is like an enchanted forest. But I cannot persuade Elinor to believe that. The naughty creature thinks of nothing but her fine new hat and her blue dress. Did you make all those clothes last night? I am very much obliged to you.'

She had dressed herself more neatly than could have been expected of a child who for some months had been a doll in the hands of Miss Wilcox. We went downstairs together, and she ran to fetch and distribute her missionary-basket purchases, which we all professed ourselves delighted to receive. There were parcels for her on the breakfast-table, such simple gifts as I had been able to procure in the village, together with a book and a dissected puzzle from Mr Ellin. They gave, I could see, infinite satisfaction to a child so long deprived of personal possessions. When Jane, Eliza and I attended morning service in the parish church, I was perfectly content to leave her in the company of old Annie who, too infirm to venture forth on a snowy day, sat in her own little parlour with her large-print Book of Common Prayer on her knee. I returned to find the two enjoying a companionable silence. Tina was sitting on the hearthrug with her treasures scattered round her and with one of the giant sea-shells from Annie's glass-fronted cabinet of curiosities pressed to her ear. Annie, leaning forward, was studying our guest, benignly, but with the same puzzled air she had worn on Christmas Eve, as if at a loss to account for the little apparition. I concluded she had already forgotten the explanation Mr Ellin had given; but her next remark told me that it was not so. 'Ah, Miss Arminel' — for in private Annie had never been cured of using the old name — 'I mind me how you used to do just that with these same shells that my poor brother Jack brought from overseas long, long ago. I was telling missy here how he was drowned full fifty years since —'

Tina put away the shell and scrambled to her feet. Speaking low, that she might not distress Annie — ' "Of his bones are coral made",' she said. 'That was written by Shakespeare. Diana had to parse and analyse it. She couldn't; she said it was bad grammar. But she got a black mark for presumption, taking it on herself to criticise Shakespeare, Miss Wilcox said.'

I know not whether Annie's reminiscences or the memory of Fuchsia Lodge could be held to blame, but the child shivered and grew pale. Asking no questions, I hurried her away.

Later Jane and Eliza were going to be busy with final preparations for a grand supper to be given to their relations. We all dined early therefore; and then Tina and I settled down to a quiet afternoon, during which I read to her, helped her to solve the dissected puzzle and wrote my own letters of thanks while she was amusing herself with her Christmas acquisitions. How unlike that Christmas to the merry Christmases of my youth or to the Christmases I had spent, an unhappy exile, wherever I could find temporary refuge! As far as I could tell, the solitary sprite by my side seemed happy enough; and indeed she once broke into positive mirth when Mr Ellin, taking his lonely constitutional, dropped into my letter box a missive addressed to 'Miss Martina Fitzgibbon'. She sat reading and re-reading the few lines in which she was thanked for her 'most acceptable' Christmas present; and presently, seizing her doll, she read the letter aloud to it. 'There, Elinor, you have heard what Mr Ellin says. He liked my watch-pocket, he truly liked it!'

Annie, who was not for joining a lively and perhaps noisy supper-party, spent the evening with us; and after tea I persuaded her to tell some of the Cornish stories that had charmed my childhood and that of my brothers and sisters.

What wild, strange tales they were! In the flickering firelight, I once again trembled deliciously to hear of Jessy Varcoe's Leap, wicked Tregeagle, the white rabbit of Egloshayle and the mysterious doings of enchanter Milliton of Pengerwick, whose silver table laden with golden goblets and dishes has lain beneath the waters of Mount's Bay ever since his princely barge sank there with all his guests. Often did we wonder whether a daring voyager had ventured to utter the magic formula, 'Phrut, Haveringmere, and all those who over thee fere', knowing full well that the incantation would be followed by a storm in which he and his fellows would all be drowned.

Shrouded shapes and unearthly sounds haunted the tin mines in which Annie's father had worked. Spine-chilling, too, was the story of the farmer and his wife who lived in what had long ago been Tregeagle's mansion but was now no better than a farm-house. Returning late one night from the market-town, the farmer and his wife were amazed to see light streaming from every window of their dwelling and figures of men and women in antique dress flitting to and fro, while sounds of wicked revelry and song rang out loud and clear. The farmer, a bold man, would have rushed in to challenge the intruders who were making free with his abode. But as he laid his hand on the garden gate, the lights went out, the figures vanished, the songs ceased, and all was darkness and silence.

As my brothers advanced in worldly wisdom, I heard them saying that no doubt a drop too much cider in the market-town would easily account for all the marvellous manifestations in the decayed mansion. But no such cynical explanation entered the innocent mind of Tina, who accepted all the wonders for true except that of the sinking of Milliton's barge, which, after Annie had fallen asleep, she rejected, very properly, on grounds of logic and reason. 'For if the entire boat-load was drowned, how could it ever be known that one of them had been foolish enough to say "Phrut!"?' she argued, whispering lest Annie should awake.

But the slumbers were too deep to be disturbed, even when I explained that Annie had confused two of her stories, one of which came from the Welsh border and not from Cornwall at all; it was a warning given to anyone who proposed to cross a certain haunted lake, Haveringmere. 'I hope I never have to cross that lake,' said I; 'for I am sure that I might be tempted to cry "Phrut!" just to see what happened.'

Tina laughed quite merrily. Then we sat awhile in the dusk to watch the moon glimmering above the snow-covered fir trees in Dr Percy's garden on the opposite side of the road. Once I heard Tina say softly to herself, 'Oh, this is rest.' The unchildlike words spoke, as nothing else could have done, of the strain under

which she had lived for so long. Rest, tranquillity! — they were
what both of us most desired, the woman and the girl.

I had always found enjoyment in translating from the French;
and soon after beginning my widowed life at Silverlea Cottage
I had been much struck by the sentiments expressed in some
verses of Justin Maurice. My translation was weak, free, clumsy,
void of the finish, the delicacy, the fine point of the French
original; but the making of it had nevertheless given me comfort
and ease of spirit. As is the habit of lonely persons, I murmured
some of the lines, forgetful that I now had an auditor. Tina
enlightened me.

'Please to say that again. I like it.'

I complied with the request.

'Leave me, I pray, my thoughts and dreams,
My lovely vales, my crystal sky,
My woods, my gliding meadow-streams,
My hills, where many a flower gleams,
My river with its azure waves.

And while I dwell hard by the riverside,
Heedless what care the morrow hath in store,
May there be no dark depths in life's pure tide!
By all the clamours of the world untried
So may it flow to its appointed end.

O bid it flow, unhasting, mild,
Among the flowers, by gentle hills,
Sporting with mosses, like a child,
Pushing aside the herbage wild
Where the long boughs of willows droop!

Lulled by all winds that blow, my hours
Pass onward, hand in hand,
And beauteous thoughts, like opening flowers,
From their light footsteps spring in showers,
Making life's pathway fair to see.

Men say that life is bitter fare.
Dear Lord, it is not so with me;
For poesy and constant prayer
Like mother's or like sister's care,
Will keep it spotless, Lord, for Thee.

The future lacks all meaning for a child,
Who looks no further than a single day.
He recks not that the sea of life is wild,

Pursuing, on a shore still calm and mild,
The butterfly of hope, the golden dream.

Like silver raindrops fall the days,
Each sweeter than the honeycomb.
Naught fears the soul: it can but praise.
O gracious Lord, these are the ways
That angels walk in highest Heaven.

Life's flower must fade and fall at last.
What's Death? 'Tis but to shut the eyes,
To ask forgiveness for the past,
To trust the Love that holds us fast,
To sleep — and wake in Heaven's light.'

'Yes,' said Tina, gravely judgmatical, 'that is good poetry.'
'Hardly. The original was good.'
' "The original"?'
'It was a French poem that I translated into English.'
'Like a lesson?'
'No, I did it for pleasure, and the result does not please me. However, the poet's thought is still plain to see.'
'Yes, but I don't know the word for his thought. Would it be "quietness" or "peace"?'
'Tranquillity would be my choice, I think.'
'Tranquillity, tranquillity.' She repeated my choice two or three times. 'That word has a beautiful sound.'
'It was used long ago in an ode written to the memory of a friend.' I quoted some lines from one of John Oldham's *Pindarics*:

'Thy soul within such silent pomp did keep,
As if humanity were lull'd asleep;
So gentle was thy pilgrimage beneath,
    Time's unheard feet scarce make less noise,
Or the soft journey which a planet goes;
    Life seem'd all calm as its last breath,
A still tranquillity so husht thy breast,
    As if some halcyon were its guest,
        And there had built her nest;
It hardly now enjoys a greater rest.
As that smooth sea which wears the name of peace
        Still with one even face appears,
    And feels no tides to change it from its place,
    No waves to alter the fair form it bears;
        As that unspotted sky,

Where Nile does want of rain supply
Is free from clouds, from storm is ever free:
So thy unvary'd mind was always one,
And with such clear serenity still shone,
As caus'd thy little world to seem all temp'rate zone.'

Tina said, 'That is beautiful too, though I don't understand it very well. Please say some more.'

'There is no more that is worth remembering. He died young.'

'Well then please say the French *Tranquillity* again.' I obeyed. At the end — 'Do you often do that?'

'Do what?'

'Do you often translate French poems into English?'

'Not often. Sometimes.'

'Say another one, if you please.'

'I will choose something livelier this time. Do you know the French word for "cherry"?'

She hesitated. 'I only know "pomme" for apple and "poire" for pear.'

'It is *la cerise*, and there is a poem of that name. I translated it for two of my little nieces, whose papa has many cherry trees in his orchard. Margaret and Bertha always have a holiday for the cherry-gathering.'

'I should like to hear the cherry poem, if you please.'

'Here you are, then:

'In soft springtide
    Blossoms pure white
On branch abide
    Oh, what delight!

Falls the white grace;
    Then, without sound,
There in its place
    A fruitlet's found.

In summer gay,
    Children, draw near.
Good news to-day:
    The cherry's here!

To the trees, quick!
    Where fruits so sweet
'Midst leaves I pick
    For you to eat.'

As I was speaking, snow began to fall softly clouding the window-panes.

'I like that cherry poem,' said Tina. 'It is a tranquillity poem too, but a different sort of tranquillity. Mr Ellin has a cherry tree in his garden, I have heard him say so. Have you a cherry tree?'

'No.'

'Has Mr Ellin ever given you any cherries from his garden?'

Truth compelled me to admit that he had done so.

'Last year?'

No, I think he did not give away any cherries last year except to Mr and Mrs Randolph. He had not been long in Clinton St James, and the Rector and his wife were his only close friends.'

'But he gave you some this year?'

'Yes.'

'There were not many cherries on his tree this year. The cherry crop failed. I was not here at that time; it is what I heard. Not many cherries — but it was to you he gave what he had. To you, to nobody else.'

I detected a little note of triumph that indicated, clearly enough, the identity of 'nobody else'. Making haste to change the conversation — 'That was very kind of him, was it not?' I said. 'Look how fast the snow is falling! Tomorrow you and I have been asked to dine with Dr and Mrs Percy, and Annie is to dine with their old housekeeper while Jane and Eliza take supplies of beef and plum puddings for a St Stephen's Day dinner in their own homes. Do you think that you and I and Annie will be able to cross the road without tumbling into a snowdrift?'

Like this year's cherry crop, my device failed; it did not turn Tina's thoughts away from the kind deeds of Mr Ellin. 'Oh, if we did fall into a snowdrift, all three of us, I am positive Mr Ellin would see us from his house only a little way further down the road, and he would come running very fast to help us out.'

I left her blissfully contemplating this interesting possibility while I studied the contents of a second missive that had arrived at the same time as the letter to Tina.

Until that moment I had thought that Mr Ellin was perhaps over-hasty in purchasing cloak and dress material for Martina without giving the absent Mr Conway Fitzgibbon a further opportunity either to communicate with Miss Wilcox or to present his explanation in person at Fuchsia Lodge. Nor was I by any means sure that Mr Ellin had done all he could to persuade Miss Wilcox to surrender some, at least, of Martina's own clothes. His letter, while it could not entirely exonerate him from the first of my accusations, quickly convinced me that his sauntering manner was not to blame for his failure to induce Miss Wilcox to relax her hold on Martina's property. She had, it appeared, refused two separate requests so heatedly as to leave him in no doubt that the refusals were prompted by an unholy desire to punish the unhappy little Martina for so-called 'obduracy'. Diana's cast-offs, she had proclaimed, were far too good for such an appallingly naughty, disagreeable child.

However, Mr Ellin had had better luck in certain negotiations over the snake-bracelet, an article that might prove to be of use in establishing Martina's identity. After escorting Mr Cecil to his lodgings on Christmas Eve, he had paid yet another visit to Fuchsia Lodge, in the course of which he had persuaded Miss Wilcox to sell him the bracelet — conditionally, subject to the continued non-appearance of Mr Conway Fitzgibbon — at a jeweller's valuation. ('Ha, Mr Ellin!' was my thought on reading this, 'generous to a fault, as usual. That bracelet is going to cost you a pretty penny. Taking the loss of his daughter's wardrobe into consideration, Mr Fitzgibbon can consider himself no longer indebted to Miss Wilcox for non-payment of fees. Indeed, I should not wonder' — such was my uncharitableness — 'but that she has acquired a handsome something to set against the quarter's notice that he ought to have given.')

Mr Ellin then went on to say that as he had thrust Tina upon me willy-nilly he was fully prepared to pay her expenses while he was making all the inquiries in his power. 'I rather fancy myself as a private investigator.' he wrote. 'I believe I can do as good a job as the gentlemen in Bow Street. It may, however, take some time; for I am resolved not to press Tina, who, I am convinced, has been as near breaking-point as a child can be. True, our perplexities may be resolved by the reappearance of Mr Fitzgibbon armed with a satisfactory explanation of his conduct; but should he fail to write or present himself in person, weeks and even months may pass before we work out the puzzle. The immediate question is, what can be done with Martina, for whom Miss Wilcox disclaims all further responsibility unless she is allowed to have her way about questioning the child until a confession is forced out of her. I have already imposed on your kindness by asking you to entertain Martina during the holidays, during which time I propose to find a school for her somewhere in the neighbourhood. I should be most grateful if you could give me your advice. Would she, do you think, be happier residing in some clergyman's family? The Randolphs would no doubt take her; but as you know nearly all of them are down with mumps . . .'

I spent the last hours of that Christmas night in pondering how best to answer Mr Ellin's unspoken appeal. It was abundantly plain that he wished me to take charge of Martina, not for the next fortnight, but for an indefinite time that might be short enough or very long indeed. After a brief three days' acquaintance, was it safe, was it wise, so to bind myself? The charge was no light one, although Tina was not repugnant to me as she had been to Miss Wilcox. She might be a human oyster; but I believed myself already to have caught glimpses of the pearl within. Was this, I asked, the mysterious quest that had haunted my thoughts for so long? — this caring for and training of a young creature whose history could not be other than strange and sad? To consign such a being to a school would be to separate her from her only friends and to condemn her to continue wearing the hard protective shell that had repelled and disgusted her former preceptress.

Long I thought and prayed. Then I answered Mr Ellin's letter. After mildly reproaching him for what I guessed was extravagance in the bargain over the snake-bracelet, I declared myself willing to undertake, not for the holiday period only but for whatever length of time might be necessary, the care of a child whose misfortunes had touched my heart. I professed myself fully able to bear the cost of clothing, feeding and educating her; but if it would make him happier to contribute to these expenses, I had no doubt we could come to some amicable arrangement (as we eventually did). I welcomed his intention of setting up as an amateur detective, in which occupation I wished him every success and promised him all the help I could give. I trusted that the blessing of Almighty God would attend our joint efforts for the welfare of a seemingly deserted child.

The letter, signed and sealed, awaited despatch on the morrow. My 'quest' had begun.

Chapter Seven

Mr Ellin accepted my offer with satisfaction, nay, with unconcealed delight; but it must not be supposed that the arrangement was made over Martina's little head, as if she were an inanimate object that need not be consulted about its choice of abode. As she already knew that she was to spend the holidays at Silverlea Cottage, we decided to put off talking to her about her future until the day before the young ladies returned to Fuchsia Lodge. However, on New Year's Eve, when the holidays had still a week to run, a small incident made us change our minds

Hitherto, Tina had been a prisoner in the house — save for a few steps across the road to the home of Dr Percy — but on that day a sturdy pair of shoes, made in haste by the village shoemaker, had replaced the thin slippers in which she had come to the Cottage. I would have preferred the privacy of the back garden for the snowman she was anxious to build: but I yielded to her earnest pleadings against the injustice of depriving invalid Mrs Percy of such a splendid spectacle. With the assistance of Mr Ellin, she and I had spent the morning in erecting the snowman and in concocting snow ice-cream from a mixture of snow and raspberry jam. We were busy about these pleasant pastimes when our attention was distracted by the sight of Miss Wilcox stalking by, very tall and dignified, with a young girl on either side.

Tina stood rigid, a grey stony look on her face. 'Are the holidays over, then?' she faltered. 'Do I have to go back *there*?'

'No,' said Mr Ellin, 'the holidays are not over. Those girls are new pupils, Mr Cecil tells me, whose parents were obliged to go to Scotland to visit a sick grandmother. The children had therefore to be sent to school a week early. And you are not going back "there" unless you particularly wish to go.'

'Oh no, oh never! It was horrible. The girls whispered about me. They called me "Miss Popinjay" and "Mr Peacock's daughter"; and Diana said Miss Wilcox was a toady and I was her little toad — —'

'Well, never mind about that,' said Mr Ellin, cutting short these revelations. 'Toads are useful in the garden, and they make agreeable pets. I have a toad named Ned. You shall see him some day. Would you like to know what Mrs Chalfont and I are planning for you?'

She nodded, and we took her indoors.

'Do you know what is meant by "a guardian"?' asked Mr Ellin.

She nodded again. 'A guardian guards people. Takes care of them.'

'You have two guardians now, Mrs Chalfont and I. We appointed ourselves because there was nobody to appoint us; and we shall continue to act until your papa either comes or writes. And we have resolved that you shall choose between staying here at Silverlea Cottage or being sent to another school, not to Fuchsia Lodge. You need not decide for some days yet. Think carefully before you make your choice.'

Her answer came swiftly. 'I don't need to do any thinking. I want to stay with Mrs Chalfont — I want it so much.'

'You may change your mind later. At any time you will be quite free to do so.'

'I shall never change.' She added, after the shortest of pauses: 'Now shall we go back to the snowman?'

The question of her future residence being settled, Mr Ellin turned his attention to the unearthing of the vanished Mr Conway Fitzgibbon, late of non-existent May Park, Midland County. Were ever such difficulties put in the way of an amateur detective, not only by his own judgment but also by that of the medical profession? — for Dr Percy, having observed her closely when she dined at his house on St Stephen's Day, had warned me against pressing Tina to reveal her secret. Pressure of some sort had been put upon her to such an extent that her mental health might suffer irreparable damage if, even with the best intentions, any person tried to make her disobey the instructions she had received. Let her, said good Dr Percy, have plenty of play and sleep, put lessons aside for the present, and keep her as much as possible in the open air.'

As if the elements were in league with Tina's missing parent,

62

heavy snowfalls kept Mr Ellin from trying to find the abandoned playbox in the hope that it might afford some clue either to the gentleman's whereabouts or to Tina's identity. Six roads entered Clinton St James, by any one of which Mr Fitzgibbon might have approached the village, though nobody could be found who remembered having witnessed his arrival. For over three weeks those six roads were blocked by snow, by black ice, by melting sludge. They were no sooner clear than Mr Ellin was off, visiting one inn after another, but at present confining his inquiries to hostelries within riding distance; for it seemed probable, from what Tina had admitted, that it was during the last part of their journey that the box had been condemned as 'too heavy' for the carriage.

From the last of these excursions he returned triumphant. When questioned, the landlord had promptly produced the playbox from the cupboard in which his customers' goods were bestowed to await future claims by the absent-minded owners. He had been in no hurry to dispose of the box, having been sorry for the distress of the little miss whose papa had decreed that it was an encumbrance; and he had hoped that perhaps she might be permitted to reclaim it when returning that way for her holidays.

Good-hearted fellow, he displayed hot indignation when Mr Ellin told him Tina's story. He was able to provide an item of intelligence that was not without some value: the carriage in which Mr Conway Fitzgibbon had appeared at the school was not his own, but had been hired from the inn. It was a sufficiently stylish equipage, which the landlord had bought at a bargain price from the executors of a gentleman recently deceased, and which he let out to customers who for one reason or another were desirous of 'cutting a dash'.

This piece of information gave Mr Ellin, as he said, 'something to think about' when he gloatingly returned with the box. We neither of us saw what practical use could be made of it, except that we were more firmly established in the belief that Miss Wilcox, no judge of character, had been taken in by a showy and pretentious rogue.

The playbox had been found within a day or two of Tina's tenth birthday. Restraining his impatience, Mr Ellin agreed that it should not be presented to her until the five o'clock birthday tea, to which he had already accepted an invitation.

The important day arrived, bringing to the breakfast-table the gifts Mr Ellin and I had provided. These were received by Tina with every appearance of satisfaction, but with none of the exuberance of childhood, though we had reason to believe she had been happy enough in a quiet way during the weeks at Silverlea Cottage. Certainly there had been no tears or fears save once or twice at night when she had awakened screaming after a dream of horror.

The birthday dinner was over, and tea was being prepared with pink-and-white cake and snowdrops in a floral bowl. Then came Mr Ellin's well-known knock, at which Tina's sedate looks were replaced by the little consequential airs befitting the queen of the day. At the end of the feast, when birthday tributes had been proudly displayed and riddles and conundrums asked, Mr Ellin, at a sign from me, drew back the curtains from a recess where a tall pot-plant now shared the space with an elderly battered playbox. Tina's eyes opened wide. For a moment she gazed incredulously, then sprang forward and dropped on her knees by her recovered treasure. 'My playbox!' she cried, 'my playbox! But how did it get here — how?'

'Young lady, I went in search of it,' said Mr Ellin, 'and a fine dance all over the county I have had! But restrain your transports awhile; for as the key is missing, I apprehend we shall have to break the lock.'

'Oh no, no!' said the delighted Tina. 'See here, I have the key!'

She ran to fetch her purse. Out came the key, and with trembling fingers she fitted it into the lock.

Alas for Mr Ellin's hopes and mine! The playbox contained — as far as we could tell — nothing that could afford us the clue we sought. What could we hope to gain from an investigation of painting materials, a musical box, and a number of small jointed dolls such as I believe our gracious Queen and her governess used to dress in all manner of silk and satin scraps long ago? There were books, but most of them were sixpenny and threepenny booklets in Dutch flowered paper covers with gilt edges. While Tina was rejoicing over and hugging a large favourite doll named Rosamond, Mr Ellin contrived to look at the flyleaf of three or four bound books, only to find that they were innocent of any inscription, the owner's name having been all too plainly cut out.

It was a disappointment to us both, though we could not but look with an indulgent eye on Tina's raptures as one dear plaything after another came to light. After she had rushed off to show some of the precious objects to Annie, Jane and Eliza, I ventured to express a hope that their reappearance might give her such a sense of security and well-being that she would begin to volunteer confidences about the past. Mr Ellin hoped so too.

We were in part mistaken. The sense of security was soon plain to see; but only one confidence was forthcoming — and that by accident. Some days later we were playing, she and I, a game called *Ships at Sea*, with pieces in the shape of miniature sailing vessels labelled 'The Fly', 'The Crocodile', and the like, moving over a dangerous cardboard ocean dotted with rocks, sharks, whirlpools, water-spouts and cannibal islands at the whim of a numbered teetotum. When Mr Ellin was announced, Tina eagerly invited him to join us. 'It is a very good game,' she explained, 'and quite new. It was given to me because we were going to New — —'

She caught herself up. 'The Fly' dropped from her hand and fell under the table. For what seemed a long time she groped for it, apparently in vain. At last she brought it to light and sat stiffly in her chair, her face expressive of the utmost alarm.

I could see that Mr Ellin was longing to ask her to complete the name of her destination; but he refrained, took his place at the table, and made some casual inquiry about the rules of the game, which Tina answered, hesitantly at first, but with gradually increasing confidence. Leaving her all smiles after a victorious voyage in which she had wrecked both Mr Ellin and me on a cannibal island, he bade me farewell in the hall.

'That child was about to sail to New York,' he said. 'Where else? And what changed her father's purpose? — what urgent reason caused him to leave the child at school under an assumed name?'

It was a rhetorical question, addressed to one who knew no more than he did. I could, however, tell him that within the last few hours Jane had thought good to rub and polish the playbox. In the course of her activities, some faded letters or portions of letters had manifested themselves; and she and I had made them out to be a 'T' followed at a short distance by a 'D' and other letters, nine in all, none of which could be read.

Mr Ellin followed me into the kitchen, where the playbox still stood; but he was no more successful in deciphering the nine letters than Jane and I had been: nothing remained of them save a few disconnected strokes, the last of which might or might not have been the tail of a 'y'. However, the 'T' and the 'D', coupled with Tina's involuntary disclosure, had given him a clue, albeit a slender one. ' I shall consult all available passenger lists of sailings to New York within the last six months,' he said. 'Miss Wilcox certainly understood the father to be a widower, so it is possible that at the last moment he resolved to leave Martina in England at school. Who knows what may have hindered him from sending word home?'

'But why the false name and address?' I protested.

'I fear there may have been some urgent reason for the voyage to America. It may, for example, have been a flight from creditors or from the consequences of a criminal act. Whatever the reason for Mr Conway Fitzgibbon's departure from these shores, it is now obvious why he refused, almost at the last, to allow the child to take her playbox to school with her. Having removed her name from her books to prevent detection, he suddenly noticed his own name on the box-lid, and he could not be sure that the faded letters might not be pieced together and used to trace him...Well, I must away to the perusal of passengers lists.'

I did not seek to detain him; for I was already uncomfortably aware that in his double role of guardian and amateur detective Mr Ellin called at my house oftener than was desirable. The censorious eyes of the neighbourhood would soon be turned upon me, notably the eyes of the three Misses Wilcox, at whose tea-table Mr Ellin had now become more cautious in his attendance, though he had made his peace with them after a fashion. But it would have been a relief to speculate once more in his company on what lay behind Tina's terrified silence. What arguments or threats could her father have used sufficiently powerful to ensure that so young a child would remain mute as Tina had done, wavering in her secretiveness only twice, once in her passionate rejection of the name Emma and once in her caught-back mention of a voyage to New York? Silent she might have remained while in unsympathetic surroundings — but what was to hinder her now that she found herself with those whom she loved and trusted?

For by this time the February snowdrop did love and trust us. She was no longer the frozen little image of despair that had attracted Mr Ellin's notice when it walked alone, ignored by its companions, disliked by its schoolmistress. I was strongly convinced of this when, a week after her birthday, she awoke shrieking from one of her recurrent nightmares. I hastened to comfort and reassure her; and with my arm about her shoulders, she presently sobbed out some incoherent words about a witch at the window, scratching to be let in, and 'those books, those awful books, they are here in Annie's parlour'. Patient questioning soon revealed the truth. Long since, Annie had brought from Cornwall half a dozen volumes of Mr John Wesley's *Arminian Magazine*, one of which contained a frightful account of the persecution of witches in Sweden in the year 1682. I soon made out that Tina had been frightened almost out of her wits by the savage story, which she had read when, at an unknown time in the past, she had been staying in a farmhouse for the good or her health. The fate of the witches had haunted her ever since and had no doubt played a part in her nightmares; but it was only when she caught sight of another set of the same volumes that the terror returned upon her tenfold.

I had a partial recollection of the account, which I, less sensitive than Tina, had read in my own childhood with a distaste that never became real fear. In vain I tried to soothe Tina by assurances that the Swedish witch trials had happened so long ago that there could be no possibility that a Swedish witch could come scratching at her window in order to carry her off to Blockula, the witches' meeting-place. Tina assented to all I said; but her continued quivering told me that my words had fallen on deaf ears. At last, I had a happy thought. 'Listen, Tina,' said I. 'Did you know that Mr Ellin once lived in Sweden? He doubtless knows all about those Swedish witches, and he will be able to prove to you that they cannot come over to torment you in England.'

'Oh! I did not know that Mr Ellin had lived for a long time in Sweden,' said Tina, relieved. 'Who told you?'

'Mrs Randolph.'

'Are you sure he will come to tell me about the witches?'

'Quite sure.'

Tina stopped shuddering. 'It is a very good thing that he once lived in Sweden, if he will now be able to tell me for certain that none of the witches escaped and came to live here. A great many were killed, of course, but some of them may have been clever enough to escape. Even one escaped witch could do a great deal of harm, could she not?'

I did my poor best to convince Tina that no witch had escaped; but it was the best of a person who had not lived in Sweden, and I could see that it was little accounted of by Tina. However, she snuggled down into her white pillows and only roused herself to ask drowsily, 'Why doesn't Mr Ellin live in Sweden now?'

'I suppose he prefers to live in his own country.'

'Miss Wilcox wondered what he did for his living. Do you know?'

'My Tina, Mr Ellin would tell us himself if he wanted us to know.'

'It would not be polite to ask?'

'I'm afraid not.'

'But I can ask about the witch that perhaps escaped and came to England,' said Tina, and on that assertion she fell asleep.

I left her and went downstairs to refresh my memory from Annie's book, wherein the seventeenth-century witches were shown blowing through the keyhole of the church door and assembling in a gravel pit after they had collected filings from church clocks and scrapings from altars. They then put vests on their heads, anointed themselves with troll oil, and cried three times, 'Antecessor, come and carry us to Blockula!' Straightway they were whisked off to a building in an endless meadow, where they feasted. This they did nightly, besides plaguing ministers and good people who had no part in witchcraft. They scratched at windows — alas, poor Tina! — and, themselves invisible, stuck nails into innocent heads, milked cattle to death, took children from their beds and forced them to join the rides to Blockula, clad in coats and doublets of red and blue.... Again I read of the Commissioners appointed by the King 'to root out this hellish crew by means of humiliation days and a great examination of suspected persons'. They did their work thoroughly, those Commissioners, arresting seventy full-grown witches and three hundred child-riders, of whom twenty-three adults and fifteen children were instantly condemned to death and many more were expected to die later...

The narrative, which had shocked me when I read it in my healthy, merry childhood, now shocked me inexpressibly. No marvel at the effect it had had on Tina! But I trusted that Mr Ellin would be able to dispel her fears.

On the next day he answered my summons promptly, and I learnt that he was fully acquainted with the old story. Nay more, he had visited the traditional site of 'Blockula', the Blue Island that rose like a blue knob from its surrounding waters. His comment — 'Unfortunate creatures, they paid dearly for a few rough practical jokes and some horribly indigestible suppers of broth with coleworts and bacon in it, milk, cheese and oatmeal bread spread with butter' — made me for a moment afraid that he was going to treat the matter lightly. I need not have feared. When he spoke to Tina, it was with a grave sweetness that at once met her need. The poor Swedish witches — troll-women, he called them

— were to be pitied, not blamed: in those far-off days their judges did not understand that the accused persons ought not to be punished; for they were suffering, grown folk and children alike, from an illness of the mind as infectious as the epidemic of mumps that had lately made so many people ill in Clinton St James. No one knew for certain what had caused the illness; but it might very well have been the result of eating bread made from diseased rye. Those who ate such bread had been known to behave oddly, in other times and places. The people who had not caught the illness were as much to be pitied as the sick ones; they went about fancying they heard rappings and scratchings and scrapings when there were none, and they believed the fantastic tales the sick people told them about the rides to Blockula and the feasts in the endless meadow. It was a sad, sad story — Martina must be thankful that she lived in an enlightened age. It was beyond the bounds of probability that any so-called witch had ever escaped to England — and if she had, she must have died at least a hundred years ago. Nor was it possible that such a witch could have power over a Christian child who put her trust in God.

Seeing that Tina was satisfied with the explanation, Mr Ellin entertained us with a lively description of his childhood and youth in Sweden, country of deep silent forests, silver birch trees shimmering by blue lakes, marshes golden with cloudberries, hills yellow with mountain violas, and everywhere vast lonelinesses. Tina was particularly pleased to hear of the visit he always paid to his old nurse when he went back to Sweden to see his friends. She lived in a little red house among the pines, he told us, and wore a black skirt, scarlet bodice and striped apron. In summer she gave him wild strawberries and cream; in winter he would go skimming over the snow on a curious pair of snow-shoes, the like of which were never seen in England.

'Did she tell you fairy tales when you were little?' Tina asked.

'She did indeed.' said Mr Ellin. 'Not about English fairies, though. Hers were stories of giants, trolls, elves, dwarfs who could be heard hammering in the hills, and Nekan playing on his golden harp.' He drew a book from his pocket. 'Here are some of the tales known to all Swedish boys and girls, told in English for English children.'

Gone were Tina's fears! She pounced upon the book. 'Why,' she exclaimed, as she examined her prize, 'the man who wrote this book did not put his name on it but only his initials, which are the same as yours, W.R.E. for William Roger Ellin. Are you him?'

'Are you he?' said Mr Ellin, trying to turn his question off by giving the questioner a lesson in English grammar. But his secret was out; for his self-conscious look gave him away; and I fell upon him in great indignation for daring to conceal from his friends and neighbours that he was the W.R.E. whose history of Swedish literature had long been regarded as a standard work, and who was so much admired for the power and brilliance of his prose and verse translations of the writings of Swedish authors. It was remarkable that none of those neighbours had identified the apparently idle Mr Ellin as the celebrated W. R. E.; and I now began to feel vainglorious for having entertained strong suspicions of the truth, into which I had refrained from inquiring lest I should show myself inquisitive about his personal concerns.

Mr Ellin was not minded to become a literary lion, and he made Tina and me promise not to tell what we knew. After a little further conversation, he shed his customary reserve and proceeded to give me some account of his life. His father had held various diplomatic posts in Russia and Sweden and had been active in efforts to promote good understanding between our country and Scandinavia. After studying at Upsala and Oxford, he had worked in the Foreign Office, being employed — as he observed with a grimace — in the preparation of draft agreements on such lively subjects as the promotion of Swedish fur and timber trading. In his spare time, which was ample, he had indulged in the literary pursuits dear to his heart, but always preserving his anonymity in obedience to a regulation introduced in his youth by his superiors and only recently rescinded.

Having told me so much, he seemed doubtful whether or not to say more; but at last he told me, very simply, that about two years earlier he had inherited from a maternal uncle a considerable estate, Valincourt, about twenty miles from Clinton St James. Hearing the name, Tina looked up from her folk tales.

'I know Valincourt,' she said. 'I mean, I have seen a picture of it, standing in its big park. It was the most beautiful of all the houses.'

'Most beautiful of all the houses?' we questioned.

'Yes. In a book at Fuchsia Lodge. There were no books to speak of, at Fuchsia Lodge,' said Tina, scornfully. 'But on the table in Miss Wilcox's company parlour there was a great fat book with pictures of historic houses. I had nothing to read, so I used to make up stories about the people who lived in the houses. I liked Valincourt best.'

'I am honoured,' said Mr Ellin.

Tina smiled and returned to her book. He went on to explain that he could not take up residence on his property, as under the terms of his uncle's will the widow was entitled to remain in the house for her lifetime if she so desired; and there was also an agent whom it would not be just and right to turn away. But, having sufficient means of his own, he had resigned his post at the Foreign Office and had come to live at Clinton St James so that he might be near enough to supervise the estates of Valincourt. (I learnt later — but not from Mr Ellin — that the aunt-by-marriage was an unamiable elderly lady who bitterly resented her husband's choice of his own nephew as heir rather than hers.) Seeing that he had in part conquered his shyness of talking about himself, I told him how much I had enjoyed his translations of Geijer's *Odalbonder* and Stagnelius's *Liljor i Saron*, the lovely *Lilies of Sharon*. Did he, I asked, contemplate translating the novels of Frederika Bremer?

He shook his head. 'No, Mrs Mary Howitt is already in possession of that field. I must not intrude. By the way, I understand that you too are a translator, from the French.'

'Not for publication. Who told you?'

Mr Ellin indicated Tina, curled up in a chair, oblivious of time and space. 'So you understand the delights and frustrations of rightly rendering other men's thoughts in your own language?'

'In a small way, yes.' And we plunged into an animated discussion of the merits and defects of translators in general and of Chapman, Pope and Cowper in particular. (I had sewn and embroidered my way through the immense number of hours devoted by Mr Chalfont to the reading aloud of these gentlemen's dealings with Homer.)

After that day, we fell into the habit of talking about books whenever we met, exchanging opinions and arguing vehemently when our opinions differed. Tina was particularly impressed by one of these argumentative discussions in which I hotly defended James Macpherson's translation of the poems of Ossian. In vain did Mr Ellin, calling on Dr Johnson to support him, proclaim *Ossian* to be a palpable and most impudent forgery; in vain did he ridicule the prose-poems as a farrago of dark winds sighing, lamenting ladies, moss-covered rocks, grey mists, beamy spears, streamy isles and a thousand thin ghosts shrieking at once on the hollow wind. The sole result of his efforts was Tina's announcement made after his departure, 'I should like to read those poems. Have you an Ossian book?'

Laughing, I found the small book in its green and gold tooled binding. A frown of disapproval crossed her face as she opened it. 'Somebody has been scribbling on the pages. The margins are covered with pot-hooks and pot-hangers, and so are the pictures. Who did such a dreadful thing?'

Tina was as likely as any other child to spill tea and splash paint, but she was remarkably careful in her handling of books; they were treated as tenderly as if they had a life of their own. I smiled as I answered, 'My stepson Guy when he was very little.'

'Why didn't you rub them out?'

How could I tell her that those pencil marks were my only links with the boy I had wanted to treasure as my own? She did not wait for an answer.

'It was very naughty to spoil the book. Pray what did you say to him when you found out what he had done? Oh no, you could not scold him because ——'

She stopped in some embarrassment.

'Of course Mrs Chalfont could not scold him,' said Annie, who was with us. 'You cannot have forgotten that she never set eyes on any of her stepchildren.'

Shrinking as I did from the revival of old memories, I had never inquired how much of my story had been made known to Tina during her schooldays; but I more than suspected than any gaps in her knowledge had been abundantly filled by Annie, who now seized an unexpected opportunity of once again giving vent to her disapproval of my stepchildren's behaviour.

'He was put up to it, baby that he was, by Miss Emma and the other two, who were angry because they wanted their holiday extended so that they could visit a big travelling circus that was coming to the neighbourhood. But their papa said no, Mrs Chalfont was coming home on that very day and it was now too late to write and put her off as she would already have started on her homeward journey. In their spite and malice they — led by Miss Emma — avenged themselves by going into their step-mother's boudoir and drawing ugly pictures and writing insults in some of her books. Little Master Guy was four years old then, and he couldn't write or draw like the others; but he had been taught to make pot-hooks and pot-hangers, so that was what he did, thinking, poor child, it would annoy his stepmother just as much as his sister's and brothers' insolence. Miss Arminel did not complain, bless her! The children's ill-doing never would have been brought to light if their papa had not happened to wish to consult one of Miss Arminel's books. He was a gentleman that kept his own books spick and span — and when he found the book shamefully defaced he opened others and saw they were in the same plight. Oh, what a state he was in, to be sure! He went straight off to Parborough Hall — and those bad children paid dearly for their nasty trick. Not one farthing of pocket-money did they see until every one of those books had been cleaned and handsomely rebound at their expense. It was the last prank Master Augustine ever played in his life, I've been told; for he was at school by that time, where it was very awkward and humbling for a lad to be without money and everybody knowing why, whereas at home with tutor and governess Master Laurence and Miss Emma could keep their disgrace hidden from the world. As for Master Guy, Miss Arminel contrived to push his book out of sight — and Mr Chalfont never even suspected such a little one of being in league with the others.'

'If Guy was old enough to make pot-hooks and pot-hangers, he was old enough to know right from wrong. I think it is a great pity he was not caught and punished with the rest of his unpleasant family. I do not like to read a book spoilt by his scribblings — I have a good mind to ask Mr Ellin to lend me his *Ossian* — I know he has one.'

And Tina strutted off with a self-righteous air.

Chapter Eight

Mr Ellin's not being immediately available, Martina contented herself with the book that Guy had disfigured; but she found consolation in displaying it, with many expressions of horrified disapproval, to Elinor and Rosamond, whom she harangued at considerable length on the care and respect that should be shown to all printed matter. Thereafter they were obliged to listen to many readings aloud from those shadowy chronicles, Tina's choice resting always on the pathetic passages in which maidens with red eyes and heaving bosoms mourned the fallen heroes. How often did those poor dolls patiently endure the recital of her favourite page from *Carric-Thura*, wherein the warrior-maid Crimora, bright in the armour of man, followed her much-beloved Connal to the fight, her yellow hair loose behind, her bow in her hand. Having observed the approach of Connal's enemy Dargo, 'she drew the string on Dargo; but erring she pierced her Connal. He falls like an oak on the plain; like a rock from the shaggy hill. What shall she do, hapless maid! He bleeds; her Connal dies! All the night long she cries, and all the day, "O Connal, my love and my friend!" With grief the sad mourner dies! Earth here encloses the loveliest pair on the hill. The grass grows between the stones of the tomb; I often sit in the mournful shade. The wind sighs through the grass; their memory rushes on my mind. . . .'

The small doll inhabitants of the playbox were not compelled to be mute auditors: theirs was a more active part. Renamed for the nonce Fingal, Shelric, Selma, Oscar, Hidallan, Malvina and I know not what, they rushed madly into battle at great cost to their jointed arms and legs and to the robes fashioned by Martina from my rag-bag's silks and velvets in what she fondly believed to be the styles prevailing in remote antiquity. The study of *Ossian*, however, was only one among my young charge's multifarious occupations; for she had become the busiest of creatures, reading everything she could lay hands on, drawing and painting on every scrap of paper that came her way, digging and planting in her garden plot, learning to cook under kindly Eliza's supervision and devoting herself to the education of Elinor and Rosamond, whom she taught to count in the Cornish numerals — un, du, tri, padzher, pemp, wheth, seith, eith, nau, deig — that she had picked up from Annie, and for whose edification she devised miniature paper books containing, I was given to understand, much that it was necessary for them to know.

She began, also, to make advances toward friendship, unlooked for in a child who, stiff and silent, had held herself aloof from schoolmistresses and schoolfellows alike. After Larry, gardener as well as handyman, had prepared a plot for her, she confided to me her regret that she had not given him a Christmas gift. 'For I was new at Silverleà Cottage then, and I did not think of it. Besides, there was not anything in the basket that was suitable for him except the watch-pocket that was Mr Ellin's. You do not suppose that Larry was hurt in his feelings, do you, Mrs Chalfont? I should not like him to be hurt.'

I assured her that Larry's feelings were intact; and she sped away to hold a conversation through the garden hedge with the Rector's children, who for so long had been seen but as swollen faces peering through the windows. Mr and Mrs Randolph's elder children were out in the world or at boarding school; but there were three still at home; Anselm, a boy of eleven, who studied under his father; Elizabeth, an invalid of Tina's own age; and the little Anna, four years old. Tina's attention had first been drawn to them when with pitying eyes she watched Anselm trundling Elizabeth down the garden paths in her wheel-chair. They had spied her and called to her — and before I knew that a friendship had been established Tina was crawling back through a hole they had made in the hedge to proclaim the amazing news that she and Elizabeth shared the same birthday. 'And think of it, Mrs Chalfont, Elizabeth could not have a party on her birthday because the house was full of mumps. I had a party with you and Mr Ellin — a splendid party! Was it not sad for Elizabeth, missing hers? Anselm went to a party just before they all fell ill — oh, such a party! He described it to me. It was a boy's party: there were no girls. They would not play any of the games that had been arranged for them except a game of bobbing for apples in a tub, when they pushed one another's heads under the water. And they threw jam tarts at one another and spent the whole evening sliding down the bannisters and riding the stairs on a tea-tray. The papa and mamma were very cross. Anselm says he behaved well; but Elizabeth and I do not believe him. We know better!'

Though I sympathized with the cross mamma and papa, I kept my opinion to myself, so delighted was I to see Tina carried away by an outburst of childish glee. The friendship was well established when in late April I judged that Tina needed more in the way of lessons than a small amount of piano practice and the daily reading with me of short selected portions of the daily Lessons and Psalms. Mrs Randolph readily agreed to my request that Tina should share Elizabeth's governess; and Dr Percy and Mr Ellin, when consulted, saw no reason why Tina should not in strict moderation resume her studies. They would not have her wearied or worried; but if all strain could be avoided, they felt sure that young companionship and perhaps the spur of competition would be of great value to her.

Tina herself welcomed the arrangement, in part because it helped to remove a lurking fear that Miss Wilcox might — as she expressed it — 'try to grab her back' to an establishment now swollen to accommodate some fifteen boarders and as many day girls, with Diana as Senior Pupil and Mary and Jessy as her assistants. Willingly, therefore, she scrambled through her hole in the hedge in preference to walking sedately up or down the garden path; and joyfully she came prancing home with a vast store of wondrous adventures encountered in a lively, merry household full of comings and goings, and in which Mr Randolph, aided by Mr Cecil, regularly prepared two or three young men for ordination. Students of divinity they might be, but their presence increased rather than diminished the joyousness of that ever-cheerful Rectory; and from time to time Tina enlivened quiet Silverlea Cottage with reports of outrageous practical jokes that would have made the hair of my sisters — and in particular the hair of my excellent sister Mary — rise on their heads with horror, had the education of their daughters been carried on in such hilarious surroundings.

I cannot think that the two little maidens exerted themselves much in their lesson-hours. It was in their playtime that, urged on by Tina, Elizabeth gradually shook off the invalid habits of some years. This first became apparent when Tina, to whom Mr Ellin had presented a skipping rope, was dismayed to find herself practising her art alone.

'I am going to make Elizabeth learn to skip,' quoth she. 'I cannot have her everlastingly stuck in that wheel-chair as if she were a person of ninety years old. Anselm will not join me because he says skipping is not a sport for boys. Elizabeth and I have a suspicion that he skips all by himself when he fancies he is not observed. We mean to keep a watch — and then we shall have the laugh of him! As for that fat little Anna, she is only a baby and does not skip any better than a cabbage. So Elizabeth must.'

Thanks to the strong will and persistent encouragement of Tina, Elizabeth, somewhat to the consternation of her parents, struggled out of her invalid chair and surprised her world by walking and later by attempts at running, though the desired goal of skipping was by medical orders prohibited. In their gratitude Mr and Mrs Randolph did not know how to reward the young unknown for working this near-miracle, or me for having undertaken the guardianship of her.

I needed no thanks; for by this time the charge of Martina had become, to misquote (I hope not irreverently), 'such a burden as wings are to a bird'. It was, in truth, so deep a joy that I was obliged to take myself to task for selfishness in that I had never, in the five years of my loneliness, bethought me of welcoming to Silverlea Cottage some neglected orphan who would have been glad of such a refuge from the storms of life.

It was not to be supposed that Mr Ellin was able to devote his entire life to the search for Tina's missing relatives. He had been for the past twelve months engaged in writing a *History of Swedish Poetry* in the intervals of attending to the necessary business of the Valincourt estate. Also, much to his embarrassment, he had been plagued with invitations from all quarters on its becoming known that he was a distinguished author and landed proprietor. The secret had leaked out through Tina, who, despite her promise to keep what she knew to herself, had promptly bestowed the same knoweldge on Elizabeth. 'How could I possibly tell that Mr and Mrs Randolph had not already told Elizabeth about Mr Ellin? If I had a little girl, I would tell her everything, quite everything,' she pleaded, when Mr Ellin and I taxed her with her breach of faith. 'And how was I to know that Elizabeth would go and tell Miss Spindler and so it would be spread all round the parish? A governess ought to know better than to get talking. I *had* to tell Elizabeth. She is my friend, and it is *wrong* to keep secrets from friends.'

Mr Ellin was accepting the excuses with a smile and a shrug, when a thought struck him. 'So are we your friends, Tina, Mrs Chalfont and I. But you keep secrets from us, though you have known us longer than you have known Elizabeth. Isn't it time that you told us what we should like to know?'

Tina shrank away from us, hanging her head as in the old days at Fuchsia Lodge. 'I would tell you if I could,' she said at last. 'I must not. No, I must not and — and I dare not.'

'Some day perhaps you will be brave enough to speak,' said Mr Ellin. 'And in the meantime, don't you give away any more secrets that Mrs Chalfont and I may happen to tell you. Here have I had three invitations to dinner this week, which I cannot refuse without giving mortal offence. Think what you have done, you little rascal — and repent!'

Tina smiled again. I cannot say whether or not she repented.

Though he could not, as I have said, spend all his days in trying to find out what Tina could not or would not tell, Mr Ellin had certainly done all in his power to solve the mystery. From Christmas onward he had caused to be inserted at regular intervals in the newspapers a notice requesting the relatives of Miss Martina (also known as Matilda) Fitzgibbon to communicate as soon as possible with Miss Wilcox, whose address he gave, rather to that lady's annoyance, as she was thereby obliged to postpone the selling of Miss Matilda's finery until it should become abundantly evident that the Fitzgibbons of all degrees of relationship had no intention whatever of communicating with her. As soon as the roads were clear he had searched for and recovered the playbox; and acting on the slender clues suplied by the intials 'T.D.' and Tina's mention of a voyage to New ——, he had ever since been most diligent in making inquiries at shipping-offices in all the main ports. But an exhaustive study of their passenger-lists revealed no trace of a Conway Fitzgibbon; and three passengers with the initials 'T.D.' proved to be persons of unblemished record whom it was impossible to suspect of having deserted a young female relative. He was almost at his wits' end when he discovered that a French ship, calling at the almost unknown port of Thanpool, had there picked up a few passengers of whom the port authorities had kept no list. It was rumoured, he was told, that the *Pandore* had foundered midway to New York, with the loss of all on board.

He had great difficulty in tracing the owners of the ill-fated *Pandore*, who at first refused to give him any information about the lost ship, being afraid that he intended to set up some claim against them. When finally reassured on this head, they told him that the only survivors were two brothers named Reynolds, who had been rescued from their make-shift raft by a passing American vessel, which had conveyed them to New York. The tragedy was now many months old; for the *Pandore* had been wrecked within a month of the day on which Martina had been deposited at Fuchsia Lodge.

There followed the task of tracking down the rescued brothers. They had long since left their first address in New York and had to be pursued by repeated letters to — as Mr Ellin once despairingly observed — almost every known corner of that gigantic country. In mid-July success — a sorrowful success — crowned his efforts. One of the brothers wrote to confirm that he and his brother George had made the acquaintance of Mr Conway Fitzgibbon on board the *Pandore*. It was not an acquaintance, unfortunately, to which either of them looked back with pleasure. George had lost a large sum of money at cards to the man, who was later detected by another passenger in cheating; and he, himself, had never been able to throw off the first unfavourable impression made on him by a trifling incident at the beginning of the voyage — an incident on which, Mr Reynolds said, Mr Ellin's own inquiry had thrown an ugly light. The two brothers and Mr Fitzgibbon were standing at the rails to watch the moment of departure when an old respectable serving-man came hurrying up the gangway just before it was withdrawn. Quite out of breath, he handed a packet to Mr Fitzgibbon, saying, 'For little Miss Martina, Sir, from ——'. A name followed, but was lost in a gasp. Mr Fitzgibbon took the packet and opened it, saying with a smile, 'Oh, I am going to have a peep first!' The packet, when opened, proved to contain a pretty writing-case in blue leather with silver clasps. 'Miss Martina will be charmed with this,' he said. 'She is playing with some little friends just now, in the dining-cabin. You will not forget to take our thanks, Martina's and mine, to the kind donor?' Then he fee'd the old man and dismissed him.

Mr Reynolds went on to say that the name Martina, being unusual, had stuck in his memory. Although he knew that Mr Fitzgibbon had come alone aboard the *Pandore*, he naturally supposed that Martina, daughter or niece, was already in the ship. He would have thought no more of the incident had it not been for a curious circumstance that occurred when the *Pandore* had been some time at sea. He and his brother had moved away from Mr Fitzgibbon's vicinity when they saw him pick up the writing-case from where it lay on a bench. It was then, with considerable energy, hurled into the sea by one who evidently believed himself unobserved. Later, they discovered that no 'little Miss Martina' was numbered among their fellow passengers.

Undoubtedly, wrote Mr Reynolds, there was a discreditable mystery of some kind; but unless the child could be induced to speak, the truth would never now come to light. He and his brother could positively state that Mr Fitzgibbon had perished in the wreck of the *Pandore*. Themselves adrift on their tiny raft, unable to render the least assistance, they had seen with horrified eyes the capsizing of an overloaded boat, to the side of which Mr Fitzgibbon was clinging. That dreadful sight was for ever imprinted on their memory . . .

Mr Ellin had gone to London to see the publisher who was bringing out his *History of Swedish Poetry*. On his return he found the letter from Mr Reynolds awaiting him. He came immediately to consult with me. Together we summoned Tina.

She ran gaily into the parlour, rejoicing that Mr Ellin was come home again. Something in our attitude arrested her, and she stood still, looking at us doubtfully. Mr Ellin drew forward a chair and motioned to her to sit down. 'My dear,' he said, 'Mrs Chalfont and I have sad news for you.' Then, in the gentlest words he could find, he told her of her father's death.

She sat still, her head bent; she did not weep. Presently she said, in a voice of utter desolation, 'He never wrote the letter. He never wrote it. What shall I do now?'

'You must tell us your true name,' said Mr Ellin, a little startled, I thought, at the absence of normal signs of grief. 'And I think you should also tell us why your papa's letter was so important.'

'I cannot tell you anything, not one single thing since the letter has not come, the letter that Papa said he could not write until he was safely in America. He said I must not, or I should spoil all. If I did, frightful things would happen to him and to me.'

'Nothing frightful can happen to your father now. He is in the hands of God,' said Mr Ellin reverently. 'And you may be very sure that Mrs Chalfont and I have been appointed by divine providence to protect you from harm. Be brave, then, and tell us your name and the reason, as far as you know it, why your papa left you at Fuchsia Lodge.'

'No, no, I cannot. The letter did not come.'

She repeated the words over and over as we pleaded with her to reveal all. When we suggested that her grandparents or uncles and aunts might be in anxiety about her, she stopped short in the middle of her repeated parrot cry. Here, it appeared, was something that she was prepared to say.

'I have no grandparents, they are all dead long ago, before I was born. And I have no uncles or aunts; for Papa and Mamma were both only children. I have no one. And the letter did not come. I will tell you this much; I do not know what Papa would have written in it, but he said it would make me happier than I could dream of. But I am happy now, I could not be happier. Only I must not tell any more. The letter did not come.'

We had to own ourselves baffled. Tina was silent and grave for the rest of the day; she appeared to be thinking deeply. At night she came to me in a hesitancy which presently resolved itself into words that were part explanation, part confession: 'Mrs Chalfont, I am sorry to hear that Papa was drowned, indeed I am. It must be dreadful to be drowned. I fell into a pond once, when I was little, and it frightened me very much. But you see, I did not know Papa very well. He and Mamma were often away from home, sometimes for months, travelling or visiting their friends; and when they were at home, they entertained much company. Papa never kissed me that I can remember. He never came to my nursery, or to my schoolroom when I grew too old to have a nurse. That happened when I was getting on for six years old. Mamma said I loved my nurse more than I loved her, and she would not have it; she would find me a governess whom I would not be able to love because nobody ever did love a governess —'

At the time I did not perceive how infinitely sad were these artless disclosures: the realization dawned on me only when I was alone with leisure to think. While Tina was speaking, my mind was full of the hope that I might be able to persuade her to tell me more, since she seemed to be in a communicative mood.

'So you were fond of your nurse, my dear?'

'Oh yes, yes! I loved her dearly.'

'What was her name?'

The answer was disappointing. 'She was just Nurse. I had another nurse at first when I was a small, small baby; but I don't remember her — I only remember Nurse. If Papa found me anywhere downstairs, it was always, "Run back to your nurse, Martina". I did not know Papa nearly as well as I know you and Mr Ellin. If either of you were to be drowned, I should die of grief. Will you please explain to Mr Ellin why I did not cry when he told me about Papa? I just felt strange, so strange. I could see that Mr

Ellin thought I had a hard heart.'

I told Tina that I understood, and I promised to make Mr Ellin understand also. Then, with assumed carelessness, I asked, 'What was your governess's name? Do you know where she is now?'

After a pause for reflection, Tina decided that this question could safely be answered.

'Her name was Miss Murphy, and she went back to Ireland to be married as soon as she had made enough knitted lace. I don't know where she is now.'

I could not grasp the connection between marriage and the making of knitted lace. Mr Ellin would have said that my mind whirled at it. Seeing my bewilderment, Tina condescended to explain. 'Miss Murphy was engaged to be married. She had been engaged for over four years, ever since she came to be my governess. But she and her betrothed — that is what she always called him — were resolved not to be married until between them they had saved enough money to live in comfort, not hugger-mugger in a cabin with pigs and hens, which — Miss Murphy said — was the way stupid English people thought the Irish lived. So in addition to teaching me, she made quantities of knitted lace in her spare time. It went to be sold in shops or among her friends. She was the best maker of knitted lace in the whole of Ireland, she said, and her lace was in great demand. Shawls she knitted, and petticoats and babies' clothes and edgings. I had to be as quiet as a mouse in lesson-time and in playtime too — I must never squeak my slate-pencil or ask questions or kick the legs of my chair for fear of putting her out in the counting of her stitches. She knitted in my lesson-time; but she never let anyone see her doing it. Once Mamma came in unexpectedly. Miss Murphy shuffled her knitting into her work-bag so fast that the knitting came off the pins and the stitches were dropped — oh, ever so far down! I laughed. Miss Murphy made me learn twenty lines of poetry for that.'

It seemed to me that the penalty should have been inflicted on the best maker of knitted lace in the whole of Ireland rather than on Tina, whose lesson hours, I now heard, were largely passed in learning by heart the answers to Mangnall's *Questions* and in performing the exercise commonly known as 'transcription'. I next inquired the name of Miss Murphy's 'betrothed'.

'I never heard the whole of his name; but I know his little short name. It's Pat. Once Miss Murphy's sister came over from Ireland to see her. She held a letter up behind Miss Murphy's head and she said just as we do in a game of forfeits, "Here's a thing and a very pretty thing — and what will you give me for this pretty thing?" Miss Murphy cried out, "It's a letter from my dear saucy Pat!" — and she made a snatch at it and ran out of the room. Her eyes were all shiny. I liked Miss Murphy's sister. She told me stories about leprechauns and she described the misfortunes that happened to a man her papa knew who was foolish enough to cut down a fairy thorn tree.'

'Did Miss Murphy not tell you stories?'

'No, never. She played battledore and shuttlecock with me for the good of my health; but she said she had not undertaken to tell me stories. It would have interfered with her knitting, you see. And that reminds me, I shall not ask you to tell me the next part of *Lucy and the Enchanted Castle* tonight. I think it would not be kind, so soon after I had heard about poor Papa.'

The decision showed a delicacy of feeling that I was pleased to note. On my own account I was relieved; for my inventive powers had been under constant strain for some nights, having been repeatedly called upon to provide fresh adventures for Miss Lucy in the shape of encounters with dragons, ogres and magicians. A respite was very welcome.

To my surpise, Tina volunteered yet another piece of information about her governess. 'Miss Murphy went away just before Mamma died. It was very sudden, the servants said.'

'What was sudden, my dear? — your mamma's death or Miss Murphy's departure?'

'Both. Miss Murphy was vexed because she had to leave so soon when she was not expecting it. She would have difficulty in finding another post, she said. Ladies did not like to employ a governess who was expecting to leave to be married within a few months. Mamma and Miss Murphy had a quarrel about that, very fierce it was. Miss Murphy said Mamma had no right to turn her off with a month's notice when she had accepted the post on the clear understanding that she would stay for full five years; till I was old enough to be sent away to school. And Mamma said there had been no undertaking to keep her for five years; it was all Miss Murphy's own imagination. And Miss Murphy said Mamma was not speaking the truth and she ought to be compensated for loss of earnings as the five years had not been finished but only four and a half of them. Mamma said that was a preposterous demand and Miss Murphy was to pack her trunk and go that very day and she did. I was sorry for Miss Murphy. But Mamma could not keep her because ——'

Here Tina broke off, apparently alarmed by her own loquacity. She had not explained why Miss Murphy was dismissed; but it was obvious to me — as it would be later to Mr Ellin — that the impending voyage to New York was the reason or pretext, whichever it might be.

It was also clear that Tina had seen little more of her mother than of her father, and that she grieved no more for the one than for the other. I therefore had no hesitation in asking, 'How did you come by the snake-bracelet? — was it a gift from your mamma? Was her name Emma?'

A scared look crossed Tina's face. 'It belonged to Mamma — it was given to her by a friend. Papa said I was to keep it; but Miss Wilcox took it away.'

'Be comforted, my dear Mr Ellin bought it from Miss Wilcox, and he is taking care of it for you.'

'Mr Ellin is always good,' said Tina, 'but oh pray, Mrs Chalfont, ask him to keep it always. I do not wish to see it ever again.'

I could ask no more; and I tried to put away a dim and vague suspicion that had haunted me from the first hours of Tina's coming to Silverlea Cottage: a suspicion that I knew who Emma must be. Such a suspicion was baseless, unreasonable; the name Emma was common enough — why, every tenth girl was an Emma! And even if there was ground for my suspicion, what did it matter to me that the snake-bracelet had been given to Tina's mother in token of friendship? I recollected a moment in my youth when I, Arminel St Clair, had given my silver name-bracelet to a dearly-loved Sarah whom I had not seen for over twenty years, and whose surname I had forgotten.

Tina wore a subdued air for some days after she heard of her loss; but as she made no further confidences, it was impossible to tell whether she was mourning for her father or lamenting the letter he had failed to write. The story of Lucy and her enchanted castle was resumed and continued until I had to confess that for the time being the well of imagination had run dry. Whereupon, in her thirst for tales of every kind from the historical to the fanciful, Tina betook herself to the parlour of good old Annie, whose stock of stories, Cornish and otherwise, was well-nigh exhaustless. Whether the act of listening served Tina as an anodyne, a remedy against melancholy musings, I know not; but in the succeeding weeks she was frequently to be found sitting on Annie's cushioned window-ledge, her chin propped in her hands and all her soul looking out from the brown eyes that never left

Annie's face.

It was no legend but a woeful tale of fact that Annie was relating as I approached her parlour one evening. At her first words I stood motionless in the shade of the half-open door. Turned as it were to stone, I could not speak to tell Annie that this, the saddest passage in my life-story, was not fit for a child to hear. There Tina crouched, her face white as a lily, her eyes dilating; and there lurked I, plunged once more beneath the waves of an ancient sea of sorrow.

'Ah, Miss Arminel has known sadness. She was the child I loved best of all the brood,' old Annie was quavering. 'Oh, but Mr Chalfont was a hard man, hard as the nether millstone! He would not let her have the little Guy to whom she would have been the best of mothers. No, he said, Guy must not be separated from his brothers and sister. And then long years afterwards — oh, the weary years! — she had hope of a babe of her own. She had settled it should be christened Theodore if it was a boy, Dorothea if it was a girl. Those were Greek names, she told me; and they both had the same meaning, the gift of God. I will maintain, yes, to the last day of my life, that all would have gone well with my poor Miss Arminel had it not been for Miss Emma. When the babe's birth was imminent, what does Miss Emma do but stay in the Grewby village, a mile off, along with a friend who had hired a little house there while her own house was being repaired after a fire. She would drive over constantly in her pony chaise to chat with her father "to cheer him up", she said, while her stepmother was safely out of the way. Struck for death Miss Arminel was, when she heard what was happening. "Annie, Annie, Emma hopes I will die," Miss Arminel cried, over and over again. "Emma is waiting to see me die." And so she was, I do verily believe, the black vulture in the black cloak she wore, having a fancy for that colour, though to my mind better befitting an old hag of a witch than a personable young woman. I went to the master, yes I did, and begged him on my bended knees to forbid Miss Emma the house till the babe was born. I tell you, I thought he would have struck me to the earth. "What! Forbid my daughter the house?" cries he. "You are out of your senses, woman. Get you gone, or I'll have you put in Bedlam."

'So Miss Emma came and went as she pleased; and upstairs Miss Arminel moaned on, "She has come to see us die, see us die." And at death's door she lay; and the little babe was born dead, and I looked every minute for Miss Arminel to follow it to the grave. Days went by before she was out of danger —'

'Was the baby a boy or a girl?' asked Tina, moving for the first time.

'A girl.'

'Dorothea,' said Tina softly.

'No!' Annie flung at her in angry resentment. 'Did I not tell you that it was born dead? It could never have a name. Its little coffin was brought up to the house at once; for the undertaker — the same whose funeral coach Miss Emma had once hired — had a tiny one by him. Wretched fellow! I do believe Miss Emma drove past his workshop and warned him to be ready. Poor babe, poor babe, carried away by the underlings; for neither the nurse nor I could leave Miss Arminel — t'cha, t'cha, Mrs Chalfont I should say, but the old name clings. However, there is a thing for which I shall ever be thankful: it was buried in the family mausoleum. The other servants told me so, when I could bear to listen to them. And I heard something else that it did my heart good to hear. There had been hot words between Miss Emma and her father on the manner of the burial. She said it must be buried in an unconsecrated corner of the churchyard; it was not lawful for it to lie in consecrated ground, not being a Christian. They say that Mr Chalfont turned on her like a lion, and, says he, it should rest in the mausoleum if all the bishops in Christendom said him nay. I never had any liking for Mr Chalfont save when I heard how he withstood the black vulture to her face. "Get one of the gowns your stepmother had prepared," he bade her, "and see that all is done decently. I will return shortly to carry the child to the mausoleum myself. Are you going to obey me, or shall I call some of the women to do what you ought to be glad to do for your poor little sister?"

'Amazed and shaken she must have been; for I doubt whether he had ever spoken so harshly to her before in all her wild pranks, not even when she twice took up with gentlemen that were no fit match for her. And when she said she would do as she was bid, he turned on his heel and left her.

'She wouldn't allow anyone to come near her after the babe, that had been washed, was brought to the room where the coffin stood. With her own hands she put it in the coffin and screwed down the lid. She would not wait to see her father again, but jumped into her pony-chaise and off she went — and the next thing we heard was that she and her friend had quitted the friend's rented house that same evening and taken themselves off. Right rejoiced was I to know that I'd seen the last of that black cloak flapping across the park.'

'Was Mr Chalfont sorry about the baby, then? I do believe he was; for he would not have it put where the poor suicides lie, and he carried it to the mauso-mausoleum himself. What is a mausoleum, Annie?'

'A place of dole, child, where the corpses lie above ground instead of below in a vault. The Grewby Towers mausoleum was made like a heathenish pagan temple, with yew trees all about.'

'Horrid!' said Tina, shivering. 'Did Mr Chalfont make friends with his daughter again?'

'Oh, trust her for that! A storm in a tea-cup, as you might say. They were as thick as thieves again in no time at all. Yes, I suppose he was sorry, though I was put past my patience to hear him, while the mistress still lay between life and death, making the worst kind of to-do about a book he had lost. Turned the whole house upside-down, he did. He never could find it, though, I'm thankful to say. Served him right!'

The spell that bound me was broken by Annie's little exhibition of human spite. I moved quietly away before either the narrator or the listener had seen me.

I noticed that Tina was unusually thoughtful after she had heard Annie's story. On the next Sunday afternoon, when I was hearing her repeat the *Catechism*, she surprised me by saying, 'Mrs Chalfont, is it true that at one's Confirmation, a person may take an additional name?'

'I have heard so,' I answered, 'but I am not sure whether it is true. We must ask Mr Randolph or Mr Cecil. Who told you of the practice?'

'At Fuchsia Lodge I heard Diana saying to Jessy that she did not like her name. She said she was resolved to be called Theresa when she was confirmed.'

'Indeed! And what name do you wish to take?'

In the the lowest of whispers, Tina made answer, 'Dorothea'.

There was no need to ask her the reason for so unusual a choice. I knew it.

Chapter Nine

At the earliest opportunity I acquainted Mr Ellin with the information I had gleaned from Tina, scanty though it was. When I mentioned Miss Murphy's marriage, Mr Ellin forgot his manners as far as to whistle. 'Whew! here's another problem to add to our host of insolubles. How do you propose I shall trace one saucy Pat in an island that swarms with them? Faith, it will be as easy to find the former Miss Murphy as it would be to pick a particular potato out of a sack! However, I'll do what I can. Are there not agencies to which ladies go when they are seeking instructresses for their children? Such places would probably keep a register of their clients.'

I said that these agencies might very well exist, although personally I would never employ a governess who had not been recommended to me by my friends.

'I shall have recourse to the London directory,' said Mr Ellin, 'and if that fails, to the Dublin one. A short sojourn in Ireland would do something towards consoling me for the loss of you and Tina, who, I understand, are proposing shortly to disport yourselves at the seaside. And it strikes me that these directories may be useful also in providing the names and addresses of shops likely to purchase the wares of the celebrated maker of knitted lace who taught Tina in the odd minutes left over from that absorbing occupation. I don't propose myself to conduct investigations in the lace shops — I'll bring or send you likely names.'

After we had disposed of Miss Murphy, I consulted Mr Ellin on two matters in which I needed his advice. One was the desirability or otherwise of putting Tina into mourning. Mr Ellin dissuaded me from doing so, pointing out that Martina had made her appearance at Fuchsia Lodge in the resplendent apparel that was to have suitably impressed the natives of New York. Since Mr Fitzgibbon had not chosen to provide his child with mourning for her mamma, there could be no reason for Martina's guardians thus to honour his memory. But, added Mr Ellin, he supposed it might be advisable to make some slight alterations in the clothes I was getting ready for the forthcoming seaside holiday, such as a black sash on a white frock, or a Sunday dress in violet or grey. I, he was pleased to add, would be the best judge of that.

This took me to the last of the matters I had wished to bring to his notice. Lodgings for the sojourn by the sea had been found for me in the village by my sister Mary and my brother Hugh, who with their families intended to spend a month in the leisurely enjoyment of the many-twinkling smiles of ocean. Was it wise or kind, I asked, to bring Martina in sight of the tempestuous element in which her father had met his death?

Mr Ellin thought that I could not in fairness break the agreements I had made; and he opined that the sudden cancellation of an eagerly-anticipated holiday would affect Tina far more adversely than the sight of the sea, surrounded as she would be by a lively group of youngsters in the best of spirits.

Thus reassured, I again set to work on my preparations, which were rendered all the more arduous in that the last item in Diana's wardrobe — the dress that Jane's aunt had dyed the prettiest hollyhock pink — was now consigned to the cupboard where the maids kept their rubbing and scrubbing rags, it having suffered grievously from a short-lived but intense devotion to the manufacture, in company with Anselm, Elizabeth and Anna, of bowls and dishes from a small clay pit they had found near the bank of the Clint. This passion having now abated, I was glad that the first few days of her holidays saw Tina engrossed in a return to a less begriming and frustrating favourite pastime, namely the compilation of yet another of her midget encyclopaedias. This new production was distinguished from its forerunners by being housed in a wine-coloured notebook larger and stouter than the previous stitched-paper volumes and paid for, moreover, at the stationer's from her weekly pocket-money. Until then she had shown me each of her 'books'; but the contents of her wine-coloured notebook were not read aloud, according to custom, in the glow of authorship; nor, being exceedingly busy at the time, did I ask to hear them.

On the sunniest of sunny mornings we set off for the most joyful holiday I had known in twenty years. Our seaside retreat was situated on a part of the coast where moorland ran down to the very edge of the shore. Those were not the sinister Grewby moors, dark, mist-wrapped, encircled by gloomy hills. Brilliantly coloured, they stretched away mile after mile to the horizon itself. At first sight, Tina cast not a glance to the blue radiance dancing in the sunlight, but — 'A purple sea!' she cried. 'A purple sea! Look, look, a purple sea!' I shall never forget her cry of ecstasy or the deep content that she showed on finding that our rooms in a comfortable farm-house faced her beloved empurpled landscape.

She showed no distaste for the sea, though her happiest hours were those that were spent in rambles and gypsyings on the moors. During the first ten days I was troubled by her propensity for standing alone to watch the advancing tide, intently gazing, silently waiting for I knew not what coveted prize. I could not find it in my heart to discourage the practice; but I was relieved when my niece Margaret said, with a giggle, 'Aunt Arminel, is it true that people sometimes put letters in bottles?'

'It has been known to happen, my dear.'

'Tina is looking for a letter, she will not say from whom. What do you think? — Dick is going to write a nonsense letter and put it in a bottle for her to find.'

'Oh, Margaret, no! Dick must do nothing of the sort. You have been told, have you not, that Tina's papa is dead? Did you not hear how he died?'

Margaret shook her head.

'He was drowned. Find Dick, and tell him how cruel it would be to play such a trick on poor Tina.'

Good little Margaret ran off at once; and I saw her speaking earnestly to Dick, who, to do him justice, looked as shocked as she was. I was touched to see that thenceforward he was constantly attempting to distract Tina's attention from her vain quest. Not that she had many opportunities for pursuing it: her days were increasingly filled with the manifold delights that a sojourn by the sea affords. Indeed, she had more of them than were permitted to my nieces; for both my sister Mary and my sister-in-law Julia professed themselves horrified that I permitted Tina to run barefoot on the sands and to go wading, shrimping and exploring rock pools with the boys. The other girls had to content themselves with decorous strolls above the tide-mark in search of agate, cornelians and sea-shells while Tina was frolicking in the waves like a veritable mermaid, watched over by the one old bathing-woman and by me.

Thus we fleeted the time. If it had not been for a solitary

untoward incident, I should have regarded that month as a period of unclouded happiness.

One morning when there was thunder in the air with a promise of rain, we ladies, the elder girls and Bertha were seated in a cove with our books and work. At a little distance Margaret was aimlessly poking among the objects cast up by the tide, apparently in search of possible treasures. Further down the beach Tina was gathering seaweeds to be dried and pressed. She wore a summer dress that had excited much amusement when she first donned it; for, all unknowing, Mary and I had selected identical stuffs and patterns, she for her daughter Bertha, I for my unofficial ward.

Our attention was attracted by the unusual sight of a gay party of riders passing by. One of them, a lady, pulled up her horse and addressed some words to Margaret, at the same time pointing with her whip to Tina, who was then closely examining the respective merits of the feathery red, olive and green beauties that she had spread on a rock for better assessment. The speaker's back was turned to us, nor were we near enough to hear either the question she put to Margaret or Margaret's answer as, shading her short-sighted eyes with her hand, she looked to where Tina stood with seaweeds scattered round her. Whatever the reply, it satisfied the lady, who put her horse to the canter, rejoined her company and was soon lost to sight behind the rocks that guarded the entrance to our cove.

Margaret ran back to join us. 'Oh,' she cried, 'did you see the tall lady in the dark riding-habit? She wished to know the name of the little girl over there. I looked — and do you know, I quite thought it was Bertha! She is just Tina's height, they both have the same-coloured brown hair, and today they are wearing the frocks that match. So I said, "That is my sister Bertha — Bertha Maltravers." The lady said, "Thank you. I had almost taken her for a child I used to know." And she rode on. Shall I run after her and tell her that I made a mistake because my distant sight is not good? Do you think I could catch her up?'

For a reason I did not choose to acknowledge even to myself, I felt thankful when I heard Mary say sharply, 'No, Margaret, certainly not! I will not have you scampering like a wild thing over the sands.'

This, I knew was a reproach directed chiefly at me for the amount of liberty enjoyed by Tina, who at that instant, unlucky child, made use of her liberty by snatching up a long leathery thong of seaweed, advancing on Dick and chasing him over the beach to the accompaniment of a whirled weapon and threats to curdle the blood. Entering into the spirit of the game, Dick fled before her. On and on went the relentless pursuit until at last, wearying of it, Dick dashed up to our sedate circle, flung himself down on the sand and lay looking up at Tina and laughing. '*Pax, Tina, pax!*' he exclaimed. 'What made you hunt me like that? What had I done to offend you?'

For a moment Tina stood over him like an avenging angel, then she threw away her thong and dropped down beside him. 'Nothing,' she answered nonchalantly. 'I was only making believe that you were an enemy that I had to get rid of. I felt the need.'

Mary, Julia and their daughters looked as though they expected me to rebuke Tina for such a display of noisy unladylike behaviour. I disappointed their expectations. It was unreasonable, no doubt; but I could not dispel an uneasy feeling that both Tina and I had indeed been menaced by an enemy. I ought to have regretted the absence of Mr Ellin: on the contrary I felt guiltily relieved by the knowledge that he was searching for the former Miss Murphy somewhere on the other side of the Irish Sea. Assuredly, had he heard what Margaret had to say about the tall dark lady, he would instantly have gone in pursuit, perhaps using Dick's younger feet to overtake and bring to a halt the riding-party.

My conscience bade me do what my fellow-guardian would have done; my inclinations urged me to let slip this possible clue to the mystery that surrounded Tina. I looked at her as she sat on the sands by Dick, her arms clasped about her knees, listening in silence to the story that Margaret was only too eager to tell all over again. At its conclusion, making no comment, she jumped up and ran away in a direction opposite to that which had been taken by the lady and her friends. I parleyed with my inconvenient conscience until I partially succeeded in stifling its voice, convincing myself that not even Dick at his swiftest could catch the riders now. And why, I asked myself, should any sane person demand of me that I should undertake a tour of all the great houses in the neighbourhood, inquiring at each of them whether it accommodated a lady who had desired to know the name of a little girl she had seen on the beach? Surely, surely, if there had been anything suspicious in that question it would have been detected by Mary and Julia, who were both sharper-witted than I! But lo, they sat sewing away, quite serene and unperturbed.

Tina returned to our group after a while, perfectly composed. In her wake she dragged a huge tangle of wet seaweed, dark and dank brown with fat blobs on its multitudinous stems. I believe the algologists have tried to compensate the thing for its ugliness by giving it some such dignified name as *fucus nodosus*. 'Look what I have found, Aunt Arminel!' she exclaimed.

Hearing the other children address me as 'Aunt Arminel', she had quietly copied them. Disregarding sundry admonitions from Mary and Julia, I had not checked her. I now sought a tactful but truthful way of responding to her obvious delight in her latest find. 'Dear me, what a very fine specimen!' I said feebly.

'Yes, is it not?' agreed Tina, well pleased. 'It will be so useful, too; for it foretells the weather. These' — she indicated the blobs — 'are always dry when the weather is going to be fine and damp when rain is coming. An old fisherman told me so. We will take it home and hang it up in the drawing-room. Then we need not be at the trouble of stepping into the hall to look at the barometer.'

My hesitation, though slight, could not fail to be observed.

'Or perhaps I will give it to Mr Ellin instead. I am sure he would like it, and I daresay it is better suited to a gentleman's study than to a drawing-room.'

I recoiled from the prospect of including that mass of slimy coils in our home-going luggage. 'But how do you propose to take it to Mr Ellin?' I objected. 'I am afraid it is too unwieldy for us to carry back to Clinton St James.'

'Oh, Mr Ellin may come to see us here!' said Tina. 'I should not be in the least bit surprised if he did. And he will know what to do with it. I will hide it in a special crevice in the rocks, so that nobody shall steal it before he arrives.'

She withdrew, Mr Ellin's destined prize swaying and slithering after her. For Mr Ellin's sake I could only hope that some malefactor, deranged beyond belief, would make off with it before our friend put in an appearance. Not that I had any reason to expect his coming.

He came, nevertheless. On the following day his arrival was heralded by a rapturous cry of greeting from Tina. My welcome was less than enthusiastic: at the sight of him my stifled conscience struggled to renew its protests, urging that he ought to be told of Margaret's encounter with the tall dark lady. I disregarded the prickings and inquired what had brought him hither.

Mr Ellin seemed a little at a loss how to answer me, inasmuch as he had taken a very long ride to bring tidings that could easily have been conveyed by letter. The term 'tidings' is ill-advised: the news he brought was nothing but a report of his total lack of success in the tracing of Miss Murphy. Before leaving for Ireland, he had enlisted the help of a married sister whose home was in London, and from her had obtained the addresses of employment agencies and of what he persisted in calling 'lace shops'. These had one and all returned civil but disappointing replies to my letters of inquiry, penned in haste before Tina and I began our seaside holiday. Bolder abroad than in his native country, Mr Ellin had investigated the Dublin lace shops and agencies in person, but with no better results. We had now to conclude that Miss Murphy obtained her posts and her sales through the goodwill of friends.

Although Mr Ellin professed to be cast down by his repeated failures, his spirits revived in a marked degree as soon as he perceived that I heard of his ill-success with a show of equanimity that effectually masked — so I trust — my inward satisfaction. He remained at the village inn for two days, 'to rest my horse,' he said; but small indeed was the amount of rest obtained by that luckless animal, employed as it was in galloping over the sands at the behest of my nephews and I suspect of Tina also, whom I once heard jealously demanding a share in those equestrian performances on the double ground of older acquaintance with the horse's owner and equal skill in horsemanship acquired during rides on the Rectory pony. Into the outcome of that dispute I did not inquire, knowing that Mr Ellin would not suffer her to run into any danger.

He was on the point of departure when Margaret must needs break out with the story of the tall dark lady, who had now mysteriously become possessed of a pair of eyes that glowed and flashed beneath the little veil that hid her face. It was a story that stopped Mr Ellin in his tracks besides visibly discomposing Tina, despite all her efforts to appear unconcerned. I saw — and grieved to see — the old stony look of despair returning to her countenance as we stood watching him ride off on the first of his endeavours to find the lady and her companions.

Again he was baffled; though he rode hither and thither for a week in compliance with a suggestion made by the landlord of an inn, many miles away, where they were found to have dined. This fellow, who had a perfect knowledge of the whole county, declared emphatically that the riders were unknown in his part of the world. They were doing, he fancied, what wealthy folk so often did nowadays, scouring the country in search of old ruins and such-like. Off went Mr Ellin in pursuit; but from each of his successive visits to ancient monuments he came back feeling, as he pathetically observed, like an old ruin himself. Defeated, he lingered with us for another couple of days, making himself very agreeable to every member of our small community, whose own stay was drawing to a close. So he went, leaving behind him two books that he had picked up during his travels, *The Parent's Poetical Anthology* for me, full of helpful guidance to those entrusted with the training of the young; and one of Mr Fisher's annual volumes, *The Juvenile Scrap-Book* for Martina, edited by the praiseworthy Miss Agnes Strickland and the worthy Quaker poet Mr Bernard Barton, and adorned with choice engravings nicely calculated to improve a young person's taste. What delicious hours we spent, Martina and I, over each other's books! I forsaking the effusions of Parnell, Mant, Milner, Collins and Gray for the melancholy tale of *The White Rose* and the *Threnody* on the death of Princess Elizabeth; while Tina, face downward in the heather of her purple sea, was voluntarily committing to memory Merrick's *The Camelion*. She intended to astonish Mr Ellin with the recitation of it on our return home; for she had heard some impertinent allusion in Fuchsia Lodge to his possession of 'chameleon eyes'. How gloriously the sun shone down from an unclouded expanse of blue; how sweetly the birds sang; and how soothingly the waves broke against the rocks! There had never been such a summer since I quitted the home of my childhood. It was a season of near-perfect bliss for me and, I hoped, for my Martina too.

My Martina! Yes, I called her mine now; for I was resolved never to part with the child who had been so strangely placed in my care. I had become convinced that Martina was the object of the 'quest' on which I had felt myself entering: her training was the life-work entrusted to me, her companionship was to be my reward. With Mr Ellin's failure to find either Miss Murphy or the tall dark lady who had briefly shadowed Tina's sunshine, I propose to bring my memoirs to an end secure in the knowledge that there is no one who can rightfully lay claim to Miss Wilcox's former pupil. Mr Ellin and I have done all that could reasonably be expected of us; we have endeavoured to trace the relatives and to persuade Martina to reveal what she had been bidden to conceal. The letter that was to have liberated her from that promise will never be written now; for the intending writer lies beneath the tumbling waves of the Atlantic Ocean. Let his secret, whatever it was, die with him! — I do not wish to hear it, nor do I wish to learn what

Tina will not tell. May she soon forget a past that should already be growing dim in her memory; may she remember only that henceforth she is my beloved adopted child.

Chapter Ten

Seven years have passed since the autumn months during which I committed to paper the preceding memoirs, recollections, reminiscences — call them what you will. Why, it may be asked, did I relate the story of my 'quest' after we had returned from Tina's blue and purple seas to Silverlea Cottage? What motives could have induced me to spend so many evening hours from September to November over what was no more than an unfinished story? This, then is my answer: Most powerful among my reasons was the 'need' — as Tina would have put it — for an occupation that might perhaps distract my thoughts from constantly pondering at this particular time on a problem that I was unable to solve.

For it had become abundantly plain that Mr Ellin wanted more from me than the calm platonic friendship I was willing to give. Our views on religion coincided; those on art, music and literature differed only enough to make argument and discussion enjoyable; our companionship was as easy and natural as that of a lock and a key. All this satisfied me, and I became restless and troubled when I found that it did not equally please Mr Ellin. He needed not to put his meaning into words: we understood each other too well for that. Moreover, he was and is a prudent man, who would not risk his fate by putting it to the touch when he could see that I was retreating, always retreating, though never retreating quite out of sight.

I wonder how King Canute felt when he saw the waves drawing nearer and nearer. He must surely have longed to gather up his royal robes and fly rather than remain in his 'siege perilous' to await the inevitable cold bath. In his place, I know that I should have edged my chair backwards, a few inches at a time, in the hope that sooner or later the tide would make up its mind to go away.

For greatly as I liked and respected Mr Ellin, I could not bring myself again to contemplate matrimony. Those bleak, black fifteen years had graven their records deep on my soul. I dared not brave the adventure of a second marriage. Was I not happy and contented in my pleasant home? Had I not my 'quest', my object in life?

So, as I have said, I strove to drive out intrusive thoughts by writing the story of Martina for my imaginary reader; and no sooner had I laid down my pen — as I did in early November — than my peaceful days were invaded by a succession of startling events that were followed by consequences more startling still. My whole life suddenly became so changed that it was long before I had time to cast a thought to the manuscript book in which I had recorded my quest. When at last I remembered its existence, I found that it had unaccountably vanished.

I regretted the loss, but it did not trouble me unduly. My days had become too full and rich to leave me leisure for dwelling on the past. So seven years have gone racing and flashing by. Then, some weeks ago, I was performing a long-neglected duty, that of turning over and setting to rights the contents of a chest bestowed in one of the attics. There lay my book! — but how it had contrived to hide itself so successfully, I know not.

Taking the book up, I perceived that a considerable number of its pages were blank. Now it is doubtless an imperfection in my character that I have never been able to endure incompleteness in any shape or measure. Those bits of trumpery that turned up year after year in the Clinton St James missionary basket! — how they fretted me till I saw their destiny as clothes for Elinor-Arminel! Therefore, reader, I have resolved to tell as much of other people's history and my own as those fair white pages will contain, stopping short on the last of them at whatever point in the tale I shall have reached, whether or not it makes a satisfactory conclusion.

I begin by stating that Mr Ellin emphatically disapproved when I told him that henceforth Tina was my adopted child. In vain did I point out that, despite praiseworthy endeavours, he had not made good his boast of being a better detective than the gentlemen in in Bow Street: he continued to insist that further inquiries ought to be made. Tina's allusion to a missing letter was proof enough for him that the mystery of her past was capable of solution. Somewhere, he believed, there must be a kindly relative of whom Tina had not heard, who would gladly welcome the orphan to her hearth and home. Since it was no longer in Mr

Fitzgibbon's power to write the all-important letter, it surely behoved Tina's friends to do what they could to give her the happy future her father had promised.

I did not agree with Mr Ellin's view of the matter. In particular, I poured scorn on his notion of a benevolent female relative lurking among the branches of the Fitzgibbon family tree. The discussion lasted long and at times waxed so warm that it almost amounted to a coolness, each of us adhering so firmly to his or her own opinion that no compromise was possible. But before either of us had admitted defeat, there came a totally unexpected turn in our affairs. The Misses Wilcox had a brother, a writer for periodicals and newspapers. Having occasion to visit Fuchsia Lodge, he received for the first time a full account of the malpractices of the pseudo-heiress and her papa — and a telling story he made of it for the most widely circulated of the newspapers to which he was a contributor! This unconscionable person did not hesitate to reveal my name and Mr Ellin's as those of the neighbours who had undertaken to support Miss Matilda Fitzgibbon after she was unmasked. The part played by Miss Wilcox was presented in the best light her brother's facile pen could bestow on it, she receiving high praise for her acumen in discovering, by means of a gold snake-bracelet inscribed *Emma*, that the child's Christian name was not Matilda but Martina; while Mr Ellin and I had to content ourselves with a somewhat grudging admission that we, too, had done some slight service by our reading the letters 'T.D.' on the playbox. In a style flowery and sentimental, he dwelt on the little Martina's tongue-tied silence and obvious dread of offending a grim unknown — perhaps the 'Emma' of the bracelet — by a frank confession. Speaking for Martina's wronged preceptress, he concluded his piece with an eloquent appeal to any relatives to come forward and do their duty by a young girl whose grace and beauty had touched the hearts of all who knew her.

I raged inwardly when I read this precious effusion; for I fancied that it would have more effect than any cautiously-worded notices sent to the newspapers by Mr Ellin. From my own family I could not hope for even lukewarm sympathy: one and all, they were of the opinion that the sooner I was rid of my ward-from-nowhere, the better: although those of them who had seen Tina were less aggressive than the others, Mr Maltravers and Mary, Hugh and Julia agreeing that she was a nice enough child but sadly over-indulged by Mr Ellin and me, who evidently did not have correct notions on the bringing up of children. I felt like a bear about to be deprived of her cub; and I was all the more savage in that I knew I should receive no commiserations from Mr Ellin. He was, like Achilles, sulking in his tent on the day Mr Wilcox's article appeared, he having been the loser in our latest battle of words over Tina. Worse still, I guessed that, far from regretting what that evilly-disposed Mr Wilcox had done, he too thought than the journalistic methods would be more effectual than his own restrained gentlemanly appeals.

Effectual they were, but not in the way Mr Ellin and I had expected. Some weeks later — indeed, the very day after I had made an end of writing Martina's story — a small closed carriage drew up outside the Rectory gates, and its coachman brought a message, ostensibly from me to the governess. Would she kindly permit Martina to leave her lessons early, as Mrs Chalfont wished to take her on a shopping expedition to Barlton Market? Miss Spindler consenting, Tina skipped joyfully out — and was seen no more.

She was not missed until five o'clock in the afternoon. I had gone that morning to visit a friend whom I found alone and so seriously ill that I could not leave her until a married daughter, already summoned, could arrive from her distant home. As I had no means of communicating with Jane and Eliza, they were puzzled when neither Tina nor I returned home at noon. Seeing Elizabeth and Anna seeking garden greenstuff for their rabbits, Jane asked what had become of Martina; had the governess kept her in? She was told that Tina had gone off, full of joyous expectation, for a holiday treat.

My mode of life had not led Jane to suspect that I was the kind of person who would whisk off a-pleasuring with small consideration for the feelings of those left behind to prepare and serve a meal that would not be needed. Although surprised, she was not alarmed by what she took to be an unprecedented freak on my part.

But when I came home, weary and sad, from the bedside of my dying friend, what alarm and confusion reigned in Silverlea Cottage! Quickly it spread to the Rectory and thence to the village at large. The Rector, Dr Percy and Mr Cecil agreed that the small closed carriage must be overtaken without delay. If Tina had been carried off by relatives who had the best right to her, we were powerless to remove her from their custody, shabby and ungrateful as their conduct had been. But if she had been criminally abducted, right was on our side and the child could be restored to us by force, if need be — and that as soon as possible.

The pursuit began in half an hour. Mr Randolph and Mr Cecil rode their own horses, Dr Percy sent his groom, Larry borrowed a nag from Farmer Giles; and the ordinands, delighted to win a respite from their graver studies, managed to obtain mounts from various quarters. Other volunteers joined them and off they went, two riders to each of the six roads out of Clinton St James. Such a scattering of the searchers was necessary; for as Mr Fitzgibbon's carriage had come and gone unseen, so did Martina's. Only one person could have provided the needful clue. That person was the little boy on whom the coachman had bestowed the magnificent reward of sixpence for pointing the way to the Rectory. But that greedy infant knew no more about the carriage than if it had dropped from the skies; for he had run off immediately to stuff himself with Dame Pettigrew's aniseed balls.

When darkness closed in, the searchers came back discouraged, no glimpse having been obtained of the missing vehicle. This, to be sure, was the result — or lack of it — that I had expected, inasmuch as the carriage had a clear seven hours' start. Early the next morning, the hunt was resumed. Again it failed of its object. At nightfall, it was evident that the searchers had done all that they could do.

Where, you will ask, was Mr Ellin, that he did not take part — and that the chief part — in the proceedings? Alas, it was known that he had gone to London, returning by way of Valincourt, where he had business connected with the estate. Fiery-cross summonses had been sent to him at both places, to which he responded as quickly as a man could who had stopped in an inaccessible part of the country between London and Valincourt to visit friends. The sixth day saw him at Silverlea Cottage. Our recent little differences of opinion were as though they had never been: his concern for Tina's safety was as great as mine. Indeed, as I was afterwards to learn, it was greater; for he knew more of the world and its ways.

He did not, however, manifest that concern in his demeanour or by any rash impulsive action. Instead, he remained calm and deliberate as ever. After hearing where and how far the chase had gone and what steps had been taken to inform the police about the abduction, he said, at his most impassive, that he wished to ask the young Randolphs whether Tina had ever talked to them about her home. We went, then, to the Rectory. Anselm shook his head when questioned. Elizabeth was able to tell us that Tina had not liked sleeping in Miss Wilcox's room at Fuchsia Lodge because Miss Wilcox snored. Pressed further, she recalled that Tina had once described the dull walks she took 'in the park' with her governess. When the governess had her holiday, Tina cut out and painted families of paper dolls. These she dressed in poppy and rose petals, and made houses for them in the hollow roots of the park's huge trees.

While this information added slightly to our knowledge of Tina's earlier surroundings, its picture of a lonely child had no bearing on the situation in which we now found ourselves. Fortunately Elizabeth had more to offer.

'For our composition lessons Miss Spindler has lately been making us write stories illustrating proverbs or popular sayings, such as *A stitch in time saves nine*, or *Look before you leap*. One week we had to illustrate the saying *Quarrelsome folk never prosper*. Tina wrote a story about two young ladies who were both in love with the same young gentleman. They were so angry and jealous that they decided to fight a duel with pistols to decide which should have him. They fought, and the young lady who had proposed the duel shot the other young lady's little finger off. And when the young man heard what had happened, he would not marry either of them. He said he would die sooner that take one of those viragoes to be his wife. When Tina read her story aloud to me, I was shocked; and I said that Miss Spindler would be worse shocked with her for inventing such a frightful tale. Tina said, "I did not invent it, on my honour I did not. It really happened. I knew both the young ladies." But she tore the story up and wrote another about two birds who quarrelled so badly in their little nest that they both tumbled out and were eaten by a cat that happened to be passing by. And when Miss Spindler read that story, she said —— '

But I could not wait to hear Miss Spindler's pronouncements on the conduct of the birds who had so signally failed to comply with Dr Watts's views on correct ornithological behaviour. I burst in with — 'Did Tina tell you the names of either of the young ladies?'

'No, she did not. I asked her, but she said their names were best forgotten.'

That was the sum total of what could be obtained from Elizabeth. As we walked back to Silverlea Cottage for a further consultation, Mr Ellin spoke suddenly. 'Had you heard that story before? — has it by any chance become public property? It might be helpful to know who those young Amazons were.'

I answered truthfully that the story was new to me; but I could not make myself resolve to inform Mr Ellin that the character of the victorious challenger sounded uncommonly like that of my stepdaughter, Emma, not all of whose numerous escapades had come to my ears, nor indeed to those of her papa. Mr Ellin said no more; but on entering the parlour, he called for the little books that Tina had been in the habit of compiling for her dolls' edification. 'There may be something useful in one of these,' he opined.

Restraining my impatience — for I could not see any value in such time-wasting inquiries — I indicated the cupboard in which the books were kept. 'I have read most of them — Tina always showed them to me — and I am certain there is nothing relevant in any of them. *Salt mines in Cheshire*, *The Legend of the Forget-me-not*, *The Little Princes in the Tower* and so on — those are her chosen topics. Why, you have read two or three of her books yourself — what can you hope to learn from any of them?'

'We shall see,' said Mr Ellin, taking the topmost book from the little pile.

I remembered a day in the previous December when, sitting near the window of a cottage I was visiting, I had observed Mr Ellin on his way to Fuchsia Lodge in response to that first plea for help by Miss Wilcox. Myself unseen, I had watched his leisured advance, unconcerned air, and moments of meditation under a tree. That was all very well when the matter was not one of vital import; but — as Annie was fond of saying — it fairly put me past my patience to see him turning over those booklets as if each had a precious jewel concealed within its pages. I had positively to avert my eyes lest the sight should drive me into begging him to drop this fiddle-faddling and hurry, hurry, hurry to rescue Tina.

As I might have expected, he did nothing of the sort, but went on with his methodical examination. Opening the last that came to hand, he drew back with a start. 'Have I your leave to read this?' he asked holding out a stout note-book in a wine-coloured cover.

I recognized the book as that on which Tina had been engaged in the days before our seaside sojourn. 'Yes, certainly,' I said.

'You are sure of that?' he asked, in visible embarrassment. 'You know what she has written?'

I recollected that Tina had not shown me the wine-coloured notebook, nor in the rush of holiday preparations had I asked to see it. 'What is it called?' I asked.

Without answering, he gave me the book. Large and plain were the words of the title, *The Cruel Stepchildren*.

No need to ask myself what would follow. One swift glance at the contents told me that there, told in accents that were unmistakably Annie's, lay the stories of the children's flight from home, of my enforced absences from Grewby Towers, of the vengeful attack on my books, of Emma's breach with her father over the burial of my babe. Shuddering, I bade Mr Ellin read. Covertly I watched him. I saw him spell-bound, fascinated, unable to lift his eyes until at last he came to the set of inky flourishes apparently intended by Tina to portray a printer's colophon. As if reluctant to return to the world about him, he slowly shut the book, keeping, nevertheless, his finger on the last page. 'You have never told me that your stepdaughter's name was Emma,' he said, with the faintest possible note of reproach in his voice.

It was as though he had said, 'I have given you my full confidence; but you have not given me yours in return.' I admitted the justice of the accusation. 'Oh, I know, I know!' I cried. 'Those stories will have shown you why. The recollection of them has been a lifelong nightmare, something I have kept hidden from the world. But now you shall hear all, all, all —' And in an overmastering torrent of speech I described the dark hours of last Christmas Eve when I sat recalling incident after incident of my life at Grewby Towers, with the spectres of the past menacing me and the dread *Emma . . . Emma . . . Emma* beating on my brain like a knell. Nor did the torrent cease till I had poured out the whole story of my disastrous marriage to the most perfect listener that anyone could wish to meet. 'Oh, what am I about, selfish wretch that I am!' I said as I ended the sorry tale. 'Here am I, moaning over my woes of long ago and forgetting about poor Tina. That book has told you much about me; but it cannot help us to find her.'

I am not so sure of that,' said Mr Ellin. 'Listen.'

He opened the book and read:

My dear dolls, there are many other dreadful things I could tell you about Emma; but in this book I have only room to mention one story very shortly, perhaps I may write it in full another day. It is a story her papa and Aunt Arminel never knew; it was hushed up very cleverly. She and Lady Sibyl Clavering fought a duel with pistols. How wrong they were to do that. Emma won.

So they were true, then, those formless suspicions and surmises were true. My stepdaughter Emma was Tina's dreaded Emma — and Tina had known the truth all along. In an unguarded moment she had let slip part of her closely-kept secret. There could be no doubt that she had done it unintentionally; for when on 'another day' she wrote the story as a 'composition', she had prudently refrained from telling Elizabeth the names of the lady duellists.

'You see where this leads?' said Mr Ellin. 'Miss Chalfont undoubtedly moved in the same circles as Martina's parents: how else could the child have heard of a scandal that had been "hushed up very cleverly"? And what if your niece Margaret's "tall dark lady" should turn out to be Miss Chalfont recognizing, as she thought, a child she had once known? We cannot avoid asking her to help us with our inquiries.'

I shrank from soliciting Emma's help; but what else could I do? In an appeal to my stepdaughter lay our sole means of finding out who Martina's parents had been, whether she was as friendless as she appeared to be, whether she had been carried off by relatives genuine (though exceedingly ill-mannered), or whether she had been stolen from us by wicked creatures unknown to Emma and ourselves.

'Yes,' I said reluctantly, 'there is no other course open to us. Shall I write, or will you?'

'A letter must certainly be written,' said Mr Ellin, 'and you are the proper person to write it. But much time will be lost if we have to wait for an answer. Miss Chalfont still lives with her grandparents, I take it?'

'At Parborough Hall, Great Parborough. Yes.'

'The railway system, spreading its tentacles everywhere, has, I believe, recently embraced Naxworth, which is within easy driving distance of Great Parborough. Would it not be advisable that I should go down by train from Barlton Market, with the letter? I could then receive and act upon any help Miss Chalfont may be able to give us.'

My eager thanks were put aside — and very eager and sincere they were. For, though the writing of a letter was hard enough, I should have found it the hardest task in the world to meet Emma in person, though I would have done it for Tina's sake if needs must.

'I can start at a moment's notice,' he said. 'May I take Tina's miniature with me?'

I fetched the purple velvet double case that held, easily detachable from each other, Tina's miniature and my own. These had been executed, a few weeks earlier by a very worthy young woman who combined the giving of drawing-lessons with the painting of miniature portraits. It had been a piece of extravagance; but I had been tempted to it not only by my desire to encourage a hard-working artist but also by the thought that in future years Tina might be glad to have a memento of her childhood. Miss Webster had been remarkably successful in capturing the likeness of my 'fair maid of February': the miniature showed, not the paragon of beauty presented by Mr Wilcox, but a little oval face, well-featured and with speaking brown eyes. Mr Ellin looked long and intently; then he closed the case and took it away with him. I did not at the time notice that my miniature had gone too; and when I did, I put its disappearance down to absent-mindedness on his part. Certainly there was no way in which my portrait could be of service in the tracing of Tina!

So methodical a man as Mr Ellin did not leave Clinton St James until he had satisfied himself that the police investigations showed no signs of slackening and might safely be trusted to maintain their present standard. But if he did not depart literally 'at a moment's notice', he came as near doing so as any man ever did. Early on the seventh day he was gone, and I was left to my lonely vigil.

There is, I am convinced, no picture that conveys in all its dreadfulness, a vision of Sorrow, despairing, remediless, supreme. If I could paint such a picture, the canvas would show only a woman looking down at her empty arms.

Chapter Eleven

Fog and the derailment of another train so delayed Mr Ellin that it was late evening before he arrived at the station at which he must alight for the half-hour's drive to Great Parborough. There he was destined to meet with a further delay; for while he and four other passengers were making their way to the exit, a tall young woman pushed past them closely followed by the porter who was carrying her portmanteau. She sprang into the waiting conveyance, rapping out an order to the driver, who whipped up his horses and set off at a smart pace. The porter shouted protests in vain; the passengers, all save one, stood bewildered. The exception, an elderly lady, proved to be a resident of Great Parborough who angrily denounced the bold annexation of what was no private carriage but a small omnibus capable of carrying, at a pinch, six persons. 'Bateson will come back, ma'am, when he has put Miss Chalfont down at the Hall,' was the only consolation the porter had to offer.

Miss Chalfont! This beginning does not augur well for the success of my mission, thought Mr Ellin.

'Why did she do it?' someone asked plaintively.

'Do it?' the elderly lady exclaimed. 'Do it! My dear madam, if you lived in Parborough, you wouldn't need to ask why Emma Chalfont did it. Everyone in this part of the world is forced to yield to her overbearing will. She saw a good chance of getting home quickly without being uncomfortably crowded or obliged to travel slowly because the omnibus was full — and being an arrogant, selfish miss, she took that good chance, knowing that Joe Bateson is as weak as a reed in her hands. What does it matter to her that we have to stand in the cold for an hour awaiting Bateson's return?'

Civilly addressing the speaker by name, the porter now informed Mrs Tidmarsh that there was a fire in the general waiting-room. She led the way thither after warning her fellow-sufferers not on any account to give Mr Bateson one farthing over his lawful dues, however penitent he might be and however assiduous he might show himself in hauling their luggage up and down.

As soon as they were seated, it became apparent that she was ardently desirous of indulging in a few more flings at Miss Chalfont; but this she was too prudent to do until she had ascertained that of her four companions in misfortune, three would be leaving the Parborough inn by the early-morning stage-coach that would take them to a distant town not yet served by a railway line, while the fourth was also a stranger to the district. He had business in Parborough (the nature of which he did not specify) which would in all probability occupy only a short time on the morrow. Having thus made sure that her animadversions would never be reported to their subject, she began the condemnatory chronicle. Little did she think, as she sat there emulating Mr Coleridge's Ancient Mariner, that one among her auditors needed not a glittering eye or skinny hand to keep him rooted to the spot. For Mr Ellin a weary hour had never been so short.

Mrs Tidmarsh began her recital by explaining that Miss Chalfont's grandparents, owners of Parborough Hall, were a wealthy old couple who had taken charge, twenty years before, of four half-orphan grandchildren whose father had married again. Then, in graphic detail, came the story of the flight in the funeral coach from a stepmother who (I quote Mrs Tidmarsh's exaggerated praise) 'was only seventeen and as pretty as a picture'. The fugitives were welcomed and made much of by their grandparents, who had resented the father's second marriage; and their father, very unwisely in Mrs Tidmarsh's opinion, resolved to let them stay at the Hall for good.

There followed an account of the complications that resulted from Mr Chalfont's injudicious decree. Mrs Tidmarsh outdid even Annie in her descriptions of my unhappy lot. Quitting my misfortunes, she painted word-pictures of the four runaways. About Augustine and Guy she had little to say. Augustine was as coldly correct as his father and his career had been impeccable. She had heard — but could hardly believe the tale — that he had once joined the others in playing a mischievous trick on his stepmother, but that was the only word ever spoken against him. He had gone through school and college irreproachably, had married a wife who was as much of a haughty icicle as himself, and had acted, for a time, as agent on his father-in-law's estate in order to learn as much as he could about the management of great properties. He had inherited Grewby Towers some five years earlier, and was now cited as a model of all that a landlord should be. Guy was a sobersides too, but quite unlike Augustine. Bookish to be sure, but friendly and unassuming where the other was proud and austere. But as for Emma and Laurence — oh, what a pair they were, to be sure! What a pair!

Their escapades, said Mrs Tidmarsh, were beyond all telling; but she gave the company a few choice samples, of which steeple-chasing at midnight was the mildest. Half their crazy deeds had been concealed from their father and grandparents, who lived the life of toads under the harrow through finding out about the bad deeds that could not be hidden. They never seemed to grow too old for madcap pranks — why, the last time Laurence was at home, two years ago, Emma had gone to a ball with him and his wild friends at the house of a young nobleman, the wildest of them all and more than suspected of being a necromancer. And she twenty-eight then, if she was a day! Terrible times her poor papa had with her before he died, owing to her propensity for falling in love with the most unsuitable gentlemen and fighting tooth and nail for her own way. She was less uproarious after Mr Chalfont's death; but it was said that more that one eligible suitor withdrew his addresses after hearing what a reputation she had.

At this stage in the monologue Mr Ellin hoped that mention might be made of Emma's duel with the Lady Sibyl Clavering. However, Tina had not been mistaken when she said that the affair had been 'very cleverly hushed up'. Mrs Tidmarsh, who knew so much, did not know all.

'What became of the stepmother?' asked an inquiring passenger.

'Oh, she went to live a long way off, in a village called Clinton St James. I had news of her a year or more ago, when a lady of my acquaintance happened to be spending a few days with a friend who has since gone to live in another part of the country. I do not suppose I shall ever hear of Mrs Chalfont again.'

This, then, was the way in which the story of my stepchildren's flight had reached Clinton St James where I fondly believed it was known to no one. The 'friend' must have been a certain Mrs Belford, who had left Clinton St James soon after the Fuchsia Lodge tea-party at which Mr Ellin had contrived to stifle the gossip about my past. In telling me, some time later, the story of that hour in the waiting-room, Mr Ellin had to be pressed to reveal what the lady of Mrs Tidmarsh's acquaintance had said about me when she returned to Great Parborough. I was not dissatisfied with her verdict that for a woman of thirty-seven Mrs Chalfont was remarkably well preserved. For some obscure reason Mr Ellin regarded this description of me as tantamount to an insult.

The stepmother having been disposed of, Mrs Tidmarsh harked back to Laurence and Emma. Parborough Hall would be Laurence's when old Mr Grandison died; but Laurence was not inclined to wait for the time when he would step into a dead man's shoes. He had found an outlet for his superfluous energies in the explorations he was for ever making to the remotest corners of the globe in company with other gentlemen as restless as himself. He could afford those wanderings easily enough; for he and the younger children had plenty and to spare from various great-uncles and aunts, to say nothing of what their father left them. Two or three days ago he and Guy came back together from a couple of years they had spent somewhere in South America, searching for lost cities. Guy had joined Laurence's last expedition not because he was an explorer by nature but because on leaving Cambridge he had not made up his mind what his work in life was to be. And when they came back, what do you suppose they found? Why, that their sister had gone off to Belgium, alone and unattended, to collect some cases of curios that Laurence had sent back to Europe in the care of a Belgian member of the expedition who had been obliged to return home early. There was not the slightest need for Emma to go scampering off like that — the cases could very well have stopped where they were till Laurence was able to look after them himself. The Grandisons were finely put about when Emma insisted on going without a maid to bear her company; but hold her back they could not, any more than they could hold back the cataract from falling over Niagara. 'The temper of a termagant, has Emma — and they were obliged to hold their tongues, poor old souls. To be sure, she's thirty now and no tender chicken — but all the same it is not seemly behaviour for one who may be a countess in the near future. I wonder what the Earl of Orlington would think of her harebrained prank, which he does not know about, being absent in Austria on a diplomatic mission.'

'The Earl of Orlington?' said the same inquiring passenger. 'You are implying ——?'

'He's a Scottish nobleman from the farthest North that Miss

Emma has had her eye on for some time. There's nothing settled; but it's thought an engagement will be announced as soon as his mission is concluded. She has been wonderfully tractable for quite a while now, and I should dearly like to know what has made her break out again. It's my belief she didn't bring those cases home with her after all. She had just a portmanteau with her as I can tell to my cost after the jab one of its sharp corners gave me in passing. I have no doubt the Belgian gentleman refused to part with Laurence's valuable property to an unknown female who bounced into his house calling herself Laurence's sister ——'

Here the saga of Emma was cut short — to Mr Ellin's regret — by the sound of wheels heralding the re-appearance of a remorseful and hang-dog Joe Bateson. Half an hour later he deposited four of his passengers in the commodious principal inn of Great Parborough. He then continued his journey with Mrs Tidmarsh. They did not envy him his companion.

As he had arrived so late, Mr Ellin did not forward the letter I had written to Emma, but kept it by him, deeming it wiser to send it to Parborough Hall as early as was practicable the next morning. How can I describe the emotions that surged over me as I wrote that letter, the first I had penned since those pleadings from which Mr Chalfont had bidden me desist? Beginning with a short simple account of the way Tina had come into my life, I made particular mention of details not known to the writer of a substantially accurate newspaper story, a copy of which I enclosed. Chief among these details were Tina's assertion that she knew Miss Chalfont (I refrained from any allusion to the duel) and her description of schoolroom life with the Irish governess, Miss Murphy. When asking for help in establishing Tina's identity, I stated that Martina's other guardian, Mr William Ellin, would wait at the Parborough inn for her reply, but would willingly come to the Hall if she so desired. I put my whole soul into the kind messages and good wishes with which the letter ended; but I was not satisfied with what I had produced. Who could be?

A lad from the inn set off with the letter as soon as breakfast could fairly be supposed over at Parborough Hall. The messenger returned empty-handed, bearing the curt message that 'Miss Chalfont would see to it later'. At first Mr Ellin waited patiently enough; but after two hours a growing restlessness took him into the large entrance hall where he had room enough to pace up and down to the no small wonder of the domestics as they went about their household duties. One of them, after looking through a window, dropped her feather duster and ran to the back premises to summon her mistress. The landlady bustled forward, evidently prepared to receive a caller of importance.

'Good morning, Mrs Sykes,' spoke a pleasant young voice.

'Welcome home, welcome home a hundred times, Mr Guy. We have missed you and Mr Laurence sorely — two years is a long time for you to be away from the Hall. Walk in, sir, walk in. What can I do for you?'

'I am the bearer of a missive for a Mr William Ellin who, I understand, is staying here. Thomas was bringing it; but I overtook him and offered to play postman as I happened to be coming this way. Poor Thomas, he has grown very much older in these last two years, I was sorry to see.'

'It's like you to think of saving Thomas's legs, Mr Guy. Yes, you are right — he is going downhill, I'm afraid, and so are most of us. But here's Mr Ellin ready to take his letter.'

A young man came forward with a polite word of greeting. For a moment Mr Ellin thought that they must have met before; then he realized that he was speaking to a stranger. 'If there is an answer I could take it back with me,' the newcomer said courteously. 'I am one of Miss Chalfont's brothers.'

If Guy Chalfont wondered why his sister should be writing to an unknown visitor at the village inn, no hint of surprise appeared in his manner. The brothers Chalfont, thought Mr Ellin, were doubtless aware of their sister's vagaries.

They went together into the parlour, where Mr Ellin opened his letter. In a bold, dashing scrawl Emma had written:

Miss Chalfont knows nothing whatever about Matilda Fitzgibbon. She had never heard the name till she read the newspaper cutting, which she returns herewith.

Mr Wilcox's article fluttered out and fell to the floor. Guy picked it up and gave it back to Mr Ellin.

'There is no answer,' said Mr Ellin. 'Perhaps I ought to explain why I gave Miss Chalfont the trouble of writing. I am an emissary from Mrs Chalfont of Silverlea Cottage, Clinton St James.'

'My stepmother?' Guy said, colouring and looking uneasy. 'I trust all is — is well with her?'

'No, all is by no means well.'

'How so? Is there anything I can do?'

'Mrs Chalfont sent me here with a letter in which she asked a question that she hoped Miss Chalfont would be able to answer.

112

This is Miss Chalfont's reply.'

He gave Emma's letter to Guy, who scanned the uncivil lines perplexedly. 'I don't understand. Who is this Matilda Fitzgibbon of whom my sister says she has never heard?'

'That is the question which so urgently concerns Mrs Chalfont. Out of the kindness of her heart, she has for nearly a year taken charge of a little girl, orphaned and apparently without relatives, who went under the name of Matilda Fitzgibbon. The child has been carried off by persons unknown. Mrs Chalfont and I have been trying to find her, but without success. She has always refused to tell us anything about herself, but we have three clues to her identity. First, she professes to be acquainted with Miss Chalfont and ——'

'Acquainted with my sister? But my sister writes that she has never heard of a Matilda Fitzgibbon.'

'— and Lady Sibyl Clavering,' Mr Ellin went on deliberately. He heard a stifled gasp. 'This child — this lost child — had heard of *that*?'

'Even so.'

'It was known to very few.'

'Nevertheless, she had heard of it.'

'Then she must indeed belong to someone in our immediate circle. But —'

'But you have not heard the other two clues. She possesses a snake-bracelet of considerable value, engraved with the name *Emma*. Her surname we have been unable to discover, but her Christian name is not Emma nor is it Matilda. She has the very uncommon Christian name of Martina.'

'*Martina!* Did you say "Martina", sir?'

'I did. This newspaper cutting, written without my leave, or Mrs Chalfont's, contains a fairly accurate record of what is known about the child.'

Guy read what Mr Wilcox had written. He laid the paper down and turned a perplexed face to Mr Ellin.

'There is a child of that name living not a mile away at The Hurst, in Little Parborough. She is the daughter of Mr Timon Dearsley. She might well have a snake-bracelet engraved with the name *Emma* in her possession. Her mother and my sister have been the closest of friends since childhood and they did at one time exchange bracelets. From my own childhood I have seen a bracelet marked *Harriet* on my sister's arm —'

'A bracelet like this?' Mr Ellin showed the gold curves and

sparkling ruby eyes.

'The counterpart.'

'It may be imagined with what a thrill of satisfaction Mr Ellin saw Guy recognizing the bracelet immediately after pronouncing a name that corresponded to the initials on the playbox with the 'y' in the right place. But he only said, 'You have not seen Martina Dearsley since your return home?'

'No.'

'She must have changed in looks. After two years, would you be able to recognize her?'

'I saw her fairly often in the past. Yes, I am sure I could.'

'I have her likeness here,' said Mr Ellin. He laid the purple case on the table. It fell open to disclose the twin portraits. A glance was enough to establish Tina's identity. 'Yes, that is Martina Dearsley, beyond all doubt,' Guy said.

His gaze lingered on the second portrait. Mr Ellin expected him to ask a question. No question came. Guy shut the case hurriedly, as though wishing to bury some unpleasant memory. With another sudden movement he pushed the snake-bracelet further away. Then he caught Mr Ellin's eye and laughed. 'I always hated that serpent-thing!' he said. 'I mean, the fellow to this one.'

Once before Mr Ellin had seen that selfsame quick movement of revulsion: the coincidence, he thought, was curious, but he had no time to dwell on it. Guy was speaking again. 'This is a mysterious business. I can swear to the likeness, and all your details fit Martina Dearsley — but how could she come to be your little lost ward? Unless, indeed, some frightful misfortune has befallen the Dearsleys . . .'

It struck Mr Ellin that Guy would not be overwhelmed with surprise if the said frightful misfortune had overtaken the Dearsleys. 'The person to ask is Mrs Sykes. She would be bound to know,' Guy continued.

Mr Ellin rang the bell and asked for the attendance of Mrs Sykes. When she came, he left the questioning to Guy.

'Mrs Sykes, Mr Ellin is anxious to have news of Mr and Mrs Dearsley and their daughter. As I have only just come home, I can't tell him anything about them. How are they all?'

'Oh, Mr Guy, Mr Guy, you don't mean to say you haven't heard?'

'I have heard nothing.'

'It happened last year, Mr Guy. Didn't your grandparents

write?'

'They find letter-writing a burden in their old age, Mrs Sykes — they leave all that to Emma.'

'And she never mentioned it in a letter or spoke of it once you were back. Ah, poor dear, I'll warrant she was too sorrowful to write or speak, having been a friend of Mrs Dearsley's ever since they were both little trots. Depend upon it, Mr Guy, that was the reason you and Mr Laurence did not hear.'

'What has happened?'

There are those whose self-importance is enhanced by being the bearer of bad tidings. Mrs Sykes settled herself more comfortably in her chair before she was ready to begin her story at the beginning.

'Why, Mr Guy, you know what upsets had gone on at The Hurst, even before the rumpus after it was badly damaged by fire, and the insurance company made all sorts of nasty insinuations and behaved very awkward about paying over the money. But perhaps you wouldn't have taken much notice of that, being only a slip of a lad and away at boarding school and not interested in grown folks' problems. However, they weathered that storm and many another; but last year the ship foundered, as you may say. Mr Dearsley had exhausted every penny of his grand fortune, what with his gambling and racing. His wife's fortune had gone long before —'

'I know.'

'So they were to go to New York "to hide their diminished heads" as Mrs Tidmarsh went about saying. Mr Dearsley had to keep out of the way for a while, his creditors being very audacious and pressing hard on him, to say nothing of a pack of ugly rumours about what he had done concerning old Miss Crayshaw's will, which I need not go into. Mrs Dearsley can't have known quite how bad things were, but she did know he had money from the will safely stowed away somewhere in America. So he went into hiding under the rose and left what ready money he had in her keeping to be spent only on necessaries and the cost of the voyage. And what must she do but spend wellnigh every shilling of it on a splendid outfit for herself and little Miss Martina so that they should make a good impression on the Red Indians that live out there. And he came out of hiding one day — and found the ready money gone. Oh dear, dear, it was the worst kind of shock to him; for what was he to do? They had a scene of violent quarrelling, and her heart was weak, and she dropped dead on the drawing-room floor. The creditors showed good feeling then. They held back till she was buried; and on the day after the funeral he and Miss Martina stole off secretly. And they sailed in a ship that went down, a French ship called *Pandore*.

'Your Thomas was the last to see him alive, Mr Guy. Miss Emma sent him all the way to Thanpool with ever such a pretty present for Miss Martina, a writing-case it was, in blue leather with silver clasps. Thomas was that grieved to think of the little maid that was playing with her friends in the cabin, so innocent, not knowing she would never come to land. Oh, it was a sad, sad end for them both, but such is life,' said good Mrs Sykes. 'And would it be something about the sale of the property that Mr Ellin desired to know? For it has had to be delayed, partly because the creditors could not get positive news of Mr Dearsley's death for months on end owing to the French people vowing nobody of that name had been on board their vessel. Old Thomas was had up before some kind of judge and jury when it became known at last that he could testify to having seen with his own eyes Mr Dearsley leaning on the ship's rail. And even when death was proved, the creditors could have no peace, what with the wrangling and jangling of Miss Crayshaw's nephews and nieces, who had taken no notice of the old lady while she was alive, but wanted her money after she was dead. They vowed they would put everything into Chancery if they were deprived of their rights. But the London lawyers have told them that they have no hope of proving their case. So the business is resolved, and the sale of the house and land and furniture began yesterday and is ending today.'

Martina's identity was now established beyond all question. In thanking Mrs Sykes for her help, Mr Ellin told the sad little story, to which she listened with cries of 'Well, well, who ever would have thought it?' She could not reconcile herself to the fate of the blue leather writing-case: its watery end offended her best feelings even more than the subsequent disappearance of the case's young owner. 'What a shocking thing!' she kept saying. 'If ever I heard the like! Oh, what a shocking thing!' When her excitement had so far abated that she was able to look at the miniature and to accept a spare copy of Mr Wilcox's article, Mr Ellin was able to ask her whether she knew of any relatives who might have claimed the child.

No, Mrs Sykes had never heard tell of anyone belonging to Mr or Mrs Dearsley other than their respective parents, and they had been dead years and years. If Miss Chalfont and Mr Guy did not know of any relatives, then assuredly there could be none. Whereupon Mrs Sykes hurried off to unfold her tale to all and sundry with the least possible delay.

Left alone with Mr Ellin, Guy stammered incoherent apologies for Emma's abrupt dismissal of her stepmother's appeal. Looking oddly like a boy detected in a fault, he urged that she could not be blamed for trusting the evidence given by Thomas, who had vouched for Martina's presence on board the *Pandore*. 'She knew nothing about the letter written by Mr Reynolds. It was not mentioned in the newspaper article.'

'No, it was not mentioned, and for a very good reason,' said Mr Ellin. 'When Mrs Chalfont and I learnt of the death of Martina's father, we did not consider it necessary to tell Miss Wilcox and the general public anything more than the bare fact. I dare say Mr Wilcox would have liked to include a pen-portrait of the callous father in his highly-coloured account of Martina's fortunes, but he never had the opportunity. When Mrs Chalfont wrote to your sister, however, she quoted the relevant passage from Mr Reynolds's letter in full. Miss Chalfont *did* know what he wrote. She could not have failed to know.'

Guy found no immediate answer to this pronouncement. He was still pondering how best to defend Emma when Mr Ellin spoke again.

'Well, are you proposing to tell me that your sister answered Mrs Chalfont so churlishly because she is still keeping up the disgraceful vendetta against her? That merely to gratify her spite she kept her knowledge of Martina's identity to herself and was prepared to leave an innocent child at the mercy of her captors?'

Mr Ellin expected an angry outburst from Guy. He did not hear it.

'No,' said Guy, looking down, 'I can't believe she was prompted by any such base motive. I — I, well, the truth is that she is in rather a ruffled state of mind at the moment and perhaps she did not want to be troubled to answer questions about Martina, who was nothing to her. Yes, I know she and Martina's mother were close friends; but she and the child always disliked each other, I can't say why — there's no accounting for tastes —'

'Of all the lame excuses!' said Mr Ellin, for once in his life thoroughly irate. 'Miss Chalfont sent your man Thomas all the way to Thanpool with a farewell gift for a child who was "nothing to her" — and yet refused to answer vital questions about that child merely because her temper was "ruffled" at the time she

117

received a letter of inquiry. If that is the best defence you can make for your sister's conduct, you had very much better make none at all.

'No, hear me, sir,' Guy pleaded, in no wise, it seemed, put out by Mr Ellin's onslaught. 'By your leave, I had not finished. My sister has just returned from a long and tiresome journey that ended in failure. My brother, Laurence, had entrusted some cases of curios to a friend who returned early from the exploring expedition in which we have been engaged. She thought she would surprise and please Laurence by collecting the cases herself, so that he might be saved the trouble of going to fetch them. But her journey was to no purpose; for my brother's friend was absent from home, and his servants flatly refused to deliver up the cases without his authority. She came home tired to death and empty-handed, and — and — well, my brother showed himself rather ungrateful for her exertions on his behalf and my grandparents were vexed with her for going off like that against their wishes.'

Mr Ellin had no difficulty in interpreting all this as meaing that Miss Chalfont's return home had been followed by a grand family rumpus, the reason for which was already known to him through Mrs Tidmarsh's allusions to a semi-betrothal to the Earl of Orlington, who might be expected to look with an unfavourable eye on any wild doings by his intended bride. He noticed that Guy, presumably to guard his sister's reputation, had avoided mentioning that the 'long journey' had Belgium as its destination. The displeasure shown by the grandparents and the ungrateful Laurence struck Mr Ellin as somewhat exaggerated: surely in the enlightened nineteenth century a rising diplomatist, a bold explorer and even elderly persons must be aware that it was now allowable for young females to travel unprotected to the Continent for the purpose of studying languages or music? Why, then, should it be considered the height of imprudence for Miss Chalfont to follow their example when wishing to do her brother a service?

Mr Ellin did not trouble to answer his own question. For his part, he was not prepared to accept the consequences of a domestic upheaval as justification for Miss Chalfont's lack of humanity; and he said so in no measured terms. 'You will pardon me for saying, Mr Chalfont, that I still consider your sister's conduct disgraceful and totally inexcusable. However, that is now a matter of small moment, as, thanks to you and to Mrs Sykes, I have obtained the information I came to seek. I am obliged to you both for your valuable aid.'

Again, Guy showed no resentment. He said, in dejected tones, 'I am sorrier than I can say about... what has happened. I will try to get something more satisfactory out of my sister — I mean, about Martina's relatives, whether she has any or not.'

'I beg you will do nothing of the sort.' said Mr Ellin. 'I do not choose to be indebted to Miss Chalfont for any further information you might be successful in extracting from her. Indeed', added Mr Ellin, who thought Emma was more than a match for Guy, 'since she is, as you say, in a "ruffled" state of mind, I should strongly advise you not to mention our meeting; for you have contrived pretty thoroughly to thwart her unkind treatment of your stepmother's urgent request.'

Mr Ellin felt certain that his prudent advice would be followed to the full, although Guy said only, 'But you would not object, sir, to my asking my brother Laurence whether he has ever heard of any relatives the Dearsleys may have had?'

Reluctantly Mr Ellin resolved to postpone his departure from Great Parborough rather than risk the loss of a possible clue. Moreover, he recollected that in her lightning-sketch of Laurence's character, Mrs Tidmarsh had alluded to a time in Laurence's early youth when he had, as she expressed it, 'burnt his fingers finely' at cards with an unscrupulous gamester of that neighbourhood. His father had consented to pay the boy's debts only on condition that Laurence gave his solemn promise never to play with that gentleman again. If the unscrupulous gamester happened to be the man who had cheated George Reynolds and others on board the *Pandore*, then Laurence might very well be acquainted with the Dearsley kith and kin.

'I shall be obliged if you will do that,' said Mr Ellin. 'How soon can you let me know?'

'Not till about half-past three, I'm afraid. My brother is not at home, but he will return before three o'clock.'

'Very good. Half-past three, then.'

Guy paused on his way to the door, He said, hesitatingly, 'You spoke of my stepmother's grief. She was, then, much attached to Martina?'

'Mrs Chalfont is the most tender-hearted woman in the world,' said Mr Ellin (I quote his opinion without endorsing it). 'She had learnt to love Martina, and Martina returned her love. It was delightful to see them together. If I should fail to find the child, I do not know how Mrs Chalfont would bear the loss. She has had a sad, lonely life.'

He saw Guy flinch at the implied reproach.

'I would be glad to help in the search. Is there any way in which I could be of use?'

'I think not. Mr Laurence Chalfont's answer to your question will be all the help I shall need.'

Mr Ellin did not remain inactive after Guy had left him; for he had already resolved on paying a visit to The Hurst. Such a visit could hardly be expected to have any practical results, but it would at least serve to fill the vacant hours. Having obtained directions from Mrs Sykes, he trudged through a succession of muddy lanes to the sound of the November wind gusting through the trees. A weed-grown drive brought him to a fine old mansion standing desolate and forlorn in extensive but badly neglected grounds. Its doors stood wide; and within the great entrance-hall a few last-minute buyers were chatting together as they arranged for the transport of their goods. The sale, it appeared, was over; for the house was dismantled, nothing remaining save one large handsome bookcase-cum-cupboard, a carved chest, a moon table, ornamental shelves and a heap of books and toys surmounted by a couple of schoolroom chairs. As he stood by the melancholy medley, Mr Ellin needed not to be told that he was looking at Tina's property. He picked up the nearest book and read the title with a smile and a sigh.

A clerk approached with an explanation of the disarray. By an unaccountable piece of carelessness on the part of those responsible, the schoolroom, situated at the end of a wing, had been overlooked when an inventory was made of the contents of the house. The oversight had been discovered that afternoon, too late for the goods to be catalogued and included in the sale proper. The remaining buyers were not disposed to make an offer for the lot as it stood. Would the gentleman care to do so?

Mr Ellin has never been able to determine what motive impelled him into behaving as he did: was he inspired by the title of the book in his hand or by the sight of Tina's ruined world? For he made an offer then and there, without ever stopping to ask himself whether he had any authority for depositing — without my permission — a whole roomful of furniture in my house. Did he ask himself whether I had space for it, or what use I could possibly make of it if by some ill chance we never saw Tina again? No! Such minor considerations never even occurred to him —

until it was too late!

A disengaged carrier was in attendance. Mr Ellin paid for his purchase and arranged for its journey to Clinton St James as soon as the packing of the smaller articles had been done by a former domestic, who, with her husband, had been left in charge of The Hurst by the solicitor acting for the creditors. She took a morbid pleasure in telling Mr Ellin that he had purchased the possessions of a drowned child. When he set her right on that head, her mingled rejoicings and lamentations showed that after all she was not without heart. 'Poor little Miss Tina, poor litle Miss Tina!' she kept saying, 'who could have been so wicked as to steal her away from the kind lady who was looking after her? And when one thinks of all she had been through already, poor lamb!'

Mr Ellin asked the meaning of the last words. In answer, he heard again the story Mrs Sykes had told, ending with the same mysterious murmurs about 'old Miss Crayshaw's will'.

'Yes,' said the caretaker, concluding her doleful narrative, 'if ever there was a child to be pitied, it was Miss Tina. A miserable moping life she lived, shut up in a schoolroom with no play-fellows and nobody but the governess to bear her company. True, she was not present at the moment of her mother's shocking death; but she heard all about it afterwards and went creeping here and there like a little white ghost till Mr Dearsley took her away directly the funeral was over.'

Mr Ellin strove to banish a mental picture of Tina skulking alone and unfriended in the playground of Fuchsia Lodge, afraid to mingle with the playmates who had no dark places in their lives. 'Was she always so unhappy?' he asked. 'Surely there must have been times . . .'

'Oh, she was happy enough in a quiet way as long as the nurse was with her. A good, kind Christian young woman was Pleasant Partridge —'

Mr Ellin tried not to smile. The caretaker laughed. 'Pleasant Partridge! — yes, sir, you're right, it's an odd name and no mistake. Poor Pleasant, she was so ashamed of it that she hid it up as well as she could. Folks used to twit her, I'm afraid.'

'Too bad of them,' said Mr Ellin. He took out notebook and pencil. 'Can you give me her address? When we find Martina, I am sure that she would like to have news of her dear nurse.'

'I don't know where she is now, sir, though I did hear she would soon be leaving her present post as the children are nearly old enough to do without a nurse. But her home is Buttercup Farm,

Berrydale, near Naxworth. That should find her.'

'Thank you. And Miss Murphy's address, if you happen to know it?'

'I don't suppose Miss Tina is pining after *her*,' remarked the caretaker, with a sniff. 'But I have the address, which she sent from Ireland after she became Mrs Moriarty, in case any letters should come for her. Though who she thought would be at the trouble of forwarding her letters, I don't know.'

Mr Ellin copied the address, thanked and rewarded the caretaker and began to walk back to the inn. He ought to have spent the time in regretting his late extravagant purchase and perhaps he would have done so if his thoughts had not been in a curious turmoil, a state from which they had not emerged when, soon after his return, Guy was ushered into the inn parlour.

'You have seen your brother?' Mr Ellin asked.

'Yes, Laurence knows of no one who could lawfully lay claim to Martina. Timon and Harriet Dearsley were only children, and their parents were only children before them. They used to boast that they were not "afflicted with relations". I wish I could have brought better news. Are you quite sure that there is no way in which I could help in the search? I should be glad to be of service to Mrs Chalfont.'

At that, Mr Ellin's hostility to the whole tribe of Chalfont, repressed with no very striking success during his previous interview with Guy, now gained the victory over his good manners. Raising his eyebrows, he uttered a sarcastic, 'Indeed?'

Guy coloured. 'I deserved that,' he said, without resentment. 'It is late in the day; but I am anxious to make what amends I can, and — and I should have been glad of an opportunity to do so.'

'Your stepmother never blamed you,' said Mr Ellin, a little less stiffly.

'You are in her confidence? You know her story?'

'I have that honour.'

'I thought you must be. No, at first I was not to blame. I remember nothing about our flight from Grewby Towers.'

'Have you not heard that your stepmother was so far from blaming you that she tried her hardest to obtain her husband's consent to your being brought home to be under her care?'

Guy's dumbfounded look told that this was news to him. Mr Ellin went on, 'She would have had the others brought back also; but again consent was refused, nor were they willing to return. You knew that?'

122

'Not for a good many years. As a small child, I was always silenced when I asked why we did not live always at home. For some time I believed — you will, I hope, pardon me for the error — that Mrs Chalfont was so wicked we could not be permitted to see her. You have her miniature there, with Martina's, I saw it this morning. She looks not a day older than she did in the portrait painted just before her marriage and returned to her after my father's death. As a small boy I used often to steal into the picture-gallery to look at my beautiful stepmother, wondering what crime one so lovely could possibly have committed.'

Mr Ellin, still smouldering with indignation over the epithet 'well-preserved', was considerably mollified by what he considered Guy's juster appreciation of my person. He said, more amiably,

'A very natural result of what you will allow me to describe as your father's grievously mistaken decision. How did you discover that your belief was unfounded?'

'I don't know. It changed, little by little, into a later belief that Mrs Chalfont disliked children and would not remain at home during our holidays. The subject was always avoided, both here and at Grewby Towers, and all questions were discouraged. I learnt the full truth last year when Laurence and I happened to be alone one night over the camp fire. He himself had not clearly understood — and I am afraid he had not troubled to find out — that it was our father's decree alone that prevented our return home: we had made our choice, he said, and we must abide by it. Laurence had been under an unclear impression that Mrs Chalfont was somehow responsible. But he found out his mistake shortly before we left for South America. Two of the men on the estate had always shown themselves unfriendly to us. Respectful, but silent and aloof. They were in attendance on Laurence once when Augustine asked him over for the shooting. Laurence rounded on them and asked them what they meant by their behaviour. Then it all came out. Mrs Chalfont had been kindness itself to them and their families ever since she tended them when they were injured by a collision with the funeral coach. The men were her devoted adherents and they knew a great deal that was uncomfortable hearing for Laurence. He told me all he knew. By his desire, I wrote to our stepmother. Write himself he would not, since he said he was the elder and totally without excuse. My letter remained unanswered.'

'Mrs Chalfont did not receive your letter!'

'How do you know that?'

'Mrs Chalfont has told me that she had never had a letter from any of you, save the formal letters written by Mr Augustine Chalfont on the occasion of your father's death.'

'I cannot understand why the letter failed to reach her. Other letters, sent at precisely the same time, arrived safely.'

'You directed the letter to Silverlea Cottage, Clinton St James?'

'No, I was not sure of the address. It was sent home to be forwarded.'

'By "home", you now mean ——?'

'Parborough Hall.' Suddenly Guy's voice held a trace of uneasiness.

'I see,' said Mr Ellin, in tones that he endeavoured to render expressionless. 'A pity. Yes, I see.'

There was a pause. 'I will write again,' said Guy.

'No, do not write,' said Mr Ellin. 'Mrs Chalfont is alone and unhappy. I shall be absent, I know not for how long, continuing the search for Martina. Go to her.'

'Would she receive me?'

'Find that out for yourself,' said Mr Ellin, smiling.

They shook hands and parted on cordial terms.

For reasons of his own, Mr Ellin thought it wise to tell no one how he proposed to continue the search for Martina; and when Guy turned at the door to ask the question, the answer was to the effect that he had 'something in mind'. Left alone, he spent the next hour or two in consideration of that 'something'; and then, having come to a settled conclusion, he wrote a letter to me. He had plenty of time at his disposal; for he knew that he could not reach his intended destination any the sooner by leaving Great Parborough that night.

The letter was not easy to write. He had brought Mr Coleridge's *Aids to Reflection* with him to occupy his leisure moments; but not one page of those admirable aphorisms did he read the whole evening through. He particularly desired that Guy should not hear of the 'something' and therefore, if I was to feel perfectly at ease with my visitor, I must not hear of it either. For hours he struggled to produce a letter that should be a masterpiece of caution and candour combined.

Picture to yourself, reader, the emotions with which I received the result of his struggles, shorn as it was of nearly everything I most wanted to hear. It was the baldest, driest communication I had ever had from him. Enclosing (without comment) Emma's scrawled lines, he said that through a chance meeting with Mr Guy Chalfont he now knew that Tina was the daughter of the late Mr and Mrs Timon Dearsley of The Hurst, Little Parborough, who were in grave financial difficulties at the time of their deaths. Mr Laurence Chalfont had confirmed Tina's own statement that she had no relatives. He had himself gone to The Hurst, where a sale of the whole property was nearing its end, and had obtained from the caretaker the addresses of Tina's nurse and of Mrs Moriarty, *née* Murphy.

Then followed the most human passage in the letter: an exceedingly meek and humble apology for being about to unload a quantity of furniture on Silverlea Cottage without consulting the owner. He was quite abject about this.

He ended by telling me that he did not expect to be able to return to Clinton St James for ten days or a fortnight. A postscript bade me write to Mrs Moriarty asking her to tell us anything about the Dearsleys that she felt justified in telling. It was not, he thought, advisable that the nurse, Pleasant Partridge, should be questioned.

That was all. No mention was made of the entertainment provided by Mrs Tidmarsh for the passengers in the waiting-room at Naxworth station; no mention of Guy's confidences or of his suggestion that Guy should go to Silverlea Cottage; no mention of where he, Mr Ellin, was betaking himself, or why.

He was, as the future would reveal, on the point of adventuring on what might prove to be the wildest of wildgoose chases. His trust was in his own intuition, for no man the surest of guides. Hence the secrecy with which he had surrounded himself as with a cloak.

Mr Ellin was bound for Belgium.

Chapter Twelve

Even the most unsatisfactory letter can contain news of vital import. So it was with this one. Matilda Fitzgibbon was no more; Martina Dearsley reigned in her stead. How often in the waiting-time did I read and re-read the lines that gave Tina a habitation and a name, and how often did I look again at Emma's rejection of my attempt at reconciliation. The motive seemed plain enough: her hatred of me must be still aflame within her bosom, else she could never have refused the help for which I asked and which she could so easily have given. What other motive could there be, was my question. I knew of none.

My anxiety was little, if at all, allayed by the possession of enlightenment on Tina's mysterious past. Till I lost her, I had not, I think, fully realized how far she had crept into my heart, the engaging creature who now bore no resemblance to the cowed, cringing child of Fuchsia Lodge. Day and night I was at the mercy of a thousand thronging fears. If I had been able to take an active part in the search, those fears would have been endurable — but what could I do that Mr Ellin and the police were not doing already? Futile seemed the only task that was assigned me: the writing of a letter to Mrs Moriarty. Nevertheless, I punctually fulfilled it, though telling myself it was worse than useless to make inquiries of a woman who had no time to spare from her eternal knitted lace.

There was a duty laid upon me during the seven or eight days after Mr Ellin quitted Great Parborough, and hard indeed was the doing of it. My old friend had died soon after Tina's disappearance. Her daughter, engaged in the sad task of disposing of her mother's effects, needed all the comfort and consolation I could give; and daily I went to keep her company in the house of mourning. How I dreaded issuing forth on those visits! — for every time I ventured out of Silverlea Cottage I was surrounded by a sea of faces peering into mine as they asked the same weary questions. What of Martina? Have you any news yet? Where is Mr Ellin? Why does he not write? What, what, of Martina?

Aye, what indeed? I had not dreamt there were so many concerned persons in the world: the Randolphs, Dr Percy, Mr Cecil, the Misses Wilcox and a dozen others including the pupils of Fuchsia Lodge, headed by Diana Green, who said, during their afternoon walk, 'I am sorry she is lost, poor thing. She had changed, Mrs Chalfont, she was more like you.'

More like me? — I had no heart to ask in what way a fairy child could come to resemble a staid middle-aged woman. But Diana persisted. 'Yes, she was. And there's a strange thing, I've seen another grown-up person who reminded me of Martina. He and another gentleman were riding down Rose Lane not two minutes ago.'

Miss Mabel Wilcox, who was escorting the school, here broke in with horrified chidings. 'For shame, Diana!'

'Oh, I was not staring at the gentlemen,' cried Diana, prompt to defend herself. 'It was the beautiful chestnuts they were riding that attracted me. We are a great family for horses, Miss Mabel. But I did happen to notice that the nearest gentleman had a look of poor Matilda-Martina. Was not that odd?'

Miss Mabel hustled Diana away before she could make any more ill-advised remarks; and I continued my dreary way home without dwelling on what the girl had said about the rider's likeness to Martina; it was, I thought, a silly fancy that a more tactful young miss would have had the sense to keep to herself. Some days had passed since the postman delivered Mr Ellin's curious letter; and although the month was still November, December loomed close, clad beforehand in mists of grey, silver and pearl. Through the gloom I presently perceived a scene of bustle and confusion at Silverlea Cottage. A carrier's cart had halted at the garden gate, Jane and Eliza were carrying parcels indoors; and Larry and the carrier were consulting how best to dispose of a large and stately piece of furniture that had shown decided objections to being lodged in my humble abode.

Oh, Mr Ellin, Mr Ellin! Not a single thought had that misguided man given to the width of my passages, the height of my ceilings and the size of my rooms. Though I could have wept to think of this set of treasures arriving when their little owner was far from home, I had to collect my wits and set about finding accommodation for bigger things than Mr Ellin's letter had given me reason to expect. In the end a little-used room, known as 'the sewing-room', was hurriedly called upon to house Tina's goods, which were bundled in pell mell to await more leisurely treatment on the morrow; and when the carrier had been rewarded, refreshed and sent on his way, I prepared to spend yet another evening in a dismality intensified by the presence in my house of objects I could not look upon without a shudder.

What an evening that was! — how unlike anything I could have foreseen! As I was sitting, listless and despondent in the fast-gathering twilight, Jane announced the last visitor I should have expected to see. Methinks I hear, even now, her voice proclaiming in accents breathless with excited importance: *Mr Guy Chalfont.*

My stepson advanced a step or two, then stood still, uncertain of his reception. Jane, sorely against her will, shut the door behind her. He spoke, low and stumblingly, 'I have come to ask your pardon, Mrs Chalfont. Will you — can you forgive me?'

I rose and held out my hand. What answer I made, I have never been able to recall; but it satisfied Guy. When next I was able to think clearly, we were sitting together by the fire and Guy was asking the oft-repeated question, what of Martina? But it did not hurt when I heard it from him.

For answer, I said that Mr Ellin had written to tell me of his discovery of Tina's parentage but without giving any indication of how that discovery was to be followed up. Where he was at the moment I did not know. There must be some reason, equally unknown, for his secrecy. The police inquiries were continuing, but so far had produced no result.

We fell to talking of Martina, whom Guy remembered as a shy little girl walking demurely in the lanes with her governess and visiting the Hall in the company of her mamma, when it had sometimes been his duty to keep her amused while her elders were conversing. He remembered lifting her up long ago to look at a robin's nest, when she had been quite indignant with him for not knowing which of the gaping beaks belonged respectively to Dicksy, Flapsy and Pecksy. And in the late summer before he went to South America, Mrs Dearsley had sent to beg blackberries from the Hall, The Hurst's supplies for jam-making having failed. He had gone down to the Hall meadows to help the governess and her pupil with the filling of their large baskets. That was his last sight of Tina.

So in my turn I told him how Tina had come to me in all her forlornness, changing with incredible rapidity into a child of promise, sweet-natured, generous, imaginative, a lover of books and flowers and all things beautiful; but resolutely, immovably silent about her past.

'Mr Ellin has told you about Mr Dearsley's money troubles?' Guy asked.

'Very little. He spoke vaguely of "certain financial difficulties".'

'That was a mild way of putting it. Before leaving home, Laurence and I heard from our grandfather that Mr Dearsley was so heavily in debt that it was thought the sale of his property would not go far towards repaying his creditors. Also, he had fled the country just in time to save himself from being arrested for the alleged forgery of a will. He must have strongly impressed on Martina the need for keeping her true name secret.'

'Surely he could not have told the child why he was leaving England!'

'I should think he must have spoken to her of "enemies" who were bent on harming him.'

I told Guy of Tina's long waiting for the letter that never came. He said, thoughtfully, 'I suppose Tina was a hindrance while he was escaping from creditors and criminal charges. Probably he meant to send for her as soon as he was safely on the other side of the Atlantic.'

'That we shall never know.'

'Save perhaps from Martina herself, when Mr Ellin brings her back.'

'You think he will?'

'Certainly. I haven't a doubt of it. If only there was something I could have done — but Mr Ellin wants no help.'

I wondered whether Guy would make any allusion to Emma's rejection of my appeal, not then knowing that the poor boy had been so thoroughly daunted by Mr Ellin's rough reception of his apologies that he shrank from making any further attempts to extenuate her conduct. When he did not speak, I changed the conversation by inquiring after his grandparents, Augustine, Emma and Laurence. At the mention of the last name, Guy sprang to his feet. '*Laurence!* I forgot all about him. He is down at the King Charles's Head, where we put up our horses.'

I recollected the existence of a second rider.

'Laurence did not wish to come with you?'

'Oh, he would have come fast enough! — but he dared not. I was to venture here first and go back at once to fetch him if you were willing to overlook the past. But all that went clean out of my head. I was frightened too, you see.'

'Guy, you have kept Laurence waiting an unconscionable time. Go and fetch him while I am consulting with Jane and Eliza about supper. For I insist that you sup with me.'

I remember how Guy stood looking at me as if he could not quite believe that the past was wiped out. Then he smiled, suddenly confident. Just so, in the early days of our companion-ship, had Tina's doubting heart been set at rest.

He went to summon Laurence while Jane and Eliza and I made our hurried preparations for a meal that was neither dinner nor supper, but a combination of both. All being in order, with beating heart I awaited the arrival of a second unknown. The doorbell rang; they were admitted.

'This is Laurence,' said Guy. He hesitated, then said diffidently, 'Have we your permission to call you — Madre?'

'By all means,' I answered, craning my neck to look up at the tawny-haired giant who now came forward with outstretched hand and a mixture of audacity and alarm on his genial, hand-some face.

'I wonder you don't throw us both out of the house,' he said. 'We deserve it. I — I'm sorry, Stepmother.'

'"Madre",' I corrected gently, scarce able to keep from laugh-ing. It was such a speech as a boy might have made when seeking forgiveness for some childish offence. And indeed in many ways Laurence's nine years' seniority and life of adventure had left him more boylike than his younger and more thoughtful brother.

He was youthful too in the ease with which, once assured of forgiveness, he cast off care and sat down to eat the hearty supper of which he and Guy stood in need after their long ride from Parborough. The journey, which they had made on horseback, had taken them three days in leisurely stages. Accustomed as they were to being in the saddle, they had disdained the comparative comfort and speed of travel by rail.

I have somewhere read of a woman who had to wait thirty years before marrying the man to whom in youth she had plighted her troth, but who had been parted from her by circumstances over which neither he nor she had any control. When once she was happily married, the thirty years, which in progress had seemed a vast illimitable desert, dwindled in retrospect to a tiny circlet of sand. Thus it was with my stepsons and me. Laurence began at once to tell me what they had been doing in their two years' absence from England. There was no need to speak of what lay behind those two years: of course I knew all about that!

'And your next expedition?' I asked, when the recital of their adventures came to an end. 'But perhaps you will be staying at home to rest after your strenuous exertions in South America?'

'No,' said Laurence. 'I shall be off again as soon as I can. If I stay at home I shall only get into mischief. My grandfather keeps the reins in his own hands, and there's nothing whatever for me to do. We should have come to you some days sooner if I had not previously arranged to see a man whom I hoped to enlist as a *compagnon de voyage*. He was no earthly use; but I shall be seeing two or three others after I leave here.'

I was rash enough to ask whether the grandparents knew that I was to be visited on the way to Laurence's tour of discovery. From his answer it was plain that the Grandisons' hostility had faded away as they grew older: the placidity of age had so descended on them that they not only refrained from objecting to the visit but even declared it to be right and proper that inquiry should be made about my welfare. 'Had we informed Augustine, he too would have approved of our coming,' added Guy. 'Since our father's death he has more than once expressed regret for the past; but he thinks it unfilial to question our father's wisdom in acting as he did.'

Truly, Augustine was his father's son. So would Mr Chalfont have spoken, had their positions been reversed. I could hear the very tones of Ashley's voice.

I judged it prudent not to inquire whether Emma had been told of the proposed descent on Silverlea Cottage. My stepsons' attitude — their slight uneasiness of manner, the glances that they exchanged — were sufficient assurance that she knew nothing about it. I had, moreover, a strong suspicion that the grandparents would keep their own knowledge of it to themselves. Being at that time unaware of the explosion caused by Emma's trip to Belgium, and of the family's subsequent care to avoid a renewed 'ruffling' of her temper, I drew the erroneous conclusion that she had been allowed to remain in ignorance on account of her undying hatred of me.

Avoiding, therefore, the putting of an awkward question, I again asked Laurence to which quarter of the globe his next expedition was taking him.

'I have not decided yet,' Laurence answered. 'As you have heard, the last expedition began just after Guy came down from Cambridge and before he had made up his mind what his work in life was to be. So he joined us. I was in hopes to have him with me this time; and knowing him to be parsonically inclined, I gave him his choice between a search for Noah's Ark on Mount Ararat or an attempt to find the site of the Garden of Eden. There! What could be more appropriate? I thought a Sim would be safe to jump at one or the other of them. He was a regular Sim at college, I've heard. But he wouldn't be tempted. Said that henceforth he ought not to give the first place in his life to the gratifying of his intellectual curiosity — or some rubbish like that. A thousand pities! — he's an explorer wasted.'

My older nephews had long since enlightened me as to the meaning of the term 'a regular Sim'. I looked at Guy, who said, almost inaudibly, 'I did not mean to disparage Laurence's interests, it was just my clumsiness. But I believe myself to have received a call to Holy Orders.'

'Provoking, don't you think?' said Laurence.

'No, it is the greatest honour that can be bestowed on a man,' I responded warmly. 'You know that, Laurence.'

'I suppose I do. All the same, it's highly inconvenient for me.'

The conversation turned, I know not how, to the subject of Mr Ellin, about whom Laurence desired to be more fully informed. Who was this gentleman who was championing the cause of Martina Dearsley, and why had I been chosen as partner in the enterprise? The explanations were, as may be imagined, somewhat embarrassing; and I twice caught Laurence bestowing a roguish look on his sober brother. Breaking off in confusion, I blundered into an admission that I was distressed by Mr Ellin's continued silence. 'My anxiety is foolish and excessive,' I confessed. 'Mr Ellin warned me that he might be away for as much as a fortnight. This is Friday and the fortnight will not be up till next Wednesday. But I cannot keep my mind from picturing every imaginable disaster.'

Laurence and Guy were all sympathy in a moment. Their business was not urgent, they said, nor were they tied for time. If I needed support, they would be delighted to remain at the inn till news came of Mr Ellin or Tina or both.

I did need support, faithless woman that I was. 'But there is no need for you to remain at the King Charles's Head,' I told them. 'You can easily be put up here. My disrespectful nephews and nieces say that Silverlea Cottage is a perfect rabbit warren of little rooms.'

They protested against giving me trouble, but were easily

persuaded to accept the invitation, which, Laurence said, would give him an opportunity for seeing something of the countryside and for visiting certain of his old friends, some of whom might prove to be potential explorers. That night we parted affectionately, a mother and her sons; and the next morning the beautiful chestnuts were received in triumph by Larry, who had always regretted the absence of horses from his stables. Jane and Eliza were in their glory, waiting on those whom they persisted in designating 'the young masters'. Only Annie held aloof: she did not find forgiveness easy. But her aspect of silent disfavour relaxed after a while: she could not resist Laurence's boisterous *bonhomie* and his brother's quiet friendliness. Soon indeed she took to studying Guy much as she often studied Tina, for no reason that I could see.

Small support had I from Laurence on that first day, or on most of the days that followed! He began his survey of the neighbourhood within an hour of his arrival at Silverlea Cottage, and did not return from it till dusk, when it appeared that a most improper curiosity had taken him all the way to Valincourt, which he declared to be inhabited by 'an ancient tigress'. It further appeared that, tempted by the sight of much magnificent timber, 'sadly in want of the owner's hand', he had ventured — accustomed as he was to prowling where he would in other people's countries — to proceed to an inspection of the tigress's lair. Her he had encountered as she hobbled on her stick through her late husband's woodlands. Brandishing the said stick in her feeble hand, she wrathfully asked what business he had there. His answer did not satisfy her — as indeed, how could it? — and he found himself ordered off the premises for an impudent trespasser. Very different was the day Guy spent with me. Having heard of Mr Ellin's visit to The Hurst and its sequel, he volunteered to help me in setting Tina's new abode to rights. A herculean task we found it; for in addition to worthwhile books and playthings, Tina's parents had bestowed on her a vast collection of gay, useless trifles, gaudy Punchinellos, glittering baubles, most of which had been put away unused in their boxes. Tina had no taste for the grotesque, though the elder Dearsleys must have revelled in it to judge by their gifts of grimacing dolls, hideous masks and picture-books with menacing illustrations — all of foreign origin and purchased, we thought, during visits abroad. When all was in order and I had brought in winter flowers and pots of coloured leaves from my greenhouse, we looked with satisfaction on the result of our labours: no little girl, we were convinced, could wish for a prettier playroom.

Throughout the morning our talk had been of chairs and tables and such mundane matters; but the afternoon, quiet and firelit, was the time for confidences. Shyly and simply, Guy told me how to him, uncertain of his future, the call to Holy Orders had come one night as they were camping near a ruined city, lost in a forest's deep loneliness. There had been neither speech nor language; but the Voice was heard . . . and obeyed. He had tried, as opportunity offered, to prepare himself by meditation, prayer and the study of the Scriptures; and now that he was at home again, he hoped to receive further instruction from some clergyman skilled in training young men for their sacred Office. Before leaving South America he had written to a like-minded Cambridge friend asking to be supplied with the names of such clerical guides. The friend's answer was among the letters awaiting his return home.

'But I could not make any use of his list until I had made another attempt to win your forgiveness,' Guy said. 'Mr Ellin came to Great Parborough before I had a chance to write again. Did he tell you that nearly two years ago I wrote a letter that you never received?'

'No, he said nothing about that. I wish he had.'

'I did write, from Laurence as well as myself.'

'Dear Guy! And you waited in vain for an answer? Never mind now.'

We clasped hands. Before we spoke again, Mr Randolph was announced. He had come with that oft-repeated query, 'What of Martina?', but he had also brought a piece of news, which he related after I had introduced Guy, of whose coming and Laurence's he was already aware — I think everyone in Clinton St James was engaged in discussing the whys and wherefores of it.

'Mr Cecil has received the offer of a living,' was the startling intelligence he imparted to us. 'I don't know what I shall do without my valuable colleague; but I am rejoiced that his prospects are so materially improved.'

The allusion, discreet as befitted the occasion, was interpreted by me to mean that Mr Cecil's marriage with Miss Mabel Wilcox would be facilitated by the presentation. Turning to Guy, I explained that Mr Randolph, assisted by Mr Cecil, had for some years undertaken to train a small number of ordinands in the theological and practical aspects of their intended ministry. 'You have three or four with you at present?' I said, addressing Mr Randolph.

'Three at the Rectory — all that I can find room for in the house,' he answered, 'and two more in lodgings in the village. They all hope to be made deacons at the approaching Advent ordinations; and in the New Year I begin again, God willing, with another five.'

'I know it is work that you thoroughly enjoy doing,' I said.

'It is work very near my heart,' he answered as he took a kindly leave of Guy, at the same time expressing his pleasure in perceiving that my stepsons were standing by me in my trouble. When he had gone, Guy showed me the Cambridge friend's list. The first name on it was that of Mr Randolph, accompanied by a recommendation couched in the warmest terms. Guy said that he intended to apply to the clergyman whose name followed the Rector's.

'Why are you passing Mr Randolph over, Guy? I am sure no one could give you wiser guidance. Did you not like him?'

Guy smiled at me, a little sadly. 'It doesn't matter whether I liked him or not. You wouldn't want me almost on your doorstep.'

"I should not have the smallest objection. No, not the smallest. It would please me very much to hear that you had reconsidered your choice.'

Guy gave me a grateful look. 'But I don't suppose Mr Randolph would consider accepting a sixth pupil, now that he has lost that fellow — Claudius, Cyril, or whatever his name was.'

'Mr Cecil? Oh, he will not be leaving immediately, and I presume his place can be quickly filled. Six or five could make no difference to Mr Randolph. And he would not have to find lodgings for you, Guy, unless you prefer independence. There is, as you know, plenty of space in Silverlea Cottage, and I should be glad to give you house-room.'

'Madre, you don't mean it?'

'Of course I do, my dear.'

His thanks were so eager that I was obliged to remind him, half laughingly, that he had had only the briefest glimpse of Mr Randolph. On Sunday he would have further opportunities for making sure that he had chosen aright in a matter so important. To which he replied that he could trust my judgment and his friend's. I think, though, that in the end, he exercised his own.

That was a pleasant Sunday, made more so by a mysterious lightening of the spirit, a conviction that Mr Ellin either had succeeded or would shortly succeed in his search for Tina. With a stalwart stepson on either side of me, I was able to face the congregation bravely; although I could not help feeling that every worshipper there had as many eyes as Argus. Guy found the services entirely to his mind; and I could perceive that he already looked on Mr Randolph as his future mentor and guide. On Monday he called on the rector and came home some hours later to tell me he had been accepted for the course that was to begin with the opening year.

Laurence, having expressed his qualified approval of Guy's future, spent that day in looking up the friends whom he wished to cajole into taking part in his next expedition. His blandishments were in vain; and he returned to Silverlea Cottage disappointed but not so cast down that he was not ready to ride off on Tuesday with Guy to the cathedral city of Valchester, where Mr Randolph had advised Guy that books necessary for his studies could be found in the bookshops old and new with which the place abounded. They came back laden with as many stout volumes as their horses could carry, Hooker's *The Laws of Ecclesiastical Polity,* Herbert's *The Temple,* Pearson's *Exposition of the Creed,* Paley's *Horae Paulinae* and I know not what besides. On Wednesday the postman brought me a letter from Mrs Moriarty.

It was a precise and formal epistle, in which she expressed, in the correctest of terms, her distress at hearing of Tina's misfortunes and her hope that the child would soon be restored to the kind guardians of her welfare. She regretted that she was unable to give any information that could lead to the recovery of Martina. There was, however, an old lady living in Great Parborough, a Mrs Tidmarsh, who was possessed of intimate details of the history of most families in the neighbourhood. Mrs Chalfont and Mr Ellin might find it worth their while to consult her.

I gave the letter to my stepsons to read. Guy laughed when he came to the mention of Mrs Tidmarsh, who knew he said, a little more than everything about everybody. Laurence did not laugh. He knitted his brows and muttered something uncomplimentary under his breath before saying, quite savagely, that Mrs Tidmarsh was the most arrant old gossip on the face of the earth and the sooner she was under it the better. He then swung out of the room and went down to the stables in readiness for the ride to Barlton Market, where Guy was to purchase a desk and some bookshelves for the room that had been chosen as his study. Guy was slightly taken aback by his brother's outburst; but he accounted for it by telling me that Laurie had never been able to forgive Mrs Tidmarsh for writing, half a lifetime ago, to complain to their father that he had nearly demolished her grandson in a fight at school. At the time I accepted Guy's theory of a hidden grudge as being a reasonable explanation of Laurence's display of resentment. Later, I was not so sure. Laurence was still frowning heavily as they rode off, nor had the frown left his forehead when they returned. By dint of ceaseless activity I had kept at bay fears and torments concerning Mr Ellin, whose promised fortnight would expire that very night: and now I could not wait to show off the various improvements I had made in the study, into which I had introduced several objects calculated to give it an ecclesiastical aspect, such as a black oak inkstand, my own treasured antique *priedieu* chair, and an hour-glass, so useful for measuring the length of sermons. Guy was full of admiration for these additions and was particularly struck by the discovery that the window, beautifully encircled with choice variegated ivy, looked down on a secluded path in the Rectory grounds where an ordinand was pacing in solitary meditation. But Laurence, advancing to that same window, declaimed against the folly of allowing the wall of the house to be damaged by a pestiferous creeper that he would, if permitted, get rid of forthwith.

I let him have his way. And for an hour he hacked at and hewed my precious ivy as if he were demolishing a Mrs Tidmarsh in every leaf. His good temper was restored by the exercise, but not his usual liveliness. At eventide, he was still unlike himself. I could see that Guy, too, was wondering what could be the matter with Laurence.

Chapter Thirteen

In his methodical way Mr Ellin had travelled first to London and obtained from the Foreign Office the papers empowering him to search for and bring away Miss Martina Dearsley, aged ten, who had been unlawfully removed from her guardian, Mrs Arminel Chalfont, of Clinton St James, ——shire, England. Thanks to his years spent at the Foreign Office, this was achieved without difficulty and he had then to wait, with what patience he might, for the next of the steam-packet's twice-weekly crossings from Dover to Ostend. On arrival there he made his way to the *Règistre des Etrangers* in Brussels to declare his business in Belgium. Much to his chagrin — for he firmly believed that he could manage the affair far better without help — two police officials were bidden to accompany him on his search and, worse still, to direct it.

Their proceedings would have driven any other man wild; but Mr Ellin had always endeavoured to live in accordance with the maxim that fretting and fuming never furthered one's purposes. So he resigned himself, only observing afterwards (with a singular lack of originality) that the three of them then began a journey round the sun to get to the moon.

From the first, he had been of the opinion that Tina had been deposited in a convent orphanage; but the two officials insisted that she must have been left with one or other of several disreputable persons who were known to have been involved in child abduction in the past. They would not allow Mr Ellin to approach the orphanages until all these persons had been questioned and their protestations of innocence thoroughly investigated. This done, the officials conducted Mr Ellin to precisely those orphanages that were furthest from the capital city, instead of beginning at the centre and working their way outward. Back they had to come, empty-handed. On the return journey they visited a small town a few miles from Brussels. This they reached on a Saturday afternoon — the day before my own sudden lightening of spirit.

Very unlike was the state of Mr Ellin, trudging through ugly streets under a dark and lowering sky. The long high wall of a convent came in sight. On the other side of the road stood the parish church, its illumined windows showing that a service was going on.

It ended as they drew near, and out streamed a procession of orphans in black cloaks and pinafores, escorted by half a dozen nuns. Holding herself stiffly erect, one child lagged behind. Mr Ellin had barely time to note that there was something familiar about the pose when with a shriek and a kind of flying leap Tina was in his arms.

The nuns were about them instantly, like a flock of fluttering doves. Tina raised her face. Inexpressibly shocked, Mr Ellin saw, not the joyous countenance that was wont to greet him in Silverlea Cottage, but the pinched screwed-up lips and aloof eyes of the little girl whom he had pitied at Fuchsia Lodge.

'All is well, my child,' he said. 'You are safe now.' She did not weep. Still clinging to him, she pulled back the hood from a head cropped close as were the heads of the other orphans. While the two officials were making voluble explanations to the Mother Superior, she was feverishly trying to unfasten the buttons of cloak and pinafore.

It was over in less than half an hour. The procession wended its way into the convent buildings and rescuers and rescued were led into the Mother's Superior's office. Mr Ellin kept his arm round Tina while he was presenting his credentials to the Reverend Mother and receiving from her a curious missive that had been given to her by the woman who had brought Tina to the convent.

In execrable French the writer stated that Matilda Fitzgibbon was an orphan whom the good Sisters were desired to receive and educate until she should be old enough at fourteen to earn her living in some respectable way. For very good reasons she must not be allowed to communicate with her English acquaintances. A hundred pounds in Belgian money accompanied the letter; and a postscript indicated that a second hundred would follow in two years' time, when Matilda would be twelve years old.

The Mother Superior was positive that the letter could not have been written by the woman who had charge of the little *Matilde*. Though well dressed, the woman was obviously uneducated, knowing not a word of French and unable even to sign, when requested, the name that she gave as her own. She must have been acting as the agent of some other person.

Mr Ellin and the officials agreed that it was so; and Mr Ellin added that he believed he knew the identity of the said person. He should make it his business, as soon as he returned home, to conduct a thorough investigation into the shameful affair. In the meantime, he wished to express his best thanks to the Reverend Mother and the Sisters for their care of his ward, whose name was not Matilda Fitzgibbon but Martina Dearsley.

He felt a thrill run through Tina's whole frame as he pronounced the last words. The Reverend Mother showed no surprise but composedly recorded in her great register that Martina Dearsley, alias Matilda Fitzgibbon, had that day been discharged. Which done, she accepted Mr Ellin's offer of payment for medical and nursing fees, Tina having spent most of the time in the infirmary, suffering, it was supposed, from the prolonged effects of sea-sickness unwisely alleviated by overdoses of drugs. She then asked, plaintively, what was to be done with the hundred pounds. 'Keep it, Reverend Mother, keep it. Use it for your good works,' said the Belgian officials, who stood by, beaming from top to toe.

The nuns had for sale various articles of children's clothing and an array of shawls worked in brightly-coloured stripes. Mr Ellin asked them to put up whatever his charge was likely to need during a journey that would last till the following Wednesday. On hearing this, Tina dragged at his sleeve. 'My blue cloak is stolen. That woman took it from me and put it in the pack she carried on her shoulders. She said I should not need it ever again and it was beautiful cloth and would fetch a fancy price.'

Thereupon Mr Ellin bought Tina a warm woollen bonnet; but there being no cloaks for sale, he was obliged to buy one of the brilliant shawls. Interpreting what he took to be a look of dismay from its future wearer — 'it can't be helped, Tina, you must have something to keep out the cold. You may give it to old Annie as soon as we are at home again.'

The magic word 'home' brought a lessening of tension: the lines about the mouth softened, the eyes lost their aloofness. Prompted by Mr Ellin, she thanked the Reverend Mother for her care; and then, turning to the Belgians, she said, falteringly but clearly, 'Je vous remercie, messieurs.'

Those excellent fellows were much affected by the scene. They applied their handkerchiefs to their eyes, smiled benevolently on Tina and escorted the pair to the train that would take them to Brussels. Nor did the faithful watch-dogs quit their post of duty until they had proudly deposited their two charges in the *Registre des Etrangers*, there to report the success of the mission.

A brisk exchange of handshakes, compliments and congratulations followed, during the course of which one of the chief personages whispered an order to a clerk, who ran from the building and returned with a huge *bonbonnière,* all snowy satin and white ribbons. Mr Ellin had to thank the kind donors on Tina's behalf, for she was too overcome to be able to do more than smile and curtsey her acknowledgements.

'Why did they give me this?' she asked, when they were driving to the hotel where Mr Ellin intended to spend the next two nights.

'Because, Martina, you are now a person of importance. It is not every young lady who has had the distinction of being kidnapped.'

'Kidnapped'? I don't know the word. Was I kidnapped — was that what happened to me?'

'Yes.'

'Will she ever do it again?'

'The woman who brought you to the convent?'

'No, not the woman, I do not care about her. She did it because she was paid. A hundred pounds she had, and her passage to Australia and an outfit; and besides all that, she stole my blue cloak. I mean Emma.'

'Emma?'

'Mamma called her Emma, so I always think of her as Emma. But I called her Miss Chalfont when I had to talk to her. She is Aunt Arminel's stepdaughter, that is who she is.'

Mr Ellin had never been able to pinpoint the moment at which he first began to suspect that Emma might be the culprit; but he knew that he firmly believed in her guilt not later than two minutes after he first met Guy. Here was welcome confirmation of that belief.

'Take my word for it, Tina, Miss Chalfont will not do it again. I'll make sure she does not!'

He heard a sigh, as of one casting off a burden.

'We will not talk any more till you have had something to eat. Look, we are at the hotel.'

Bright lights, fires and ornate furniture made an agreeable contrast to the bare walls and stone floors of the convent. Tina ate and drank, and the colour came back into her cheeks. She was then quite ready to talk about the kidnapping; but first she had a question to ask.

'You called me by my name twice, once in the orphanage and

once in that place where they gave me a prize for being kidnapped. How did you find out that I was Martina Dearsley?'

'Martina, are you asking me questions or am I asking you? I found out by reading one of the little books you wrote for your dolls. In it, you told them that you knew Miss Chalfont and Lady Sibyl Clavering. So I went down to Great Parborough with a letter from Aunt Arminel, asking Miss Chalfont to help us in our search for you. We thought it was possible she might know of someone — perhaps a relation of yours — who wanted you. Mr Guy Chalfont brought Miss Chalfont's answer to the inn where I was staying. In it she said that she knew nothing of any Matilda Fitzgibbon. But I had a little talk with Mr Chalfont, during which he saw your picture, recognized you and told me your surname. So I came to Belgium.'

'Is this Belgium?'

'It is.'

'I thought it was France. What made you think you would find me in Belgium?'

Mr Ellin gave a short account of the passengers' plight at Naxworth railway station.

'I know Mrs Tidmarsh. Emma once called her a talkative old parrot. I heard her telling Mamma so. But how could you possibly tell that she had come back from Belgium in a great hurry after kidnapping me?'

'It was pure guesswork. And lest I should be horribly mistaken, I did not tell anyone where I was going.'

'Not even Aunt Arminel?'

'No, not even Aunt Arminel. Only some people up in London, trained to keep secrets, who had to give me the necessary authority to bring you away when I had found you. It would be a terrible thing to accuse an innocent person of such a dreadful crime. Are you sure, quite, quite sure, that Miss Chalfont is to blame?'

'Yes, she is, she is! I could not be more surer than I am,' cried Tina excitedly. 'She was the coachman. Listen, I will tell you just how it happened. A message was brought that Aunt Arminel was waiting to take me out shopping. I ran out as fast as I could; for I love to go shopping with Aunt Arminel.'

'I'll warrant you do!' said Mr Ellin.

'I did not suppose anything was wrong — why should I? — when I first saw that the carriage was not the one Aunt Arminel hires from old Mr Todhunter, but another closed carriage driven by a tall man in a black coat with his hat pressed down low on his head. At sight of him a prickle ran down my back, I didn't know why. In I jumped. And it was dark inside the carriage, and the next instant a great thick muffler was round my mouth, and the driver had whipped up his horse and we were away. I fought and struggled and tried to leap out; but the woman who held me was too strong, and besides I was nearly choked with that frightful muffler, which smelt very musty. We drove for miles and miles — I don't know how far — and at last we came to a wild lonely heath with no houses anywhere in sight. Then she took off the muffler and I screamed and screamed; but nobody came because there was nobody to come. I went on screaming till I was so hoarse I could not make a sound and my throat hurt. Then she said, "Give over 'ollering, will you? 'old your noise and you'll come to no 'arm. I ain't a-going to murder you. The lady wot you've been living with don't want you in 'er 'ouse no more, so she 'as paid me to take you to a school where you will stay till you are old enough to earn your keep. You'll be ever so 'appy along of the other misses, so you better pipe down like a good gal and stop singing out fit to bust a pusson's eardrums."

'I did not believe a word she said. And it flashed into my mind that the man who was driving the carriage was Emma, dressed up as a coachman. I did not know why Emma was taking me away; but I did know that my papa had once said that she was his deadliest enemy and mine too, and that she had it in her power to send him to the gallows. I began to feel as if I might die, and — and —'. She faltered, stopped, and began to tremble violently. 'Oh, I forgot, I forgot! I have told you something I was not to tell.'

Mr Ellin reassured her by pointing out that Mr Dearsley was out of Emma's power now, and so was she. Brokenly she resumed her story. 'My legs and arms went limp and everything was fuzzy. I think I felt then as a jelly-fish must feel always. Mrs Smith — she told me to call her that but I am sure it was not her name — took a flask out of the big bag that she had on her shoulders, and gave me something to drink. After that, I do not remember what came next. When I woke up the carriage had disappeared and Mrs Smith and I were getting into a railway train and she was telling some other people not to come into the same compartment because I was sickening for something, she didn't know what. I tried to speak; but the muffler was round my mouth, choking me.

It was when we were alone in the train that she told me how a "pusson" — she knew it was no use for her to pretend it was Aunt Arminel — had paid her what she said was the best 'eart could 'ave wished. Her husband and son had gone to Australia long years before; and ever since she had been trying in vain to scrape together enough money so that she could go to them as soon as their time was up. I asked her why Mr Smith and his son had gone to Australia without her in the first place; it was very unkind of them to leave her behind. She seemed annoyed. "Poor folks can't help theirselves," she told me. "They was obligated to go." I don't know what she meant by that, and I could see she did not wish me to ask. So I begged and implored her to write to you and Aunt Arminel as soon as she reached Australia, telling you where I was. But she would not promise. She said she always acted square by them as acted square by her; it was ordered in the Bible, as I ought to know.'

'You won't find that text in your Bible or in mine,' observed Mr Ellin. 'Pray proceed.'

'I don't remember what happened next; it was all confusion,' said Tina again. 'I think Mrs Smith must have given me more drink to soothe my throat. When I woke up we were tossing on the sea and everybody in the ladies' cabin was as ill as ill could be, except Emma.'

'Emma? You saw Miss Chalfont? You are sure it was she?'

'Yes, yes, yes! I have not made a mistake. It was the only time I ever saw her full face. I shut my eyes quickly to keep her from finding out that I had seen her. She was not dressed like a coachman then. Somewhere and somehow she had changed into a lady's clothes. Mrs Smith was ill, but not so ill as the other ladies, and she was trying to stop me from shouting and screaming. I think Emma came and looked at me and gave me some tablets that Mrs Smith made me swallow. For ages and ages after that I seemed to be rolling in clouds.'

'You called my name repeatedly,' said Mr Ellin. 'That was why the tablets were given to you.'

'But — but you weren't there. How do you know that I called you?'

'It's very simple, Tina. When I crossed over from England, I asked the stewardess if she had seen any little girl answering to your description. She couldn't remember at first, then she recalled that on one very stormy night all her ladies were ill save one haughty young woman who sat by herself and stirred neither

144

hand nor foot to help the other poor creatures who were crying and squalling, half of them moaning that the ship was going down and the other half sobbing out that they didn't care if it did! Very much surprised was she when the callous lady suddenly decided to take notice of a little girl who was quite bewildered by sea-sickness. She gave the child's attendant some tablets to calm her; for she was calling piteously for someone named Ellin — a sister, the stewardess thought.'

'It was not a sister — it was you!' cried Tina. 'I called and called your name. Did you guess that the callous lady was Emma?'

'What I guessed doesn't matter,' said prudent Mr Ellin. 'I had no proof.'

'But you have proof now?'

'I believe so.'

'I woke up to find we were off the sea and in a train. My head was going round and round and I was so giddy I could not stand. The worst of it was — Emma came too, dressed like a coachman again. I never saw her as clearly as I did on board the ship; but she peered through windows and whisked out of sight again and again. I tried to tell passengers and railway guards that I was being stolen. Nobody understood me; for I did not know the French word for "kidnapped". Miss Spindler has a book, *French Questions,* and Elizabeth and I have to learn four questions and answers every day. Not one of those questions was of the slightest use to me. So silly they were: *Have you the good sofa with the yellow cushions? Have you the handsome cabbage? Have you the fine egg?* And dozens of others just as stupid. Do French people really talk as they do in Miss Spindler's book?'

'I am thankful to say they do not,' said Mr Ellin.

'At last Mrs Smith became very angry. She said she knew somebody who would put me in a place from which I could never, never escape. I thought she meant Emma would kill me if I did not stop trying to tell my story. And I was so frightened that I decided to wait quietly until Aunt Arminel sent you to find me. We came to a city with bright lights. It must have been Brussels. After that, another train. We rang the convent bell in the dark. I saw coachman Emma lurking by the wall; she did not know I saw her. I forget what came next. Soon I was alone in a room with many beds. Nobody else was ill, only me. The nuns were kind. They could not speak English; but when they cut my hair off I somehow understood it was the rule for all the orphans. They brought me what Eliza calls "nourishing soups" and they lent me a scrapbook full of holy pictures. When my head stopped spinning I slept in a long dormitory and went into the schoolroom with the others. I could not do any of the lessons; but the teacher-nuns only said, "Pauvre enfant!" I said my prayers and waited, waited, waited till you came.'

Mr Ellin explained the reasons for the delay. His explanation was graciously accepted by Tina. 'I see you did the best you could — but oh, I thought the days were never going to end!'

Mr Ellin soon had cause to echo Tina's plaint. It was no light responsibility to be in charge of a child who started at any unexpected sound, dreaded the sight of doors that might open to reveal an enemy, and shrank from passing a dark alleyway even in broad daylight. He deemed himself fortunate in that he was able to discover, in each of the hotels they visited, a kindly chambermaid who, for a consideration, was willing to watch over Tina and to share her room at night.

On Sunday Brussels awoke to the sound of pelting rain. A quiet and languid Martina was content to spend the morning on a cushioned window-seat, now dozing, now listening to the bells and watching with some interest the crowds hurrying to Mass under their unbrellas. In the afternoon, between showers, Mr Ellin took her for a walk, during which he happened to observe that they were not far from the house in the *Rue des Cendres* in which the Duchess of Richmond gave her ball on the eve of the Battle of Waterloo.

'Oh, pray take me to see that house!' said Tina, rousing herself for the first time. 'Elizabeth and I have learnt some verses about the ball for our recitation lesson. They were written by a man who called himself Childe Harold, though that was not his name any more than Mrs Smith's name was Mrs Smith. The verses began, "There was a sound of revelry by night". Miss Spindler said he was a great poet but a very bad man. Perhaps, as he was so bad, I had better not recite his verses on Sunday.'

'Perhaps not,' agreed Mr Ellin, unprepared at short notice to discuss this theological problem.

Dark clouds hung above the historic house in the *Rue des Cendres*; but the wayfarers returned to the hotel in safety ere the first pattering drops had become a storm. Earlier in the day Mr Ellin had sought mental food for himself and Tina among the contents of a shelf of books left behind by former travellers. An English translation of Krummacher's *Parables* proved to be just right for reading aloud; and Tina, equipped with pencil and sheets of writing-paper, was contentedly employed in drawing, for Aunt Arminel's future benefit, pictures illustrative of the various themes.

On Monday they went by rail to Ostend. Mr Ellin could perceive, though she said little, that Tina looked forward with apprehension to a second sea voyage. He cast about for some means of distracting her attention from the coming ordeal; and on their arrival at the port he was happy to espy, in a shop hard by their hotel, a number of lidded baskets, each with its lid thrown back to display three or four beautiful foreign seashells resting on an assortment of lesser shells wrapped in twists of violet and green paper. He purchased one of these baskets, giving Tina her choice.

Long and earnestly did she study those baskets, comparing and re-comparing their rival merits. Then, the decision made, how joyous were the hours of unwrapping, admiring, counting, and wrapping up again! Mr Ellin heard no more about the terrors of the deep. On the Tuesday, engine trouble detained the packet at Ostend for several hours. While the other passengers growled and lamented, Tina sat happily playing with her shells.

The crossing was so smooth and the weather so fine that she spent much of the time with Mr Ellin, glad to escape from the ladies' cabin where the stewardess was, so she declared, 'as grumpy as could be.'

'Why so, I wonder,' said Mr Ellin. 'Can you have displeased her in any way?'

'It was not I, but one of the sailors,' said Tina. 'He came in and laughed at her for being such a sawny — that was his word, not mine — as not to recognize a kidnapped child when she saw one. If she had only told the captain about me, she would now be receiving a grand reward. That's what has made her so cross.'

Mr Ellin wondered no more.

He was on deck when Tina came, wrapped dormouse-wise in her shawl, to make an urgent request. 'Mr Ellin, would you very much mind if we gave this shawl to Jane's grandmother instead of to Annie? I would rather not be obliged to see it every day of my life. Besides, Annie will not need it. If you promise to say nothing, I will tell you what Aunt Arminel is making for her. It is a Christmas secret; but I know what it is.'

Mr Ellin promised that he would be skinned alive sooner than tell Annie.

'The Christmas secret is a very special kind of shawl, knitted from a pattern that was given to Aunt Arminel long and long ago

147

by an aunt who died far away in the north of Scotland. It is a seashore pattern not like anything Miss Murphy ever knitted. There is black to represent rocks and cliffs, brown for sand, grey wool for wintry seas and white for the line of foam at the sea's edge. So Annie will not need the nuns' shawl, but Jane's grandmother will be pleased to have it. And perhaps Eliza might like my bonnet for one of her nieces.'

'Dispose of both bonnet and shawl as you wish,' said Mr Ellin. 'Then you will have nothing to remind you of what you would prefer to forget.'

'I shall still have my short hair,' sighed Tina. 'What a set of frights we looked in the orphanage, to be sure! I look just like a boy. Anselm will insist on calling me Martin, I know he will. He is such a tease! Aunt Arminel will be so upset. How long will it take my hair to grow again?'

'Can't say,' said Mr Ellin. 'But I can vouch for it, Aunt Arminel will be so glad to have you at home again that she would not care if you returned to her as bald as a fine egg!'

'Do you really think so?' said Tina, delighted.

The dormouse then disappeared into the folds of its shawl, emerging after a while to mourn her near approach to the study of *French Questions.*

'Ah, that reminds me,' said Mr Ellin. 'I know how dearly you loved your Mangnall's *Questions* in the old days; and happening lately to come across a copy, I bought it for you to give to Miss Spindler. You once told me that she regretted not being able to procure a copy for your use and Elizabeth's.'

'I never did love it, never!' cried Tina, performing a dance of indignation as she spoke. 'I will not give it to Miss Spindler, I won't, I won't. I cannot be beset by questions in English as well as French.'

'Keep it yourself, then,' said Mr Ellin, 'and study it diligently in playtime.'

She ran off in mock fury; but before long she was back again. Mr Ellin's meditations were interrupted by the sound of a small voice asking, 'What are you thinking about that you look so solemn?'

'I was thinking,' said Mr Ellin, 'of the time when I shall be all alone in my big house in Valinwyk. A few days before I set out to find you, Tina, I heard from my old aunt, my late uncle's widow, that she does not wish to live at Valincourt any longer. She has a house of her own near a nephew whom she loves very much, and she is going to move into it and leave Valincourt to me.'

Tina was dismayed and confounded. 'No, no, you must not go away to Valincourt, Mr Ellin, that will be dreadful. Pray don't leave us. Make your old aunt stay where she is.'

Mr Ellin spoke reassuringly. 'I shall not be leaving Clinton St James immediately, my dear. Old ladies do not usually move house in the cold winter-time. I shall be a fixture till next spring.'

To Tina's young mind 'next spring' was a season infinitely remote. She was consoled. 'Oh, then, there is no need to think about your big house yet,' she told him.

'Indeed there is,' said Mr Ellin. 'I always like to make my preparations well in advance. Do you know, Tina, my aunt will take the whole household with her when she departs. She will take them all, I tell you, from the coachman to the kitchen-maid. And there shall I be alone in my big house. Is that not enough to make anyone look sad?'

'You will have the Browns,' suggested Tina.

'No, I shall not have the Browns. Mr and Mrs Brown have served my family faithfully for many years, and now the time has come for them to rest and live happy ever after in a snug little house that I know of, in Valinwyk.'

Wily Mr Ellin had his own reasons — I do not choose to say what they were — for gaining the sympathy of soft-hearted Martina. He could not foresee the embarrassment that his proceedings were destined to cause me. Tina was all eagerness to help.

'Oh, but you could have Larry for your coachman! Aunt Arminel would certainly let you have Larry. Do you know his story, Mr Ellin? It nearly made me cry when Jane told it to me. He was coachman to a grand family, and one day he had to drive the lady of the house many miles to a ball. He drove through the rain and then he had to wait for hours and hours in his wet clothes and then drive back in worse rain than ever. So he was very ill, and the lady turned him off and would not keep his place open. Did you ever hear of such a wicked, cruel thing? All his little savings went, and he could not get another place; for nobody wanted to employ a sick coachman. In the end he had to take the first job that offered as gardener and handyman. It was a sad come-down, Jane says. He is quite strong again now, and Aunt Arminel has been trying for a coachman's place for him among her friends; but so far she has not heard of anything. Oh yes, you could have Larry! He would be so glad!'

'I shall be very willing to employ Larry if Mrs Chalfont can spare him. I have a high opinion of Larry's capabilities,' said Mr Ellin. 'But you have not considered, Tina, that Larry will be no company for me. He will live with his wife and little Charlotte in the coachman's rose-covered house, and I shall still be alone in my big house.'

'Aunt Arminel is so good, she would perhaps let you have Jane and Eliza,' said Tina. 'Eliza is an excellent cook, and Jane polishes silver to perfection — I have heard Aunt Arminel say so.'

Mr Ellin declared that he was much obliged for the kind offer, but begged to decline it. 'Eliza would be in the kitchen wielding her rolling-pin and Jane in the silver pantry dabbing at her plate powder — and I shall still be alone in my big house.'

'Unless —' began Tina.

At this juncture Mr Ellin perceived — too late, as I was destined to discover to my cost — that it behoved him to stop making sentimental allusions to his hypothetical loneliness next spring. Saying that no doubt he should do well enough when the time came, he hastened to direct Tina's attention to the horizon where the white cliffs of Dover might be supposed to be about to show themselves. 'Who will see them first, Tina, you or I?'

At the hotels in Brussels and Ostend Mr Ellin had thought it unnecessary to give an explanation of his relationship to Tina; but had, he believed, been taken for an eccentric English papa who, being himself impeccably clad, troubled not at all about the odd spectacle presented by his young daughter. All that was changed when they came to the Ship, where Mr Ellin was well known and his errand to the Continent was known also. Much to her surprise and gratification Tina found herself an object of the liveliest interest to guests and domestic staff alike, all eagerly demanding to hear about her rescue and treating her with the honours due to a princess. Though secretly uneasy, Mr Ellin did not remonstrate when he saw her being regaled, soon after their arrival, on crumpets, gingerbread and plumcake; but before the evening meal he took care to warn the head waiter that his ward would require only the lightest of light suppers.

The head waiter, however, interpreted the request in the most liberal spirit, having, no doubt, his own opinions as to the fare that ought to be provided for a rescued damsel. Mr Ellin, charmed unexpectedly to meet and converse with an old acquaintance, failed to ascertain whether or not his orders had been carried out. It was well for his peace of mind that he did not know Tina was supping sumptuously on lobster patties, ice pudding and other dainties, in an atmosphere of universal admiration.

A political meeting and a grand assembly were taking place in Dover that night, with the result that Mr Ellin and Tina had the coffee-room to themselves after supper. Never has the comfort of the coffee-room of the Ship Hotel, Dover, been better pictured than by the American author Mr N. P. Willis in his entertaining book *Pencillings by the Way*. The blazing fire, the thick Turkish carpet, the gleaming mahogany tables with their burden of English newspapers, the rich red damask curtains — all were there in their perfection. Mr Ellin looked across at Tina in her padded leather chair on the opposite side of the hearth; and it occurred to him that now was the hour to try whether he could obtain fresh light on puzzles that must not wait till next spring for solution.

'Martina my dear,' he began, 'you recollect that when you first came to live at Silverlea Cottage Mrs Chalfont and I promised not to torment you by asking questions you did not wish to answer.'

'I remember,' said Martina.

'You were forbidden, were you not, to disclose your name and address or anything about your home life. I hold that you are now at liberty to speak freely since your father has not fulfilled, and now will never be able to fulfil, his promise to write that very important letter.'

'If I had told you sooner, would Emma have been kept from kidnapping me?'

'Probably.'

'But what do you want me to tell you? When you went to Great Parborough you found out everything for yourself.'

'Not quite everything, Tina.'

'Who told you? Mr Guy Chalfont knew my name and where I lived, but he did not know the rest. He was away in South America when it happened.'

'One of the people who talked to me was Mrs Sykes of the inn at Great Parborough.'

'Did she tell you that Papa and Mamma and I were going to New York because Papa owed so much money he could not live in England? I nearly told you about New York myself, by mistake. It was when we were playing my game *Ships at Sea*.'

'Yes, Mrs Sykes told me. We need not go into that now.'

'Did she tell you that Papa had a deadly enemy?' Mr Ellin took a moment to consider whether the body of creditors or the next-of-kin of the late Miss Crayshaw could be designated by that title. 'No, Mrs Sykes spoke of persons who were for their own reasons displeased with your papa; but she did not mention any enemy in particular.'

'I know more than Mrs Sykes. Papa did have a deadly enemy. It was Emma.'

Tina looked all round the room as if afraid of the sound of her own voice. 'It was Emma,' she said again, in a whisper. And a third time, more loudly, *'It was Emma.'*

Mr Ellin waited.

'Papa never could bear Emma. I guessed it long ago; but until the day Mamma died I did not know she was his deadly enemy. I was in the room when he said it. And when Mamma heard what he said, she died.'

Mr Ellin said, with difficulty, 'My dear little girl, you must be mistaken. Mrs Sykes told me that you were not present . . . at the time.'

'Mrs Sykes was not present herself, so how could she say? It happened like this. Papa was from home, I think he did not want to be caught by the people to whom he owed money. But he came back a day or two before we were due to start for America. I was in the drawing-room with Mamma, who was altering one of the dresses that had been made for me. It was too long, and there was no time to send it back to the dressmaker. We heard a bustle in the hall. Mamma thought a visitor had called. My frock was off, so Mamma said, "Run behind the Japanese screen and wait till I call you." I ran as she bade me. In came Papa. He had found out that Mamma had spent a very great deal of money that he had asked her to take care of. And they — they quarrelled. It was the worst quarrel I had ever seen, and it went on for a long time. At last Papa calmed down and stopped shouting. Then he asked Mamma how on earth she expected him to pacify the servants and pay our fares to America. "Oh, don't trouble! We can borrow from Emma," said Mamma. "Emma has plenty, she will lend us whatever we need." Papa raged again, angrier than ever. He said, "Borrow from *Emma?* — Borrow from the deadliest enemy I have in the world!" Mamma said he was exaggerating and talking nonsense as usual. He said in a voice that made me shake so much I nearly knocked over the screen — "Very well, Madam, I've spared your feelings long enough, and now you shall know the truth about your beloved Emma. Know, then, that she has it in her power to send me to the gallows!"

'I knew what Papa meant when he said "the gallows"; for I had read *The Fairchild Family* and Miss Edgeworth's *Popular Tales*. But I do not know what Papa had done wrong, except that it had something to do with an old lady named Miss Crayshaw whom we used to see quite often. Papa talked fast and very low, and I heard the words "Crayshaw" and "Emma". Mamma cried out, "No! No! I will not, I cannot believe it! Oh, what is this? Oh!" — and she fell on the floor. Papa rang the bell and called for the house-keeper. Mrs Blades and all the servants came running. Some of them screamed and fainted. I crept away to my room; nobody saw me go. Through the window I saw a groom riding fast down the drive. He was going to fetch the doctor, but I did not know it then. I was afraid to be alone, so I put on another dress and went down to the kitchen. By and by Dr Vincent came calling, "Tina, where are you?" He was gentle and kind, like Dr Percy. He told me that Mamma was very, very ill, and presently I understood that she was dead... All that week I stayed in Mrs Blades's room — she was the housekeeper — or in the servants' hall or the kitchen as often as they would allow me to come; for I was still afraid to be alone. The servants talked in front of me as though I were not there. They were worried about how they were to get their wages and the mourning that was their right. Papa, they said, had not a shilling left in England, owing to Mamma's extravagant spend-ing, however much of Miss Crayshaw's money he had tucked away in America where it couldn't be got at. I don't know exactly what they meant about Miss Crayshaw or how they contrived to find out all that they did find out. But there was one thing I knew and they didn't. I knew that Emma was Papa's worst enemy who could send him to the gallows if she chose. I did not tell them what I knew. I thought it was better not.'

'Much better not,' agreed Mr Ellin.

'Then something very strange happened, and I do not under-stand it yet. Papa managed to find money from somewhere to pay the servants all that they said was due to them; and they went about with smiling faces, trying their hardest to discover where in the world he had got it from. They even suggested that Emma might have given it to him, seeing that she and Mamma had always been as thick as thieves and she had come to the funeral looking like a dark statue of Grief, a very unusual thing for a lady to do, they said. I could not believe that Emma had lent or given the money since she was Papa's deadliest enemy — I thought some-one else must have done it. Mrs Blades was shocked that Papa would not buy me any mourning; he said, very shortly, that I had new clothes enough. He scarcely spoke to me all that week; but in the evening after the funeral he came to the schoolroom and said, "Did your mamma mark your clothes with your name?" I wondered why he should ask such a thing; for it is not a gentleman's business to see to the marking of clothes. I told him, No, Mamma had said that it would be employment for the voyage.

'My playbox was open on the floor; for I was making some changes in the things I wanted to take to America with me. He called for my scissors and cut my name out of my books. I did not see him do it; for he sent me with a message to Mrs Blades. When I came back the box was shut and locked and Papa said it was not to be opened again till we had left home. He did not tell me why he wanted the scissors; but I found out when the box came back to me on my birthday.

'The next day we left The Hurst. As soon as we were alone, Papa said that he did not intend to take me with him to America. Instead, I was to be left for a time at a school he had heard of. But because he had a bitter enemy, who was my enemy also, it was necessary that I should be called by another name and never, never tell anybody any single thing about myself. He made me say Matilda Fitzgibbon, May Park, Midland County over and over till he was sure I would not forget it.

'I felt — I don't know how. Papa said, "Well, well, don't be foolishly timid. If you keep silence, your enemy cannot harm you or me. I wish I need not impose this hard condition on you; but it is a matter of necessity. You have only the one enemy; but I have many, and secrecy must be observed till I am safely in America. Listen now. As soon as I land I will send you a letter that will make you happier than you have ever been in all your life. In it there will be a great and wonderful piece of news. Show the letter to your schoolmistress, who will tell you what to do next. But till then — not a word!"

'He did not tell me who the enemy was — but of course I knew it was Emma. We travelled by secret ways for fear the enemies might be on the look-out. When we stopped at the last inn, he said I must leave my playbox behind. I know now that he was afraid people might be able to read his name printed very faintly on the lid. Poor Mamma had meant to buy me a new playbox, but she had not time to do it. Because she died.

'Some time later we stopped at a greengrocer's shop in another town. Papa ordered and paid for a great box of fruit to be delivered at Fuchsia Lodge six weeks from that day. He told the greengrocer that I was being taken to school, and that the fruit was intended "to keep the schoolmistress sweet". The greengrocer laughed and gave me a ripe pear, which afterwards Papa would not let me eat for fear the juice should drip on my frock. So we came to Fuchsia Lodge... and poor Papa was drowned... and the happy letter never came ...'

'Is that all you have to tell me?'

'I have told all that Papa forbade me to tell. Oh, it was so hard to keep the secret! I dared not talk or play with the girls lest they should ask questions that I must not answer. I was not myself. I had turned into another girl whom I disliked. Till then, I did not know it was possible to have two selves, one of them a sort of cold stranger. When you took me to Silverlea Cottage, Matilda Fitzgibbon began to disappear. She vanished slowly, a little at a time. Now that I have told Papa's secret, she is gone for evermore.'

Mr Ellin had long revolved questions that he wished to put to Martina; but the framing of them was exceedingly difficult and delicate. To his surprise and relief, she saved him the trouble.

'I never was Matilda Fitzgibbon,' she said, 'and I do know I am Martina because I saw a paper that said so.'

'A baptismal certificate?'

'Is that what you call it? When we were getting ready for going to America, Mamma gave me a bundle of old letters to tear up, and this paper was among them. Mamma was vexed when I asked why I had been baptized in a strange church in a town I had never heard of. At first she said I was a tiresome child, and then she said I was born while she was travelling to France to join Papa. The church was only three doors away from the inn where she was staying; and as I was not very strong, the landlady made a fuss and said that I ought to be baptized at once. I was named Martina after my grandfather Martin Lestrange, who was dead.'

'Well? — as she paused for thought.

'So I know for certain that I am Martina, but I do not know whether my surname is Dearsley. For I am not quite sure that I belong to Papa and Mamma.'

'What makes you think that, I wonder,' said Mr Ellin. He took pen, paper and safety ink-pot from his writing-case.

'There were voices talking, always voices that whispered. I was very little, I did not understand what the whispers meant, I don't even now. Yes. Soft voices, saying things.'

Mr Ellin waited.

'They did not whisper all the time, but sometimes. When I grew older, I used to see people looking at me and whispering again. Old Mrs Tidmarsh was the worst —'

'So I should suppose,' said Mr Ellin.

'How do you know?'

'I have met the lady,' said Mr Ellin. 'Pray continue.'

'Once I heard her say to her friend Miss Pattison, "I am not given to making rash statements; but I must say that the family likeness grows every day more pronounced. I would stake my life that the child is a ——' And Miss Pattison said, "Sh-sh!"'

'I tried to think who I could be like, and I came to the conclusion that the voices meant I was like Mamma's friend Emma. I don't know what made me think it; for I did not see how I could possibly belong to Emma instead of Papa and Mamma.

'One day something happened that made me very much afraid I was Emma's. Mamma had quarrelled with Emma. She and Emma were friends; but they often quarrelled, just as she and Papa often quarrelled. After Emma had called for her horse and ridden away, Mamma came to me, still angry, with the snake-bracelet in her hand. She threw it on the table and said, "There, child, take that and put it in your jewel-case — I've done with it!"'

'I said, "Please, I don't want it." For indeed I never had liked those snake-bracelets, Mamma's and Emma's —'

Unconsciously, Mr Ellin spoke his thoughts aloud. "You are not the only one to feel like that.'

Tina looked at him inquiringly, 'Do you know somebody else who didn't like them?'

'Miss Chalfont's brother, Guy, saw the bracelet when he recognized your picture. His sister had a bracelet engraved "Harriet".'

'Yes, that was Mamma's name. They wore each other's bracelets, but I did not love Emma and Emma did not love me. Mamma cried, "What, you little monster, you don't want a gift any other girl would give her eyes for? Take it and be thankful. You have a better right to it than I." And she rushed out of the room.'

'Then again I was afraid that somehow I was Emma's. And a long time after that another quarrel happened. This time it was between Papa and Mamma, and I do not know what it was about. But it began when I was lying on the drawing-room sofa wrapped in a rug because I had ear-ache and Mamma had forgotten I was there. Papa said that Emma had been the curse of his life, and why should he be saddled with a child who was neither his nor Mamma's. And he stormed out of the room and Mamma ran after him.'

'Martina, are you sure that those were his exact words?'

'Positive-certain-sure, because they frightened me so much. You see, it seemed there was nobody left for me to belong to, save only Emma. Soon after that I was ill. The doctor could not tell what was wrong; but he said I needed fresh air and no lessons. Miss Murphy took me to a farm where there were animals and chickens and wild flowers. I was happy there, except when I found the book that told about the Swedish witches. Secretly I thought that Emma might be the Swedish witch who had escaped to England. It was silly of me, was it not? I came home quite well, but not happy. One afternoon Mamma found me crying. She insisted that she must know why, so in the end I told her. Not about the Swedish witches, though. I said I was crying because I was afraid I belonged to Emma, that I was Emma's child.

'Mamma was extremely angry. She said I was a very naughty girl ever to have thought of such a thing and she would not answer for the consequences if Emma ever came to hear what I had said. And she shook me as if she meant to shake me all to little bits, and she said I should go to bed without tea or supper and she would ask Miss Murphy to give me the longest and hardest punishment-task any girl ever had. In the middle of the shaking and scolding, in walked Papa. "What's all this?" said he. I was frightened out of my wits; for I thought he would be worse than Mamma. He had never been unkind to me; but I had seen him angry with other people. But he was not angry, not in the very least. He put back his head and roared with laughter. "So you thought that, did you? Oh, what a little goose!"

'"Mr Dearsley, Mr Dearsley, it is no laughing matter!" said Mamma; but Papa only laughed the more. I thought he would never stop. "It isn't true, my dear," he said at last. "I tell you plainly, it isn't true. I would take my dying oath it isn't true. Now run away and play, and think no more about it. Be sure to ask Cook to send you up her best cake and jam for tea."

'And as I went out of the room, he laughed again and he said to Mamma, "It serves Emma right that the child thought so. Ha, ha, it serves Emma right a thousand times!"

'So after that I was no longer afraid that I was Emma's child. But I still do not understand why she should be my enemy and Papa's. What had we done to make her our enemy? And I cannot make out why Papa said I was not his child or Mamma's. Do you think I am like the girl in a book I once read? She was left on a doorstep when she was a tiny baby; and the kind people in the house took her in and looked after her. But how can that be, when I was born when Mamma was on her way to join Papa in Paris, and I have seen — what did you call that paper — my certificate of baptism? When I think, my head spins round and round, just as it did in the convent.'

'If I were you, I wouldn't spin my head any more tonight,' said Mr Ellin, who had been writing busily while Tina was speaking. 'What you have told me is very interesting, and I have written it down as nearly as I could in your own words. I will read it to you; then I shall ask you to sign your name at the end if you are satisfied that what I have written is correct.'

'Why did you write it all down? Is it for Aunt Arminel to see?'

'For Aunt Arminel, certainly. But it may have other uses. At present, I do not propose to tell you what they are,' said Mr Ellin.

She read, leaning against the arm of his chair. Gravely and with an obvious sense of her own importance, she signed her name.

Chapter Fourteen

When darkness fell on that fourteenth day, I gave up all hope of the home-coming of the two I longed to see. What then were my sensations when I heard a conveyance drawing up at the garden gate, a murmur of voices, footsteps on the path! I darted out of the parlour, followed by Laurence and Guy. Jane had the front door open before the bell could be rung. There they were in the doorway, dazzled by the light. Mr Ellin, with his hand on her shoulder, propelled Tina forward, while she, shawl-less and bonnetless, raised a brown head with dancing brown eyes in a face flushed with excitement! That same little oval face! — where had I seen it before? Beside me, Laurence gave a suppressed sound of dismay. Mr Ellin's voice rang out. 'Here we are, safe and sound!' was his triumphant announcement. 'Convent orphanage in Belgium. All's well.'

Coming in from the dark garden, Mr Ellin had not seen my stepsons, who now made a sudden involuntary movement as if startled by one word in his greeting. Tina saw them first. She stopped midway in her rush to embrace me. Gazing on the strangers doubtfully, she retreated momentarily to Mr Ellin for protection, then with a bound and a leap threw herself upon me, crying, 'Send them away, send them away!'

Guy was the first to recover his wits. 'Don't be frightened, Tina. You have forgotten us, but we know you. We used to play battledore and shuttlecock with you and Miss Murphy. My brother Laurence and I have come to see Mrs Chalfont.'

She looked at them steadily. 'I have not forgotten you,' she said in a loud voice. 'You are the cruel stepchildren.'

Guy winced. Laurence uttered a half laugh, uneasily.

'Yes,' said Guy, 'we were very unkind, but Madre has forgiven us.'

Tina glowered. 'Why do you call her that?'

He was a little at a loss for an answer. '*Madre* is the Spanish word for "mother". Grown-up people use it sometimes instead of "mamma".'

'Oh.' said Tina, indignation throbbing through the monosyllable. Turning, she hid her face. I kept my arm round her while we were all — Annie, Jane and Eliza included — welcoming, thanking and congratulating Mr Ellin. As soon as the first stir was over, he told me that Tina had found the day-long journey uncommonly tiring, delayed as they had been by lengthy waits at junctions and by the cancellation of trains. It would be wise, he thought, to let her retire to rest as soon as possible.

I thought so too; for I could feel her trembling as she clung to me. Having begged Mr Ellin to stay to the evening meal, I left him with the two young men to act as hosts, and gently led Tina away. Ignoring Laurence and Guy, she looked back to wish Mr Ellin good-night. At the foot of the stairs, she faced about. Then, without warning, she hurled her thunderbolt. 'Did you know that your wicked sister kidnapped me?' she demanded. 'Dressed as a man she did it, yes she did!'

Motionless, horrorstruck, stood Laurence and Guy. Their eyes met Mr Ellin's. Answering the unspoken question, Mr Ellin bent his head. I had just time to perceive that the revelation came to Guy as a shock unmodified by any previous intimations, while Laurence was not completely unprepared for it. Some cryptic meaning had obviously been conveyed to him that day by the cautiously-worded allusion to Mrs Tidmarsh in Mrs Moriarty's letter. Whatever that meaning might be, it accounted for his subsequent moodiness.

I had no leisure to ask myself what Laurence either knew or surmised: all my attention was perforce given to Tina, who was in a sorry state of mingled wrath and terror. When she was at last satisfied that Laurence and Guy meant her no harm, she sobbed out her sad story, to which Jane and Eliza came to listen with all their ears whenever their duties downstairs permitted; any gaps in the narrative were filled in for them as need required by Annie, who sat leaning forward on her stick, the better to catch every word. The tale told — and there was no staying it — we hoped she would sink peacefully to sleep. But no! — as soon as we had heard all she had to tell, she cried out that Emma was hiding in the house, disguised as a Swedish witch, waiting to pounce on her and carry her off. We succceeded in quieting her irrational fears of witchery; but worse was to follow. For, sitting up in bed, she wept bitterly, not for her own misfortunes but for the wholly imaginary griefs of Mr Ellin alone next spring in his big house.

'I said that I was sure you would let him have Larry to be his coachman, and he said he would be quite delighted to have Larry, of whom he had always had a high opinion; but Larry would live in his own house with roses and he — Mr Ellin — would still be alone. Then I suggested Jane and Eliza; but he said they would be busy about their work and he would still be always alone. And oh, Aunt Arminel, it was you he wanted to be company for him in his big house. I know it was, though he did not like to say so.'

Whereupon Jane, who was in attendance, hurried out of the room and I could hear her laughing uncontrollably all the way down to the kitchen. I felt that I should never be able to face her or Eliza again; and how I contrived to pacify Tina I was never afterwards able to recollect. Soothe her I did by degrees; and she fell peacefully asleep while I was repeating a favourite evening hymn. Leaving Annie to watch over her slumbers, I prepared to join the company downstairs, apprehensive of what I should find there.

I was met in the hall by Jane and Eliza. No trace of former untimely mirth was visible on their troubled countenances. They were, on the contrary, seriously perturbed. 'Oh, Madam,' said Jane, 'the gentlemen have barely touched their dinners. They hardly ate a thing!' — 'And it was the beautifullest dinner that ever was!' added Eliza dolorously.

I reminded them that bad news invariably affected the hearer's appetite. Such news, as we were all aware, had been brought to my stepsons. Were they and Mr Ellin still in the dining-room?

No, Jane and Eliza told me, they had been in the drawing-room for a long time.

I should have preferred to encounter them in the informal surroundings of my parlour rather than in the seldom-used drawing-room. Entering, I beheld them sitting by a table on which were laid out some closely-written sheets of paper, the snake-bracelet, the double miniature, and Tina's wine-covered *The Cruel Stepchildren*.

As they rose, the look on the younger faces told me that awful truths had come to light. Mr Ellin was almost as pale and distraught as his companions. After we were seated there was a pause, which I knew I must break. I cast about for the most tactful way of introducing a painful subject, but could find none. Therefore I asked a direct question. 'Why did Emma take Martina away?' (I could not bring myself to use the hateful word 'kid-napped').

Not receiving an immediate answer, I changed the question. 'Did Emma take Martina away? You are quite convinced that she did? There is no possibility of a mistake?'

It was evident that Mr Ellin had desired Laurence to be spokesman. Laurence remained obstinately silent. Mr Ellin therefore assumed the role.

'No possibility whatever. An additional proof was provided to-night. Miss Chalfont's brothers have admitted that she was wearing male attire during part of her visit to Belgium. On her return she instructed her maid not to unpack her portmanteau. The maid, mistaking the instruction, did unpack it and gossiped about what she found within. Mr Laurence Chalfont, who had returned from South America sooner than his sister expected, heard that she had been making free with his property. Her grandparents, already sufficiently displeased with her for insisting on going unaccompanied to Belgium, were naturally much distressed. She refused to give any reason for her mad freak.'

'How did you come to suspect that Martina had been taken to Belgium?'

Mr Ellin answered me much as he had answered Martina when she made the same inquiry. He then said that he would not trouble me with an account of his search for Martina, who had no doubt told me all I at present needed to know about her adventures. More important was a certain disclosure she had made to him while they were together. He had written down what she said. Mr Laurence and Mr Guy Chalfont had read her statement, and they had also read *The Cruel Stepchildren*.

With that, Mr Ellin gave me the paper Martina had signed in the coffee-room of the Ship.

How quiet it was as I sat reading those fateful lines! Even the fire ceased its crackling, and the wind no longer tapped cold fingers on the panes. When I laid the paper down, my three companions held their peace. Again I had to speak. I reverted to my first question.

'Why did Emma do it?'

They did not speak.

'Was she still seeking to revenge herself on me for my marriage? Or for aiding her father to put an end to undesirable attachments? But why, why, why? When I left Grewby Towers, I passed completely out of her life — why should she try to harm me now?'

Mr Ellin said, constrainedly, 'The motive was not revenge.

Dismiss that notion from your mind, once for all.'

The brothers, their voices hollow and dreary, echoed his words, 'The motive was not revenge.'

'Then what else could it be?' I asked the unanswering air.

I waited. Tumultuous thoughts made a whirlpool in my brain. Twice Mr Ellin attempted to speak, and twice he failed. At last he said, slowly and reluctantly, 'We believe that the compelling motive was fear.'

'Fear? *Fear?* How could her motive be fear?'

'Fear, most certainly. Bear with me while I endeavour to make my meaning plain. We all — Mr Laurence and Mr Guy Chalfont and myself — have been drawn to the unwilling conclusion that there is a mystery about Martina's parentage. Taken alone, some of her assertions might be regarded as the product of a sensitive child's disordered imagination. Mr Guy Chalfont tells me that he has never heard any rumours that Martina was an adopted child; but Mr Laurence Chalfont allowed — not without pressure from me — that there was such a rumour, originating he believes, from the gossiping propensities of the Mrs Tidmarsh who is mentioned in Martina's statement and also, I understand, in a letter that came this morning from Mrs Moriarty.'

I hope I did not hear Laurence saying that he would like to wring Mrs Tidmarsh's neck and Mrs Moriarty's too. Certainly I did see Mr Ellin give him a reproving look.

My heart began to race. I fancied that I knew whither all this was tending, and I was gripped by an unspeakable dread. It held me fast while Mr Ellin was resuming his measured separation of false from true. I heard his words as he pronounced them, but they were without meaning for me.

'Martina bears resemblance to more than one member of the Chalfont family; another was observed, Mrs Chalfont, by your old nurse Annie and — I now learn — by Mr Guy Chalfont when he looked at the double miniature in the inn at Great Parborough. He, like Annie, had no reason to suppose that the likeness was other than accidental. I do not propose to comment on the second likeness until we have gone a little further into the question of Martina's adoption. If we may assume that Martina heard and understood his words correctly, it follows that Mr Dearsley's declaration that she was neither his child nor his wife's was tantamount to saying that she had been adopted. If so, what more likely than that Mrs Dearsley should take pity on a life-long friend of hers who wished to find a home for her child. After Mrs

Dearsley's death, the young lady heard that Mr Dearsley and his adopted daughter had been drowned while on a voyage to America. At a crisis in her fortunes, when her prospects in life would be irretrievably ruined if her story became known, the young lady discovered that the child was living with the stepmother whom she and her brothers had so grievously wronged. She could not be certain how much the little girl knew or what she would reveal when she broke her strange silence. Terrified, the young lady resolved that the child should be disposed of in a foreign country whence it was hoped she would never return. Opportunity offered itself — and was taken.'

It sounded so reasonable, such a confirmation of my intangible fears. Had there, then, been no kidnapping in the strict sense of the word? — was Emma merely asserting her right to do what she would with her own? Would she, if challenged, claim Martina again? I was in despair.

On went Mr Ellin's level tones.

'But against this theory we have to set Mr Dearsley's laughter, his strong affirmation, his so-called "dying oath" that Martina was not, as she had feared, Miss Chalfont's child.'

'Of course she wasn't!' growled Laurence. 'Silly little idiot, what possessed her to think it? It's inconceivable. I know the best and the worst of Emma. If Dearsley and a dozen others had sworn to the contrary, I'd not have believed it of Emma. Nor would Guy.'

'And neither do I,' said Mr Ellin.

The dread, the overpowering dread, was lifted from my mind. Though all else was dark to me, one thing was clear; Emma had not the supreme claim to Martina. But Mr Ellin was speaking again.

Mr Ellin continued, 'Mr Laurence Chalfont cannot recall when or how he first heard someone say that Martina must be an adopted daughter, since everbody knew that Mrs Dearsley could never have a child. He did not give the idle rumour another thought till today, when a single sentence in Mrs Moriarty's letter made him wonder whether the same rumour had reached his grandmother. He was present during a visit Mrs Tidmarsh paid to Parborough Hall, in the course of which she observed, à propos of nothing in particular, that the little Dearsley was oddly like Guy as she first remembered him, a small boy in petticoats. Mrs Grandison, showing no sign of discomposure, replied that she had not observed any resemblance. After the visitor had departed, she observed, with uncommon tartness, that some people were very clever at detecting likenesses where none existed.

'But the likeness did exist, whether or not Mrs Grandison noticed it. Mr Laurence Chalfont saw it clearly when I brought Tina into the hall tonight. And if I am not mistaken, you saw it also, Mrs Chalfont.'

I said, with difficulty, 'There is a resemblance to the portraits of Guy in the picture-gallery at Grewby Towers, painted at seven and ten years old. I have always been haunted by a likeness that I failed to trace. It must have been a marked likeness, as it was noticed by one of Miss Wilcox's pupils when Guy first rode into Clinton St James.'

'What, then, are we to make of Mrs Dearsley's *You have a better right to it than I* when she bestowed the snake-bracelet on Martina? It indicates a relationship of some sort, though not necessarily that of mother and daughter.'

Earlier I had been mistaken when I believed I knew the direction of Mr Ellin's thoughts. Now I was all at sea. I looked at Laurence and Guy, surprised that they did not look the happier for the clearing of their sister's good name. They would not meet my gaze; for they knew what was coming, and to them it was worse than what had preceded it. Haggard and wretched, they stared steadfastly at the floor. Mr Ellin's voice came to me from a great distance.

'Mrs Chalfont, your stepsons have just read a curious story about a young lady who was staying with a married friend not far from her father's house. She had come to cheer her father during her stepmother's illness. A girl-babe was born dead, and the young lady's father desired her to see to the burial arrangements. A few hours afterwards, the hired house was left empty. The young lady returned home, the friend went off to join her husband in Paris. When the friend later brought an infant back to England, there were occasional rumours that the babe was not her own. As it grows older, a village gossip notices its likeness to a member of the young lady's family. On the other hand an old nurse notices how like it is to your nieces, Mrs Chalfont, and perhaps to you also.'

In that instant memory drew a picture of Tina sitting on the hearthrug in Annie's parlour on Christmas Day and of Annie's puzzled expression as she watched her. The same puzzled look had reappeared on Annie's face an hour ago as she gathered up the marine treasures that Tina had been proudly displaying to us before, overcome by sleep, she had put them from her with a drowsy request for her evening hymn. Those pictures dissolved, to be replaced by a vision of young Diana Green declaring, 'She had changed, Mrs Chalfont, she was more like you . . . more like you . . . more like you. . .'

I rose to my feet, only to fall back again with a cry, 'I do not understand. This cannot be.'

'I think it can,' said Mr Ellin.

I was dazed, incredulous, I could not believe that I had heard aright.

'We must presume that the childless Mrs Dearsley had an overpowering desire for a child. She was close at hand when a babe was supposedly still-born at Grewby Towers. We do not know precisely how she discovered that it lived or how she contrived to take possession of it. She left her rented house at short notice and set out for Paris. Somewhere on the way a baby was baptized in a church three doors from the inn where the pseudo-mother was staying. It should be easy to find that inn and that church if need be; but it is unlikely that the necessity will arise.'

The room darkened about me. Laurence and Guy did not move or look up. That far-off voice still spoke. It said, 'Mrs Dearsley must have had an accomplice.'

I saw Laurence and Guy lift white faces in the gloom. And I tried to speak, and could not.

'But Mrs Dearsley cannot help our inquiry now,' said Mr Ellin. 'There is no living soul who can do it save that accomplice. What would be your attitude to an accomplice who confessed to her share in the crime?'

'Merciful,' I said. 'She is safe from me.'

'You are sure of that? It is a solemn promise?'

'As I hope to be saved, yes.'

'Thank you,' said Laurence and Guy, brokenly, stumblingly.

'The accomplice may refuse to confess. But there is a way in which we can obtain proof without even seeking her co-operation. Mr Laurence and Mr Guy Chalfont have agreed with me that it would be wiser to make use of this second means of obtaining proof before confronting the accomplice and charging her with her share in the crime. Mr Augustine Chalfont's permission will have to be sought if we are to obtain proof by this means. His brothers assure me that he will give his consent.'

Gently, oh so gently, Mr Ellin told me what they proposed to do. I did not at the time take in a single syllable of what he said. A violent fit of shuddering seized me, and the room became very hot and then very cold. At last I recognized a few words spoken by Laurence: 'We must set off for Grewby Towers as early as we can tomorrow.' Then Guy spoke, then Mr Ellin, then Laurence again; but I failed to understand what they said. Language had lost its meaning. Nothing remained but a maelstrom of chaotic thought, beating and foaming in some primaeval ocean . . .

I heard the drawing-room door shut behind me, and perceived with dim surprise that Mr Ellin and I were alone in the hall, where he was putting on his great-coat preparatory to returning home. Feebly and inadequately I thanked him for all he had done. Bathos attended my poor little outpouring of gratitude; for it dwindled into expressions of regret that Tina had flown out in such an unlooked for manner at my unlucky stepsons.

'Trust a woman for spoiling a man's dinner!' was Mr Ellin's ungallant reply to that. In ordinary circumstances I should have considered it my duty to combat and confute such an erroneous opinion; but the circumstances were so far from ordinary that I judged it best to say nothing. 'Little monkey!' said he. 'If she had not let the cat out of the bag like that I could have wrapped it up nicely in silk.' Here, almost smiling, he stopped in time to save himself from blundering into any more mixed metaphors. I could see that he was tired and hungry and yet loath to go back to his solitary dwelling; I feared the aged Browns did not make it any too comfortable for him. With a mighty effort I drove my own preoccupations from my mind and thanked him all over again, this time, I hope, in terms that more appropriately matched his deserts. He lingered at the open front door.

'If you can bear to do so, say a word of comfort to those poor boys. I am afraid they did not have too easy a time with me. Laurence tried to defend his sister and Mrs Dearsley on the ground of their extreme youth. *Extreme youth!* — faugh! A child of three years old ought to know the difference between *meum* and *tuum*.'

I assured Mr Ellin that I would do what I could. He then became anxious and apprehensive about the measures he and my stepsons were about to take. 'Arminel' — I was aware that he had called me Arminel and I had recovered my senses enough to be a little surprised at the liberty — 'Arminel, you will not blame me too much if our errand tomorrow proves fruitless, a gross error? You will remember that I acted, even if mistakenly, for the best?'

'How can you doubt me, William?' I answered. 'God grant that success may attend your efforts. I shall always be deeply grateful, whether you succeed or fail.'

He was gone. I went on my errand of consolation. Of that hour I will not write.

Chapter Fifteen

There are waking dreams and sleeping dreams. In which did I pass the night? I have never been able to answer that question. All I know is that till dawn I glided alone, now over the purple moors that surrounded Grewby Towers, now among the grassy mounds and crumbling headstones of Grewby churchyard, always questing, always seeking, for some precious thing I had lost. As morning broke, I fell into the slumber of exhaustion, from which I was roused by a succession of extraordinary sounds in the room next to mine. I sprang up and hastened in, where I beheld Tina dancing like a dervish. 'I am celebrating my return home,' she explained, dropping on her bed after a final pirouette. 'Have those two, Emma's brothers, gone away yet?'

'After breakfast they are going, with Mr Ellin, to the place where I used to live, Grewby Towers.'

'Why?'

'They want to find out why Emma took you away from me. You must be kind to them, Tina; for they are not very happy. It grieves them to think that Emma behaved so badly.'

'Hum!' said Tina, making no promises. 'I shall call them Laurence and Guy in future, because you do.'

'Very well.'

'But I shall not come down to breakfast till the last minute because I do not wish to see them.'

She began her dance again and I withdrew to my own room glad that she had recovered her spirits so soon after her late tribulations. My stepsons were by no means so light-hearted; it was all too plain that their dreams, like mine, had not been of the pleasantest. I was relieved that Tina kept out of the way; for they now had an opportunity for acquainting me fully with the most urgent of the reasons that had impelled Emma to make her desperate bid to escape public disgrace. It was a reason to which

Mr Ellin had briefly alluded when he spoke of the danger to a young lady's prospects of marriage; but when we were alone, Emma's brothers had been too much ashamed to tell me what in the light of another day they had resolved I should hear: namely, that at the ripe age of thirty Emma was engaged to be married. She had been engaged more than once, they said, to highly desirable suitors, who had withdrawn their suits on witnessing or hearing about her wild behaviour. The grandparents longed to see their beloved Emma married to a husband who could, it was hoped, control her vagaries as nobody else had ever been able to do. Repeated failures had left them in a state of near despair when a candidate for Emma's hand dropped from the skies in the person of the Earl of Orlington, whose estates were in the far north of Scotland and whose diplomatic pursuits kept him almost continually abroad. 'It would be a thousand pities if this business about Martina leaked out before Emma has landed her catch,' said Laurence, whose long sojourns in uncivilized quarters of the globe had, I feared, slightly blunted the edge of his native refinement.

'She is engaged to Orlington?' I said, surprised.

'You know Lord Orlington, then?' they said, in equal surprise.

'He is my cousin,' I answered. 'But I have not seen him since we were both children. His mother, my Aunt Henrietta, died long ago, and Hamish and his late father have been little in England since her death.'

Their embarrassment was, if possible, greater than before. As Mr Ellin already knew from Mrs Tidmarsh, the engagement was private; but it would be publicly announced before long, unless —

'We must all do our best that there shall be no "unless",' I told them, and they looked their gratitude. Tina entering, no more was said.

Remembering my admonition, she greeted the unwelcome guests politely enough before taking her place at the breakfast-table; but she sat eyeing them in an attitude at once jealous and suspicious. Toward the end of the meal her feelings overthrew the dictates of decorum. To my chagrin, I heard her addressing Laurence in tones of chill severity. 'I hope you do not intend to kidnap Mr Ellin,' said Miss Tina.

I wished I had not said so much about my dear Tina's innate sweetness of disposition. Laurence was equal to the occasion. 'Shouldn't think of it. Mr Ellin would put up a better fight than you did!' said my elder stepson coolly.

'I fought my very best,' protested Tina, at once injured and crestfallen. Her eyes filled with tears; but she winked them away and applied herself once more to her bread and honey. I think she regarded Laurence as a foeman to be respected; for she made no further attack on him, and even condescended to accompany me to the front door when the conveyance drove up that was to convey the three travellers to the Barlton Market railway station.

Hardly had we waved them off when Larry advanced with a request for a day's holiday! Peter, he explained, was quite capable of looking after the young masters' horses in his absence. Peter was Jane's eldest nephew, recently employed as garden boy.

I did not need to see Larry going off to borrow Farmer Giles horse! — I knew without any telling that he was away to Valincourt to inspect his future domain, and I wished him better luck than Laurence had had when he too went on a tour of investigation. With the best assumption of ignorance that I could muster, I granted his request.

As soon as he had left me, I had to hear a similar request from Tina, who, inspired by Larry's example, begged a holiday from lessons that she might, as she expressed it, 'rearrange her thoughts'.

'For they are all upside down, Aunt Arminel, and I should like to sit down quietly and sort them out. And this afternoon perhaps I could walk with you to visit Jane's grandmother and give her the shawl. Jane says she will be riding the moon with delight when she gets it, especially as it has such a romantic history. I cannot think that there is anything romantic about being choked by a muffler and poked into an orphanage where all the children had cropped heads. But no doubt Jane thinks differently.'

As it happened, not much sitting down to meditate was done that day. Two minutes later Tina was asking the whereabouts of Mangnall's *Questions*. 'Mr Ellin told me that he had bought a copy for me,' Tina explained. 'I could not make out whether he was pretending just to tease me, or whether he seriously meant what he said. If it is true, I shall begin teaching Elinor and Rosamond at once. Their education has been neglected lately, and I must make the most of the time that is left before I grow too old to care to play with them any longer. Where is the book, Aunt Arminel, do you know?'

'In the sewing-room,' I answered without thinking. I had intended to keep the secret of the room's transformation for a few more hours in order to save Tina from over-excitement after her recent distressing experiences — but recollection came to my aid too late. Tina ran lightly into the sewing-room. A cry of astonishment rang out. 'Oh, Aunt Arminel, what is this? Am I dreaming? The schoolroom from The Hurst is here. Who sent it? How did it come?'

I explained that Mr Ellin had been able to visit The Hurst and buy the contents of her playroom-schoolroom while in Great Parborough. The carrier's cart had brought them, and Guy and I had set them up as nicely as we could.

'Guy helped you? Then I shall change everything round. I will not have Guy meddling and putting things in the wrong places.'

'Poor Guy and poor me!' I said. 'We worked so hard to please you.'

'If you will show me what you did, I will leave it just where it is. There is nothing for it but to change everything Guy did, every single thing. I do not approve of Guy. He is one of your cruel stepchildren, and he has no business to call you *Madre*. Jane tells me he is coming to live here for a time, she does not know how long. I don't see why he should come when I do not want him.'

Clearly, the spirit of jealousy still had possession of the gentle Tina. It was well that at this moment the current of her thoughts was powerfully changed by the sight, not of Mangnall's *Questions* but of the *Phantasmion* of Sara Coleridge. She seized it with a joyful shriek. 'Look, Aunt Arminel, look! My *Phantasmion*! I have got it again when I thought I had lost it for ever. Miss Murphy took it away from me. She said it was the most fantastic rubbish she had ever set eyes on, and she was shocked that the daughter of a great poet should write such nonsense. And she threw it up to the top of the bookcase where I could not reach it, and she said I was never to read it, never. But I may, Aunt Arminel, may I not? Must I obey Miss Murphy still?'

'Certainly you may read it. I have given more than one copy to my nephews and nieces. It is an exquisite piece of fairy literature, and its songs and lyrics are such as none but a daughter of Coleridge could have written. But I warn you that you may find the story a little alarming.'

'I don't mind — I like to be alarmed. Oh, joy, joy!' said Tina, beginning to prance about.

'Who gave it to you?' I asked.

She experienced a sudden check to her rapture. 'Guy did,' she said in a small voice.

'How was that?'

'Once Mamma took me with her to Parborough Hall on a hot, hot day. Emma sent me to wait in the orangery while she and Mamma were having their chat. I was in the orangery, almost boiled alive, for hours and hours and hours. I was not crying,' said Tina with dignity, 'but I was rather near it. Guy saw me through the glass door as he was on his way to the village. He fetched me a tumbler of iced lemonade and he said he was going to the bookseller's and would try to find a book for me. *Phantasmion* was what he found. He read aloud the part where a beautiful damsel came by moonlight in her little boat to a dark lake. She had a magical net made of flaming wires in which she caught many-coloured fishes that glittered like jewels. She put the fishes into a silver pitcher and took them away. After Guy left me to read to myself, I began at the beginning as Miss Murphy always made me do — she said it was a bad trick to start in the middle. But Mamma came to take me home before I had reached the pages that told of the girl with the silver pitcher. And as soon as I was back in the schoolroom with the book, Miss Murphy saw it and took it from me. So I have never been able to discover what the girl did with the fishes — not till this very day.'

All jealousy vanished like a morning cloud. I heard no more of her disapproval of Guy. Laurence too was taken into favour; for in the course of her search for prized possessions she came across a magnificent knife which he had most injudiciously presented to her, and which Miss Murphy had promptly forbidden her ever to open. I regarded the thing's innumerable blades with horror, and mildly indicated that in this instance Miss Murphy's prohibition still held good. How busy and how happy was Tina the livelong day, now dipping into *Phantasmion*, now gloating over recovered treasures, now walking with me to deposit shawl and bonnet in the homes of their new owners, and now joyously greeting her play-fellows the Randolphs, who came dashing into Silverlea Cottage as soon as their lessons were over! As evening drew on, the Randolphs departed and sweet silence prevailed. Bereft of her companions Tina followed me to Guy's study, where I was making one or two additions that I hoped would add to his comfort. She was, however, considerably disconcerted by the sight of a volume entitled *Skeleton Sermons* unearthed by Laurence in Valchester and bestowed on his brother in a spirit of mischief. She put the book down in haste and retreated to the door. 'I did not know that *sermons* could have skeletons. Oh, how horrid!'

Alone in the parlour with me, she again became curious to know more about the errand that had taken Mr Ellin and my stepsons to Grewby Towers.

'I thought you said they were going to find out why Emma kidnapped me. But Emma does not live at Grewby Towers. She lives at Parborough Hall.'

'They wished to see my eldest stepson first, before they saw Emma.'

'Why was that?'

'I cannot tell you now. It is a secret. Perhaps you shall hear the secret when Mr Ellin comes back.'

'And perhaps not?'

'Perhaps not.'

'Will they all come back tomorrow?'

'It is unlikely.'

'Is it a happy secret?'

'I do not know.'

Tina sighed, and gave up asking questions.

'I shall be very busy tomorrow, and I should like to have another holiday.'

'No, my dear, that would never do.'

'I suppose not. Tomorrow I shall have to plan what I shall give away. It seems to me that I have too much and must share some of my things with the others. Today I could not decide in a hurry.'

I have never agreed with the practice of those parents who endeavour to teach their children unselfishness by persuading them or even obliging them to surrender cherished possessions to other children or to charitable causes. Such forced generosity is to my mind utterly worthless. But when the child gives freely, spontaneously, without pressure of any kind, then indeed the gift is without price. Distracted as I was, I could yet rejoice at this evidence of a good spirit in Tina; and on the following day I rejoiced even more when I found that she did not give out of her abundance only the gay trifles that meant nothing to her; but on the contrary she presented her friends with what she evidently valued. For example, she owned a very fine red and white chess set, which she gave to Anselm, who played chess with his father but had no set of his own. Tina did not play chess but all the pieces had a personality and a life-story, even the pawns possessing names fondly remembered from the days of her life at The Hurst. Nevertheless, Anselm must certainly have the chess set because it was the best and most suitable gift for a boy, with the exception of

Laurence's knife, which must be kept lest Laurence should ask after it. A zither, on which Elizabeth was thought to have cast a single wistful glance, was at once handed to her, and little Anna was made happy with a doll's tea-set in pink fluted china-ware. Nor were the nephews and nieces of Jane and Eliza forgotten, and Larry had a boxful of treasures to carry home to his little Charlotte.

But between the day on which Tina ran into the sewing-room and the day on which she distributed her gifts, there stretched a second dread dream-haunted night throughout which I wandered again over purple mist-enshrouded moor and saw the spectral funeral coach drawing nearer, ever nearer till in panic I awoke.

Awoke! — to what? To intolerable suspense that would not end, as far as I could tell for at least three or four days; since Mr Ellin and my stepsons would have to proceed from Grewby Towers to Parborough Hall before their return to Silverlea Cottage to report the success or failure of their mission. Well, there was no help for it, I must endure the waiting-time as best I might.

My unease was increased by a visit from Mr Wilcox, who happened to be staying with his sisters at Fuchsia Lodge and who seized on the chance of securing what in his jargon he would have called 'a good story'. Before leaving, Mr Ellin had warned me not to make any kind of statement to the Press. In obedience to his orders, I denied Mr Wilcox the smallest tit-bit of information, while showing him every possible courtesy in the hope of ensuring his silence. Vainest of vain hopes! Jane and Emma had been discretion itself; but the man who drove Mr Ellin and Tina home had heard Tina say the name of Mrs Smith and had caught Mr Ellin's words of reassurance — convent orphanage in Belgium — spoken on the threshold. On this slender foundation Mr Wilcox built up an elaborate edifice of fantasy, wherein a fanatical Roman Catholic lady, a friend of the late Mr Conway Fitzgibbon and his wife, could not, for conscience' sake, suffer their child to remain in Protestant hands. In after days the public denial of this absurd tale was to give Mr Ellin and me a good deal of trouble; moreover there are persons of our acquaintance who persist in believing it to this day. Well for me that I could not know what the fertile brain of Mr Wilcox was devising as he left Silverlea Cottage after what I trusted had been an unfruitful interview!

Sympathy I had none in my unrest. There was Larry in the

garden, looking two inches taller and broader after his day's holiday, going about his duties in the lordly manner that befitted Valincourt's future coachman, and hectoring poor little Peter so shamefully that I was glad to see Laurence's terrible knife disappearing into Peter's pocket, Tina having heard and resented blame that she did not consider justified. There was Annie, drowsily content with life. There were Jane and Eliza making merry in the kitchen — I could guess the topic that merited so much animated chatter! There was Tina, who, amid her multifarious occupations, kept chanting over and over again James Thomson's description of the colours of the spectrum, which Miss Spindler had that morning caused her to learn by heart. I suppose the lines had taken her fancy; for if I heard them once that day, I heard them twenty times:

> First the flaming Red
> Sprang vivid forth; the tawny Orange next;
> And next delicious Yellow; by whose side
> Fell the kind beams of all-refreshing Green;
> Then the pure Blue, that swells autumnal skies
> Ethereal played; and then, of sadder hue,
> Emerged the deepened Indigo, as when
> The heavy-skirted evening droops with frost;
> While the last gleamings of refracted light
> Died in the fainting Violet away.

Was it possible, I asked myself, that a rainbow joy awaited me?

Chapter Sixteen

In the meantime, how fared Mr Ellin and his companions? He has since described that journey as the most depressing he ever took. Laurence and Guy hardly ever spoke; and they looked so cowed and dismal that their fellow-passengers regarded them with inquisitive interest. Mr Ellin verily believes that they were taken for a couple of harmless lunatics and he for their keeper. Arrived at Grewby, Mr Ellin was deposited at the inn, there to await Augustine's decision after he had heard what his brothers had to tell.

Quiet and composed to all outward seeming, Mr Ellin sat by a window that overlooked the moors. His attention was presently drawn to a horsewoman riding alone in the direction of Grewby Towers. As she drew nearer, Mr Ellin noted her superb horsemanship; and something in her bearing turned his thoughts to Margaret's word-picture of the tall dark lady who had questioned her on the sands. Mr Ellin caught sight of a face that might have been chiselled out of alabaster, so still was it, so set. With head held high, she passed into the winter mists.

An hour later Laurence returned, pale and despondent.

'Augustine agrees that we shall make the investigation you have suggested — and we will make it tonight, the sooner the better. It took a good deal of arguing to convince him of the necessity; but we made him yield at last. He had not seen Wilcox's article or your appeals for information about "Matilda Fitzgibbon", so the whole thing came upon him as a heavy shock. 'Twas not his fault that he held out so long.'

Mr Ellin signified his assent to the proposition. He was prepared to allow that no one could be justly blamed for obduracy induced by sheer stupefaction.

'But Augustine insists on two conditions. Should tonight's investigation prove that you were mistaken in your surmise, he will permit no inquiries whatever to be made about Martina's parentage. There is to be no suggestion that Martina is other than the daughter of Timon and Harriet Dearsley. Nor is Emma to be strictly questioned concerning her motive or motives for abducting Martina. It is to be tacitly assumed that she did so merely because she wished to remove her dead friend's child from the keeping of a stepmother she had always hated. In return for our promise that her act of criminal folly will not be made known to the world at large, she will be required to undertake that she will never again interfere in any way with her stepmother's concerns. As Mrs Chalfont's representative in this matter, do you approve and consent?'

It struck Mr Ellin that Laurence was faithfully reproducing the dicta of Augustine: the dry legalistic style was not his own. With equal formality, Mrs Chalfont's agent made answer, 'I fully approve and consent.'

His duty discharged, Laurence quickly became himself. 'I don't know whether this is going to upset the apple cart — but my sister isn't at Parborough Hall. She is here, at the Towers.'

'Miss Chalfont is here?' said Mr Ellin, not entirely surprised by the intelligence.

'Yes. Came some days ago. Can't think what could have brought her. She is not and never has been on good terms with Mrs Augustine. Her visits are few and far between — and they usually end abruptly after a battle royal.'

It was not Mr Ellin's business to comment on the relations between the sisters-in-law. 'Surely it is fortunate that Miss Chalfont has timed her visit to coincide with ours. There will now be no need for us to go to Great Parborough.'

'I don't know whether to call it fortunate,' was Laurence's glum rejoinder. To my mind, Emma has a brooding suspicious air, as if she had something up her sleeve. Three times at least she has ridden to Shardley, always unaccompanied. Is it possible, do you suppose, that she meets someone there who has knowledge of your movements?'

Mr Ellin declared this to be well-nigh impossible. He knew no one in Shardley.

'Be that as it may,' said Laurence, 'she is making ready for some black mischief or other — I know the look!'

Mr Ellin, having some slight knowledge of Emma's idiosyncrasies, thought this likely to be true. He asked whether Mr Augustine Chalfont would acquaint his wife with what was to be done that night.

'Not if he can help it — a thousand times no! We don't want her fainting away at the wrong moment. She may have to be told later — but beforehand, never! There's no knowing what might be the result of that. Females are queer kittle-cattle.'

For the next few seconds Mr Ellin indulged in lively conjectures as to the scenes likely to be enacted in Grewby Towers if Mrs Augustine heard what was afoot in the dark hours. Laurence broke in on his nightmare visions.

'Augustine has told Sophia that our stepmother has sent a friend to discuss some necessary affairs with him. He has asked her to direct that a guest-room should be prepared for the friend, who will arrive so late at night that there is no need for the servants to stay up. It has also been pretty plainly intimated that the coming of the friend should not be mentioned to Emma, who would be anything but pleased to hear that her stepmother was in communication with the Towers. I don't care to picture what will happen when she later finds out — as she is bound to do — that Guy and I have made our peace with Mrs Chalfont. However, let the future take care of itself: our concern is with the present. As I said, Emma is in a suspicious mood. She has no reason to suppose that there is anything odd about our turning up unexpectedly at our old home after a two years' absence abroad; but if she once heard of your presence here, she might stir up trouble of some kind.'

'In what way?'

'How can I tell?'

'It is impossible.'

'It would be, if Emma wasn't Emma. Enough of that: let me tell you what Augustine has arranged. We cannot do what we propose to do until the ladies have retired to rest. That will be too late for you to leave the Grewby Arms — the good folk here are early to bed and early to rise. Augustine proposes that you should dine here and come up to the Towers at about nine o'clock. One of us will come down to escort you and take you to the library, where you will wait until Augustine thinks it is safe for us to go to the churchyard. He has warned his wife that his business with you may keep him up very late indeed.'

With the departure of Laurence, Mr Ellin was left to his own devices. He dined, tried to interest himself in a newspaper many days old, and then waited with what patience he might summon to his aid. Those were not agreeable hours. He felt himself in some degree overpowered by the universal dread of Emma, whom he half expected to see suddenly confronting him, aflame with indignation against the man who had dared to oppose her will. While he could hear hearty laughter and the rumble of talk in the taproom, he had a sense of companionship; but after a time the sounds died away, and the house was quiet save for the ticking of the grandfather clock in the parlour and the hooting of an owl in the inn yard. Mr Ellin had looked at his watch for the twentieth time when his ordeal was brought to an end by the reappearance of the second of the Chalfont brothers.

One vigil succeeded another. They entered Grewby Towers by a side door, whence Mr Ellin was led to the library. There he sat waiting in the company of a number of family portraits which had not been hung in the picture-gallery but occupied spaces between the massive oaken bookcases that lined the walls. As it had been with me on a former occasion, so it was with Mr Ellin on that night: one portrait drew his particular attention. This time it was not the portrait of a girl but of a young and remarkably handsome woman whose eyes met his with malevolent purpose in their gaze. In vain did he attempt to study the other portraits: always he was compelled to meet again the baleful eyes. 'I will defeat you yet!' said the eyes, again and again. 'I will defeat you yet!'

The library, though as yet Mr Ellin knew it not, was situated in an isolated quarter of the house where readers could be free from disturbance. Now he would have welcomed the relief of hearing an owl hoot or a grandfather clock tick; but the silence remained unbroken and the eyes continued to menace. He started violently when the door opened to reveal, not Emma but three cloaked figures, the tallest of whom held a shuttered lantern.

Mr Ellin rose and followed where they led. Leaving the house by the same side door, they plunged into a shrubbery densely concealed from the house. The shrubbery ended at a gate into the park, which they crossed. A grey ribbon of road ran past the exit. On the far side Mr Ellin perceived a lych-gate and, at some distance behind it, the cloudy outlines of a church. In the churchyard was such a building as Mr Ellin had never seen before and hoped never to see again. By lantern light he beheld the object of my abhorrence, that mausoleum built in pseudo-classical style, with pillars on either side of the door. Huge yew trees dominated it with their darkness.

Augustine fitted a great key into the lock. It turned, groaning, and the door swung back on the deeper darkness within. They entered, meeting the odour of death and decay. Augustine raised the lantern and looked about him. 'There it is, as I remember it, close by my father's coffin,' he said. 'Take the lantern, one of you.' He fumbled in his pockets for a screw-driver, found it — and stopped. 'I cannot,' he said. 'Will you, Laurence?'

But Laurence, intrepid explorer though he was, shook his head, shuddering. As Mr Ellin looked at the three white faces, he began to think that he would be obliged to perform the duty that was the Chalfonts' alone. He had hardly formulated the thought when Guy came forward, inserted the screwdriver and raised the lid. All save Augustine forced themselves to look. They saw only a huddle of mouldering baby clothes, which Guy, ashen but resolute, slowly unfolded. From the remains of a babe's bedgown and flannel backcloth, a book dropped out. Laurence uttered a sharp sound between whistle and gasp; the others were silent. Guy searched the remaining clothes. Of a child there was no vestige or trace.

Laurence was the first to speak, if speech it could be called, so intermixed was it with bursts of wild laughter. 'Must be the book my father lost — the book Tina wrote about in *The Cruel Stepchildren*.' He flicked the damp, discoloured pages over. 'What's this? what's this? Whew! *Eighteenth-century Swedish Authors* by W. R. E. Mr Ellin, I declare it's one of yours! Odd to think that my father was so near finding his lost book — and he never to know it!'

Augustine spoke petulantly. 'This is neither the time nor the place for jesting. Replace the lid, Guy. We must leave everything exactly as we found it.'

Staring, Laurence laid down the book. 'But why? Since there never was a baby buried here, what need —?'

Augustine, as Mr Ellin had already noticed, was orderly and precise in all his ways. Even had prudence not dictated that all should be left in seemly guise, he could not have endured to leave the coffin open and its contents scattered. He made an impatient gesture. Guy put back the book and the clothes and Laurence re-screwed the lid, while Augustine and Mr Ellin stood waiting. They trooped out. The door was closed as gently as if they feared to awaken the dead. Augustine locked the door and took the great key from the lock.

They had gone but a few steps when, far off, they saw the small red glow of an approaching lantern. 'At this time of night! — who on earth is prowling here?' muttered Augustine. 'Into the trees, quick! We must not be seen.'

The three others obeyed, and stood silent and statue-like to watch the deepening glow of the lantern. After the first moment of uncertainty, none needed to be told who the bearer must be.

Nearer and nearer came the light, showing the tall figure of a woman wrapped in a dark mantle. As she passed by, Mr Ellin thought that he never could forget her face, iron-set, marmoreal. As did his companions, he guessed — nay, knew — what purpose had brought her to visit the house of death at an unhallowed hour, and he was unable to refrain from admiring the courage, greater than a man's, that had given her the strength to do what she had come to do.

She took a key from her pocket and unlocked the door. With no visible sign of reluctance, she went in. For perhaps a hundred seconds the light flitted to and fro. Then she was out again. They all saw what she carried in her arms.

But she did not return by the way she had come: there was a further task to be performed. Striking into a side path, she made her way among the tombs till she was hidden from sight. Laurence was the first to grasp whither she was bound. 'The well!' he whispered. 'She is going to the well!' And turning to Mr Ellin, 'It is of unknown depth. Hark!'

In the still midnight air, every least sound was magnified. The well-cover creaked and grated as it was drawn back. There followed two splashes, one lighter than the other. Again the well-cover grated and creaked. Like a red eye, the lantern glimmered as its bearer began the return journey among the tombs. Into the main path came the tall dark figure. As she neared the clustering yew trees, four other dark shapes issued forth to bar her way. 'Emma!' said Augustine, the word cleaving her shriek of mortal terror.

Mr Ellin thinks that she must have taken Augustine for her father's spirit, or something worse. But her alarm was short-lived; for Laurence's loud, 'Here, hold on, Emma, it's only us!' brought instant reassurance. She faced her accusers boldly, but in silence.

'You were a little too late, Emma,' said Augustine, coldly. 'We had already visited the mausoleum, and we can all testify to what was — and what was not — in the baby's coffin that you have just thrown into the well.'

She threw her head back, haughtily defiant. 'What do you want of me?'

'Your full confession, which you will make as soon as we have returned to the Towers. Nothing else and nothing less will save you from public disgrace. Come.'

182

'Certainly I will come. Did you think that I proposed to remain in the churchyard all night?'

Not a word was spoken as they retraced their steps. At the side entrance — 'You had better see to the fastenings of the front door,' said Emma, with perfect calm. 'I went out that way and did not secure it behind me.'

Augustine mumbled some sort of reply, in the course of which he told Emma that he intended to wake his wife and bring her to the library.

'May I ask why? At this stage in the proceedings there is no need to involve Sophia.'

'You must have the support of a female presence,' Augustine told her.

There was a metallic note in Emma's slight laugh. 'Sophia's support? I would sooner rely on the support of a broken reed.'

Vouchsafing no reply, Augustine departed in search of his wife. Laurence and Guy silently busied themselves in lighting lamps and rekindling the dying fire; Mr Ellin made entries in his notebook. It was not the moment for introductions; and Mr Ellin was not surprised that none were made during the next twenty minutes.

Mr and Mrs Augustine came at last, she in some dishevelment, with looks part incredulous, part horrified. Emma had thrown herself into an armchair, where she now faced a semi-circle of judges. She spoke no word save a contemptuous 'Well?'

Augustine said, 'You must tell us everything, from first to last. As I have already said, we will do our best to shield you if you speak frankly.'

She made a scornful motion of her head towards Mr Ellin, accompanying the movement with the monosyllable 'He?'

'Mr Ellin is Mrs Chalfont's accredited representative and joint guardian with her of the child hitherto known as Martina Dearsley. Both Mrs Chalfont and Mr Ellin are very anxious that the good name of our family should be preserved and that if it is humanly possible you should be spared the consequences of your ——'

There Augustine halted in embarrassment. He did not, it was obvious, choose to use the words 'crime' or 'sin', but was at a loss to find a suitable substitute. While he was considering, Mr Ellin observed that Miss Chalfont did not yet know of Martina's rescue from the Belgian convent orphanage. Safely restored to her guardians, she had given them certain information which had

183

led them to the discovery that had been made that night. In the circumstances Miss Chalfont would no doubt understand that in a full confession lay the only way out of her difficulties.

Emma was defeated, and she knew it. Augustine, recovering himself, left the suitable substitute unspoken. He said, 'This is what we propose. After you have given us a full account of your part in this nefarious business, you will write and sign two copies of a brief confession. One copy I will deposit with my lawyer, to remain, sealed, among the family archives; the other copy will be given to Mrs Chalfont for a similar purpose. While you are writing your confession, we will consult as to the wording of a statement to be made to the newspapers.'

Emma made a sign of acquiescence. She waited for no further prompting, but began her spoken confession at once in a level voice totally devoid of all feeling, good or bad.

'I had better tell Mr Ellin what you, Augustine and Laurence, may recollect, though Guy has probably never heard it: namely, that my lifelong friend Harriet Dearsley, having married very young, lost her reason for a short time on being told, by the best medical authorities, that she could never have a child. She had to be placed in a private asylum for a short while. Not long after her recovery The Hurst was so extensively damaged by fire as to be rendered temporarily uninhabitable. Mr Dearsley, who was — as often — in financial straits, went to France intending to make good his losses at the gaming-tables of Paris, in which city his wife was to join him as soon as she felt able to undertake the journey. At my suggestion, she and I rented a small furnished house in Grewby for a few weeks only. I welcomed the opportunity of being with my father while Mrs Chalfont was conveniently out of the way, awaiting the birth of her child.

In the event she was so near dying that I suppose little attention was paid to the babe, which was pronounced dead. My father requested me to see to its coffining. He was, I deemed, unreasonably angry with me when I pointed out that, being unbaptized, it ought to be buried in an unconsecrated corner of the churchyard. We were hotly disputing when he was called away to speak with a visitor. I was left alone, vexed and humiliated. Attendants, not the old nurse Annie, brought the babe and choice of clothing for the burial. I noticed signs of life but I did not recall the servants. Seizing a book that lay on a shelf near at hand, I wrapped it securely in some of the clothes, put it in the coffin and fastened the lid down. With the babe and part of the remaining garments under my cloak, I drove, all unnoticed, to Harriet Dearsley and thrust the child upon her, exclaiming, "This is yours!" She accepted the gift without hesitation and with extreme delight.'

There Emma paused, as if expecting to be called on to defend her conduct. Exonerate herself entirely she could not; but it was open to her to plead that a momentary madness had blinded her to the enormity of her deed, or that she and Mrs Dearsley were too young to be fully aware of their cruelty, or that she had been rendered desperate by her father's harsh reproaches and by memories of her stepmother's share in the summary breaking off of two marriages. As no one spoke to inquire into her motives single or blended, she resumed her narrative, which Mr Ellin found almost unbelievably dry and formal. He could only conclude that it was a prepared statement, held in readiness for just such a time as this. How often, he wondered, had she mentally rehearsed it in the silent watches of the night. There had been ample opportunity for preparation: nearly eleven years had passed since the hour when she burst into the little hired dwelling with a stolen treasure in her arms. That she had then been as mad as the once distraught Harriet, he had not the shadow of a doubt. He noted, with approval, that she made no attempt to cast any part of the blame on Harriet, sharer of her guilt and, perhaps, the worse sinner of the two. Facts, facts, facts, were all she gave.

'Harriet's maid, an elderly and experienced woman, knew how to care for the child. Within an hour, ourselves and our possessions had been packed into the commodious chaise that had brought up from Parborough and we were driving as fast as we dared to a distant town in which I, no less than Harriet, was a stranger. I had run to the person from whom we had hired the house, and, paying what we owed, had stated that urgent family matters necessitated Mrs Dearsley's immediate departure to join her husband in Paris.'

Augustine, who had hitherto listened impassively, here broke in.

'You must have had other servants. How did you dispose of them?'

'We had two, provided by the owner of the house. They came in by the day, and both were out when I arrived with the baby. I went to their homes, paid their wages, and asked one of them to deliver a hastily-penned note to my father, in which I told him that, heartbroken by his unkindness, I had resolved to return to Parborough

Hall as soon as I had seen Harriet safely begin the next stage of her journey to Paris.

'Having brought Harriet to a town and an inn where neither of us was known, I remained with her till the next day and then drove back to Parborough Hall. The landlady, a simple incurious soul, asked no questions that were hard to parry. She readily accepted the maid's story that Mrs Dearsley was on her way to visit a sick friend when she was obliged to stop at a miserable hovel for the unexpected birth of her child. So unspeakably dirty and vile was the accommodation that it seemed better, whatever the risk, to drive on as soon as possible.'

Mrs Augustine was heard to be suppressing gasps of horror. Emma heeded her not.

'The landlady was useful to us in one way: she was able to procure the necessary nurse in the person of a respectable young widow who had just lost her child.'

'In another aspect, the landlady's help may not have been quite so acceptable to Mrs Dearsley,' said Mr Ellin. 'Martina was baptized in a church three doors from the inn.'

If Emma was surprised by Mr Ellin's acquaintance with this part of Martina's history, she did not show it. 'Yes, Harriet feared that suspicions might be aroused if she did not yield to the landlady's insistence. She remained in the inn for a fortnight before going to Paris by slow stages, accompanied by the nurse, who was willing to quit a town that held for her only sad memories.

'The breach between my father and myself was soon healed, and neither he nor anyone else thought it strange that Harriet had gone to join her husband instead of remaining in Grewby. It was the most natural course to pursue.

'Mr Dearsley was almost beside himself with anger and dismay when his wife appeared in Paris. He was appalled when he reflected on the consequences to his wife should the theft of the child become known. As he had reason to remember, my father's temperament was hard, implacable.'

At this, Laurence shifted uneasily in his chair. Mr Ellin recalled Mrs Tidmarsh's story of the youth rescued by an indignant father from the toils of an unscrupulous gambler. Emma continued —

'No allowance would be made for the overwhelming temptation presented to a childless woman barely recovered from the attack of insanity caused by the knowledge that she could never have a child; so Mr Dearsley, not knowing which way to turn, acquiesced in what Harriet had done, thus making himself an accomplice in the eyes of the law. I think he never quite forgave her. Me he hated from that day forth; but prudence dictated that he should not forbid me the house. In the event of discovery, Harriet must not be left to bear the blame alone.

'The nurse did not return to England with the Dearsleys. When her services were no longer needed, she obtained a post with an English family resident in France. Some time later she married a man on the permanent domestic staff of the British Embassy, and it is unlikely that she will ever leave her adopted country.

'After a year the Dearsleys went back to The Hurst. There were occasional rumours that they must have adopted a child; but such rumours were to be expected in the circumstances, and were easily disregarded.'

Mr Ellin asked a question that must be answered then or never. 'Mrs Chalfont will wish to know whether the child was happy. We have reason to doubt it.'

Emma drew back. 'That is no part of my confession.'

'It is a vital part, as I see it,' Mr Ellin insisted.

'Speak, Emma.' commanded Augustine.

She yielded. 'Are children ever happy, save at odd moments? Oh, I daresay she was happy enough while she had the nurse, Pleasant Partridge, who was engaged for her after they returned to England.'

'And when the nurse was dismissed?'

'I suggest that you reserve your questions for Martina. At nearly eleven years old, she should be able to answer them.'

Mr Ellin asked no more. Emma's evasion of his inquiries was answer enough. She resumed her narrative.

'As she grew out of babyhood, Martina developed an unfortunate likeness to members of our family, and most markedly to Guy, who could not in any way be held responsible for it. People whispered, I know they did. Then, when Martina was nearly five years old, my father died. Mr Dearsley, relieved of his great dread of prosecution, scandal, punishment, immediately began urging that we should confess all to Mrs Chalfont. He was convinced that she would be lenient. The affair, he was sure, could be easily hushed up; it would be soon forgotten.

'Neither Harriet nor I would listen to him for one moment. If it had been possible to effect the restoration in total secrecy, I think Harriet would have consented. She had tired of her toy and was ready to part with it. But she knew there would be endless gossip and fingers would be pointed at her as long as she lived. That prospect she could not endure. Nor could I. We silenced Mr Dearsley. He gave way . . . but he bided his time.

'The likeness became ever more noticeable. I knew the whispers were directed at me. For years I pushed them aside, disregarded them. I cannot account for something I did some months before Harriet's death. Once, while paying a visit to The Hurst, I was alone in the library, to which I had gone to seek a sheet of paper on which to write down an address that Harriet wanted. When I tried to open a desk-drawer that I knew contained writing-paper, the thing stuck and was dragged free only after much pulling and tugging. It had been — I suppose accidentally — wedged by closely-written pages that had fallen behind it. Glancing idly at the papers, I saw a letter in the handwriting of a Miss Crayshaw, who in her senile old age had become much attached to Mr and Mrs Dearsley. With the letter were other pieces of paper, covered with imitations of Miss Crayshaw's writing and signature.

'Here was evidence of what was being almost openly proclaimed by Miss Crayshaw's relatives, that Mr Dearsley had recently possessed himself of Miss Crayshaw's fortune by means of a forged will. As I have said, I do not know why I secured those papers and hid them in my reticule. It is probable that I did so not intending deliberately to do him harm, but thinking that I now had a useful weapon should he at any time oppose me.

'The Dearsleys' affairs went from bad to worse. On the one hand were his creditors, clamouring for payment; on the other, an army of Crayshaw nephews and nieces trying — as he well knew — to collect evidence to substantiate a charge of forgery. The climax came when he was forced to go into hiding to avoid arrest for debt.

'His lawyer advised him that his best course was to abandon The Hurst to the creditors and himself fly with wife and child to America, in which country Miss Crayshaw's money was safely lodged. Mr Dearsley was most unwilling to go into what he called "exile" and "banishment". He did not believe that the Crayshaws could prove their case; and he was sure he could persuade the creditors to wait till he had retrieved his fallen fortunes at the gaming-table where — apart from a recent run of ill luck — he had always been notoriously successful. As soon as the creditors were satisfied, he would transfer Miss Crayshaw's money to England and live in splendid style as of old.

'He was ever sanguine. I did not believe — and I am sure the lawyers did not! — that he would be able either to defeat the Crayshaws or to quiet his creditors. Moreover, I was becoming desperate. I was fully aware of the harm the rumours had already done me, and I dreaded the harm they might do in the future. They had not come near the truth; but they were quite as injurious as the truth would have been. Or so I thought at the time.

'I concluded that the evil rumours would die away if only I could get the Dearsleys out of the country. Once in America, they would probably stay where they could again make a great show. Martina would, I hoped, eventually marry an American and be lost to sight. In short, all sort of contingencies might arise to prevent their return. It was then that I resolved to use my weapon. Having sought, unknown to Harriet, a private interview with Mr Dearsley, I told him of the fatal evidence I held. This I threatened to reveal to the Crayshaws unless he went to America with his wife and Martina.

Mr Dearsley was thunderstruck, appalled. Of course he vehemently protested his innocence. Those papers! — They were nothing but an idle game he had played with his half-witted old friend, whom he had thought to amuse by showing her how cleverly he could copy her writing. Was I, he asked, so simple as to suppose he would leave criminal evidence lying about? It had been a jest, a subject of merriment for them both. No, he had not told Harriet about the game — why should he? She had asked him to entertain Miss Crayshaw for half an hour while she was busy with her mantua-maker.

'It is possible he spoke the truth — how can I tell? Certainly Timon Dearsley was so careless and light-hearted that it may have been even as he said. I do not know and I did not care. One proviso I made — Harriet was to be kept in ignorance of my threat. She was to hear only that he had reluctantly agreed to accept the lawyer's advice about emigrating to America.

'Not daring to withstand me, he acquiesced. It was settled that he should go into hiding until the eve of the secret departure to America. Two especially importunate creditors suspected his intention and would have betrayed him to the rest if he had not paid them off. This left him with only just enough ready money for the fares to America and for necessary household expenses. Keeping what he would need to support himself during a fortnight in hiding, he entrusted the rest to Harriet until he should creep stealthily back on the eve of their departure.

'When he returned to escort Harriet and Martina to the ship, he found — as all the world now seems to know! — that Harriet had spent the last farthing in equipping herself and Martina for a grand entry into the New World. She had been obliged to pay in coin of the realm; for nobody would give her credit.

'There was, I understand, a violent scene, which ended fatally. As I was not present, I do not know the painful particulars; but I fear that Mr Dearsley may have broken his promise that he would not tell Harriet of my threat against him in the matter of Miss Crayshaw's will. Reproaches, even hot anger, for her extravagant spending she had often endured before — and had laughed and gone her own way. But if she heard that I ——'

Silence, charged with meaning, was the sole response when Emma paused, looking inquiringly from one to the other of her hearers as if to ascertain what they knew or did not know of her poor friend's last hour. She understood then, in one terrible moment, that something worse than a husband's indignation had contributed to Harriet's death. Paler she could not look; sign of emotion she gave none. Her voice was steady.

'As was to be expected, Mr Dearsley did all he could to keep the world from hearing the circumstances of his wife's death. Till after he had sailed for America I and others heard only that her heart, always weak, had failed suddenly. Then gossiping tongues quickly spread the story of the violent quarrel between husband and wife. But until this hour I did not know he had broken his pledged word to me.

'I had more than once remonstrated with Harriet for her extravagant spending at so critical a time; but I was unaware of the full extent of her recklessness. Hearing through friends that Mr Dearsley did not know which way to turn for money, I advanced a sum large enough to cover all immediate expenses. His creditors held back till after the funeral. As soon as it was over, he and Martina set off secretly for Thanpool. He had of course missed the ship in which he had intended to sail; but he knew of a French ship that would touch at Thanpool a few days later.

'I had feared that he might renew his pleadings that Martina should be restored to her mother; and I was prepared to resist those pleadings to the utmost of my power, using the threats that I had used before. But he did not plead. He seemed fully to accept Martina's company, and he even consulted me about which of her boxes should be placed in the hold and which taken into the cabin. I could not feel certain of his good faith, although I had assured him that he would not be burdened with Martina in future. He had only to put her into a boarding-school in New York or some other city and send word to me. I would be responsible for her keep and education until she had been fitted to earn her own living. To this proposal he assented with apparent readiness. I had no reason to distrust him, as he appeared genuinely grateful for the monetary assistance I had given — but all the same I thought it wise to send Thomas to the *Pandore* at the last moment with a gift for Martina. Thomas's report satisfied me.

'I could roughly estimate the time that must elapse before Mr Dearsley was able to write to me with the needful information about Martina's school. When no letter came, I wrote to the French firm that owned the *Pandore*. I was told she had not yet put into port. I wrote again, again and yet again. She was missing . . . she was still missing . . . she was feared lost . . . she had foundered in a gale . . . there were only two survivors, Englishmen named Reynolds. My mind was now set at rest; my secret was, I believed safe. Nothing occurred to disturb that belief —'

'Even when you met — as I think you did — a little girl playing on the sands in Moorland Bay?'

'I remember the occasion. No, I was perfectly satisfied when I was told by another child that the girl was her sister, Bertha Maltravers. Afterwards I recollected having heard that one of Mrs Chalfont's sisters was married to a Mr Maltravers. That, I thought, accounted for the likeness.

'Nothing occurred to trouble me until by chance I took up a newspaper containing an article written — as I was later to learn from Mrs Chalfont's letter — by a Mr Wilcox, brother of the schoolmistresses with whom Martina had been placed. I knew then that I had been tricked by Timon Dearsley. His apparent gratitude had been the merest sham. For over nine years he had nursed his grudge against Harriet and me — and this was his revenge!

'I began at once to consider what I could do. Martina had so far kept silence — but how much longer would that silence last? And was there any way in which I could ensure it for a year or two at the least? I need not enter into the additional reasons I had and still have for wishing to escape public censure. They are well known to you who are sitting in judgment on me.

'I made other plans; but they all failed until at last my puzzle was solved by the arrival of Laurence's curios in Belgium. The news inspired me with the thought that now it would be possible to dispose of Martina in a Belgian orphanage. To do that, I must have help. Harriet's former maid was the obvious person to enlist; for she would be very anxious to prevent her share in the theft of Martina from becoming known. Owing to a failure in health, she had quitted Harriet's service and was living with a sister in London. I did not propose to ask her to take part in the actual kidnapping — of what use would it be to employ someone likely to be recognized by Martina? But I thought it highly probable that she might know of a woman who could be bribed into acting under my direction. I was right. She readily gave me the name of a woman whose husband and son had been transported to Australia. This Mrs Smith — so called — was anxious to join them out there.'

'You always did have a taste for low company,' growled Laurence, under his breath.

'I told my grandparents that I was going to Belgium to fetch Laurence's cases. They were strongly opposed to my going, especially as I had only just returned from a brief visit to London, ostensibly for the purpose of buying new dresses, an expense of which they disapproved. I disregarded their remonstrances and set off, not direct to Belgium but first to the house of Grandmamma's old friend, Mrs Lucas, who lives about fifteen miles from Clinton St James. Visiting her in the past in Grandmamma's company, I had sometimes enlivened dreary visits to an invalid by persuading the old coachman to let me amuse myself by driving Mrs Lucas's small closed carriage round the country lanes. Leaving Mrs Smith at a distance from the house, I went round to the stableyard and told the coachman that being in the neighbourhood I would dearly like to borrow the carriage for the day. As Mrs Lucas was ill in bed, the coachman knew the carriage would not be needed. He saw no harm in lending it to the granddaughter of his mistress's friend, who had borrowed it before to take friends for drives, and who was prepared to pay handsomely for the privilege. I drove to the secluded spot where Mrs Smith was waiting, changed into Laurence's clothes and drove to Clinton St James. The rest was easy. I drove Mrs Smith and Martina to a railway station at a short distance from Mrs Lucas's house, left them there to wait for the train and drove back to the stable-yard, adjusting my dress on the way. I then took the train for London, travelling apart from the other two. Thereafter I wore male or female attire as seemed advisable. If Martina had not been so seriously ill on the crossing, she would not have had — as I now see she must have had — an opportunity of recognizing me.

'After leaving her in the convent, I endeavoured to collect the curios; but M. Romaine was from home and his servants refused to hand Laurence's property over without his authority. I saw Mrs Smith safely off to Australia and returned home. That is all I have to say. But I should like to be told how Mr Ellin discovered that Martina had been taken to Belgium. He was in Great Parborough for only one night, and as far as I know he did not meet anyone who had knowledge of my movements.'

Mr Ellin was maliciously disposed to tell her that the first clue had been given to him in the waiting-room at Naxworth after her impetuous selfishness had left him and his fellow-passengers stranded for an hour. But that clue would have been valueless apart from Guy's revelations — and he had no mind to betray Guy, or indeed to correct the misapprehension concerning the length of his stay in Great Parborough. He remained silent. Augustine put the question aside.

'That is an irrelevancy. But before you write your confession, I wish to make one further inquiry. How did you possess yourself of a key to the mausoleum? — that key which you afterwards threw into the well with the coffin?'

'If I had been able to get hold of your key, I should have used it on the first night of my stay here. But it was padlocked where it hung in the office, and I could not remove it. So I took a wax impression and rode to the locksmith in Shardley. If the stupid fellow had not been atrociously slow, I should have outwitted you all. But I was not able to obtain the key till this afternoon.'

Mr Ellin's thoughts went back to the rider who had disappeared into the mists and to the words spoken an hour later by Laurence. Though he had made the best speed possible, how nearly had those eyes on the library wall fulfilled their promise to defeat him!

Augustine accepted the explanation without comment. Rising, he placed before his sister paper, pen and a massive inkstand shaped like a griffin with staring head and curving paws. He said curtly —

'You will now write the two copies of your confession. Make it as short as you can. The bare facts will suffice.'

In a bold, dashing hand she began to write. There was not the slightest pause, no erasure; the words flowed evenly over the paper. Drawing a little apart, Augustine and his brothers composed their statement for the newspapers. Briefly and baldly it announced that Martina Chalfont, daughter of Mr and Mrs

Ashley Chalfont of Grewby Towers, was supposedly born dead, but had in reality been stolen by a friend of the family, a childless lady with a great longing for a child. After this lady's death the truth came to light on the evidence of witnesses whose testimony it was impossible to doubt. A final convincing proof was obtained when the infant's coffin, opened in the presence of four witnesses, was found to contain nothing save clothing wrapped round a book that was known to have disappeared mysteriously from Grewby Towers at the time of the child's birth.

Emma's pen, working at top speed, was the first to accomplish its task. She laughed mockingly when Augustine showed her what he had written.

'Why try to shield me?' she asked. 'It is useless — you must know that it is useless. The world will understand well enough that Harriet could never have done what she did without prompting and aid from someone — and who was there to push her into it save me?'

'The thing will be a nine days' wonder, no doubt,' said Augustine; 'but after that, talk will die away and be forgotten. It may never even reach the ears of any acquaintances at present residing on the Continent. If any such persons do not hear gossip or read this statement, then it will rest with your conscience how much or how little you decide to tell them.'

Mr Ellin easily understood that Augustine was making a guarded allusion to Emma's private engagement. He could see no future for it should Orlington hear of his betrothed's share in the child-stealing.

'Oh, you may leave me to deal with my conscience!' said Emma. 'I need none of your advice on that score.'

'Then there is nothing more to be said,' Augustine told her. 'Unless, indeed, you wish to express regret for the past.'

'What would be the use of that?' she inquired contemptuously.

Mr Ellin had no means of knowing what answer the silent brothers would have made. For his part, he deemed that words, mere words, were devoid of significance when one remembered Tina's haunted childhood, her ordeal in Fuchsia Lodge, the Belgian miseries so lately endured. Nor must the long years of my loneliness be forgotten. Should not also a pitying thought be spared for those two graves, one in the churchyard of Little Parborough, the other far off in the restless sea? Mr Ellin looked at Emma where she sat with her hard stare. Behind that blank wall, was there repentance, regret, mortification, seething anger, cold indifference or only infinite relief? Who could tell? He found himself recalling the old Russian proverb, *The soul of thy sister is a dark forest* — aye, dark, impenetrably dark, a place of fathomless gloom.

All present witnessed the confession, one copy of which was given to Mr Ellin. The three Chalfont brothers and Mr Ellin then witnessed the statement intended for the newspapers. In frozen accents Augustine made an end. 'That is all,' he said to Emma. 'You may withdraw.'

Emma rose, swept her judges a magnificent reverence, walked slow and stately from the room. For the life of him, Mr Ellin could not but admire her courage and self-control. His attention, however, was quickly diverted to a succession of shrieks, strangely mingled with laughter, emanating from the lips of Mrs Augustine Chalfont, who chose that moment for going into a bout of hysterics.

The cries must have been heard by Emma; but she did not turn back to tend her sister-in-law. The four gentlemen rendered what assistance they could. It was little enough; for none of them had the least notion how to deal with an affliction of this sort. Guy ran for a glass of water, which he contrived to spill over the patient; Laurence set a curtain on fire by opening a window that was too near a lamp; Augustine protested, adjured, implored; and Mr Ellin shut the door to keep the noise from penetrating to the servants' quarters.

The poor lady was at last restored to calmness. A stealthy procession crept up the stairs, Laurence and Guy leading the way with candles, Augustine tenderly guiding his wife, and Mr Ellin bringing up the rear.

There was not much of the night left after Mr Ellin had been escorted to his room. An hour or so he spent in committing Emma's verbal confession to paper, as nearly as he could remember it. This he did under the impression that I should wish to hear what she had said.

As he had written down one sister's story, so he wrote the other's, but with what unlike emotions! On the former occasion, the task had been a labour of love; now, the pen seemed to be weighted with lead, and he could not drive away the notion that every movement of his hand was being watched by the eyes that had menaced him from the library wall. Once he caught himself swinging round in his chair as if to confront a foe. But beyond the circle of candlelight darkness reigned.

Chapter Seventeen

Mr Ellin could not suppose that Emma would present herself at a breakfast-table from which her sister-in-law would almost certainly be absent. If Mrs Augustine kept her room, surely Miss Chalfont would not have the hardihood to act hostess in her place?

But when Mr Ellin entered the breakfast-room, there she was, chatting unconcernedly with her brother Laurence, who had, it appeared, already visited the stables. With him, she was discussing the points of her new mare. 'Where did you get the money to buy that fine creature?' he was saying. He did not add, 'After all the disbursements you have made lately, you must be considerably out of pocket!' but the direction of his thought was plain to see.

Emma was not in the least discomposed. 'Empress was a gift from dear Grandmamma,' she answered, and came forward smiling to greet the guest.

Presumably in the hope of lightening a cloudy atmosphere, Augustine had decreed that his two elder children should breakfast downstairs instead of in the nursery. With the skill and diligence of a model maiden aunt, Emma attended to their wants, removing the tops of their eggs, and sweetening their cups of milk. Nor did she fail to join in the general conversation, when her comments were so lively and intelligent that Mr Ellin could have believed that the events of the previous night were but figments of his disordered imagination.

That illusion vanished as he caught her eye regarding him with the exact stare of the portrait in the library. The hostile look was gone in an instant, and she was once more the gracious hostess and the devoted aunt of the two pale little mortals who treated her with distant respect not unmingled, Mr Ellin thought, with awe. Something of the same awe was visible in the countenances of

Augustine and Guy, whose opinion of their sister's behaviour was never revealed to him. Laurence's verdict was recorded as soon as Emma was out of hearing: 'She's the eighth wonder of the world!'

As for Mr Ellin, he did not draw a free breath till he was safely out of Grewby Towers. Almost as silent as before, Laurence and Guy went back with him to present the results of the investigation. Augustine did not accompany them; but he sent a letter expressing his abhorrence of his sister's conduct and his deep regret for what he called 'our long estrangement'. He would have come in person to greet his newly-discovered sister and her mamma, had not his dear wife been suffering from a *crise de nerfs* as a result of the late deplorable disclosures.

I was absent from home when they came to Silverlea Cottage so much sooner than I had had any reason to expect. In my restless anxiety for news, I had striven to calm myself by paying a visit to invalid Mrs Percy across the way. My absence was just what Mr Ellin and my stepsons most desired. They had wished first to acquaint Tina with the story, but did not see how they could obtain their wish until they heard from Jane that I would not be returning home for an hour. Miss Tina, Jane told them, was in her playroom.

Much surprised was Tina to behold all three marching in. She greeted Mr Ellin with effusion, the other two with suspicion. That familiar use of the name *Madre* still rankled.

'May we join you, Tina?' said Mr Ellin. 'We have something very important to tell you, and I want you to listen carefully.'

When they were all seated, Mr Ellin said what he had come to say, speaking as simply as he could, with Laurence and Guy putting in a word from time to time. Her eyes wide open, Tina sat very still.

Laurence began to read Emma's short written confession aloud. In the middle of a sentence his voice broke, and he gave the paper to Guy, who read steadily to the end. Moving nearer to Laurence, Tina laid a little hand on his arm as if to comfort him.

I came home while the reading was in progress. Jane, in a high state of mystified excitement, told me that the three gentlemen were in the playroom talking to Miss Tina. What, I asked myself, was I going to hear — good news or bad? What did this conference behind closed doors portend? With trembling hands I removed cloak and bonnet and sank into a chair in the parlour to await their coming.

They heard the sounds of arrival. Did Tina fully understand? they asked.

She said yes, she understood perfectly. There was no need for them to explain any more.

They began to suggest how she should break the tidings to me. With a dignified air, Tina put their suggestions aside. 'No, do not tell me. I know best what to say.'

The door was held open for her. They followed, keeping in the background till she had spoken.

Advancing to my chair, she touched me gently. '*Madre*,' she said, 'I am your Dorothea.'

I presume I must have fainted. I can remember nothing till I heard Tina crying out in agitation to Mr Ellin, 'Oh, did I do it wrong? Did I do it wrong?'

Making a mighty effort, I gasped, 'No, my darling, no. You did it beautifully.'

'Kiss your mother, Tina,' said Mr Ellin.

I held her in a long embrace. Then Laurence and Guy kissed me, with murmured congratulations; and Mr Ellin stood by, looking, I perceived, a trifle envious. With Tina in my arms, I heard all they had come to tell. It was an hour of ecstasy, fraught with sadness.

Ecstasy for Tina and me, sadness for the lives that had met such sorry endings and for that other life darkened by its burden of guilt. At last Guy, seeing that I was quite overcome, drew his sister from the room. Laurence followed. I feared that Mr Ellin was about to depart likewise. In a sudden dread of being alone — 'Do not leave me, William,' I murmured.

'Never, Arminel, while life shall last,' he answered.

Mr Ellin afterwards had the impertinence to suggest that I had proposed marriage to him, not he to me. I am always afraid he will some day repeat this audacious assertion to our children when they ask, as children will, questions about the words used by Papa when he made known his wishes to Mamma. Be that as it may, the news of our betrothal gave great satisfaction to all members of our little circle, and to no one more than to old Annie, who professed to find some mystical and symbolic meaning in the discovery of the lost book in the empty coffin. She set up as a prophetess from that time forth, and was held in much respect by our neighbours, though I have heard that her claims were disputed by Jane and Eliza, who averred that they had never needed Mr Ellin's book to tell them what they had known from the day Mr Ellin gave cherries to me 'and to nobody else!' And what, they asked, was the use of her boasting that she knew the truth about Miss Tina from the first, when she had never said a word to put Mr Ellin on the right track? But Annie was not to be moved from a proud consciousness of her own superiority in matters of foresight and second sight and peeps into the future of whatever kind.

Now as my reminiscences draw perforce to a close — for I have but a few pages left in my manuscript book — I must again pause to express my astonishment that seven years have galloped by since the day of wonder when my Dorothea was restored to me. Scant was the attention I at first bestowed on Augustine's letter, brought by Mr Ellin. But when I had leisure to peruse it, I fully accepted his view that a civil acquaintance should thenceforth be maintained with all members of the family. Only thus could Emma's name be protected as far as might be from ill-natured talk.

I agreed with Augustine, I say: but it was not at once possible to carry good resolutions into effect. Soon after Christmas — the gladdest Christmas I had ever known — old Mr Grandison fell ill; and though his life was never in danger, his health was so much impaired that he resigned the oversight of his estate to Laurence and with his wife and Emma went abroad for many months, during which time it was impossible to establish friendly relations. With responsibility, Laurence's character deepened and matured. He gave up his exploratory expeditions, and became almost overnight as model a landowner as his father and elder brother.

In the spring, but before Emma and her grandparents had returned from the Continent, Valincourt was empty and ready for our occupation; and at the same time a well-deserved preferment for Mr Randolph — his appointment as Dean of Valchester — took effect. Thus it came about that the later months of Guy's preparation for Holy Orders were spent partly with us in Valincourt and partly in lodgings in the cathedral city, where it was Tina's holiday privilege to drink tea with him in his rooms that looked past the Cathedral to the Val, winding like a broad silver ribbon through green meadowlands. A privilege much prized; for she quickly forgot her initial mistrust and became warmly attached to Laurence and Guy. 'They are rather old to be my brothers,' said candid Tina, 'but I do like them very well.'

All three brothers acted generously by their sister, providing for Martina as befitted a daughter of the house of Chalfont. At a later date she was to become a prime favourite with Augustine, his wife, and the nieces and nephews who were so near her own age. She is now as much a moorland nymph as ever the elder Miss Chalfont had been. Never, I trow, will she be able to understand my distaste for those dun acres.

The brothers attended my wedding, on the eve of which Tina made bold to inquire, 'Madre, when you are married, what name shall you use when you speak to Mr Ellin? Laurence and Guy will say "Sir" as they always do, and Guy suggests I should call him "Pater" if I do not care to use "Papa" a second time. But what will you call him? "Mr Ellin", or "Willie", or "William"?'

I answered that Mr Ellin must decide that question as he wished.

'Only it will not be "Will-yum",' quoth Tina demurely.

I began to be a little afraid of this child with the long memory.

By invitation of Mr and Mrs Grandison, my husband, Tina and I were present at the resplendent wedding of Orlington and Emma, which had been delayed till midsummer by reason of the bridegroom's diplomatic engagements as well as by the illness of the bride's grandfather. How, you will ask, did Emma and I first meet? I answer that I cannot tell. It is not that my recollections of those days have faded. Clearly do I remember every detail of our stay in Parborough Hall, from our gracious reception by the old people (what had they been told, I wondered!) down to the pattern on the dinner service. As in a magic mirror I see the beauty and stateliness of Emma on her bridal morn, the faces of our fellow-guests, and festive raiment of the well-wishers who stood waving good-bye to the wedded pair. Again I hear the laughter, the jests, the banter of the assembled friends and relations. Once more I watch William as he chats with Mr Grandison or strolls in the park with Laurence; once more I look on while Guy takes Tina and Augustine's children to feed the swans and the peacocks. All this, I maintain, is as vividly pictured as when I saw it first; but fugitive as a dream has been the moment when I first looked into Emma's dark eyes.

And how, during those days, did Tina comport herself? Much as Augustine's boy and girl had done at the breakfast-table on the morning after Mr Ellin came to Grewby Towers, and as they continued to do when playing their part, in Tina's company, as bridesmaid and page. The half-sisters were never alone together, even for a minute — I think Tina took good care they should not be. One unlooked-for joy she had as we were leaving the church after the wedding ceremony. Among the onlookers was a young woman who smiled at Tina. The child turned, gazed, then, heedless of spectators, sprang forward to greet with hugs and kisses one from whom it had long ago grieved her to part.

I looked at Pleasant Partridge, and I liked what I saw.

At home again in Valincourt, years of autumnal happiness have been ours. I have ever loved Keats's 'season of mists and mellow fruitfulness' above the other three. To my mind there are no roses and strawberries sweeter than October's, and no colours to match those of the dying year. William and Tina cannot be brought to agree: they are all for the white and gold of spring and the luxuriance of high summer. But I hold to my own opinion, whatever they say.

During those years there have not been many opportunities for complying with Augustine's request that we keep up a show of friendship with Emma. We have met only at Guy's ordination, Laurence's marriage, the celebrations after Augustine's election as Member of Parliament, and the banquet at which the Swedish Government honoured William for his services to Swedish literature. Orlington's chosen career has caused him to be constantly employed in posts abroad, and Emma has earned credit and renown as the spirited and brilliant wife of a successful diplomatist. Who after that, says Mr Ellin, could have the heart to blame Miss Wilcox for mentioning to prospective parents — as gossip declares she often does — that the sister of the Countess of Orlington was numbered among the past pupils at Fuchsia Lodge?

But the 'show of friendship' has become a reality. Our twin sons, Guy William and Roger Laurence, were rising three years old when Pleasant Partridge laid a second daughter in my arms. On the day before her baptism, a letter came by his wife's request from Orlington announcing the birth of a son and heir. Enclosed was a slip of paper on which, faintly scrawled, was the one word, 'Forgive'.

We did not know — we do not know now — how much or how little Emma had told her husband. If he was still in ignorance of a certain passage in her history, much damage might be done to their relationship by a letter assuring her of forgiveness. There could be only one way in which my elder daughter and I might safely tell her that our forgiveness was truly Christian, full and free. Mr Ellin consenting, we took that way. When a few hours later Guy, in his white robes, bade the proud youthful God-mother, 'Name this child,' Dorothea-Martina gave her answer in clear, unfaltering tones.

She named the babe Emma.